Moving On

KAREN
FRANCES

Moving On

ISBN 978 0 9934154 8 7
Published by: Clydeside Publishing

Cover Design by
Kari March Designs

Model
Autumn Jones

Editing by
Karen Sanders

Interior Design & Formatting by
Christine Borgford, Type A Formatting

Dedication

This is for anyone that has found themselves in Lauren Trent's situation.

We all have difficult paths to cross, but it's how we deal with them, that define us.

Acknowledgements

WRITING MOVING ON, FOR ME was harder than I had imagined. I knew the storyline I wanted to write, I knew the characters inside out. But for the life of me I couldn't get the words written. And when I did finally get some words down on the laptop I ended up deleting the first 21K. That was a lot of words to delete. Two very dear friends, Maxine and Suzie, kept me sane when I was losing all feelings for this story.

After taking a small step back, I delved back in with the encouragement and support of not only Maxine and Suzie, but also my editor, Karen. Now, finally, I have a story that I'm proud of.

Special thanks to the team I have around me that help take my story and turn it into a book; Karen Sanders, my lovely editor, you push me at every stage to go one step further and in turn you always get more out of me and my stories.

Kari March, my cover designer, you do know what I'm looking for even if I don't. Christine Borgford, my formatter, what can I say? Love you, lady.

Maxine, I don't have enough words to express how grateful I am that you came into my life. You're so much more than my PA, you're a very dear friend.

Laura and Suzie, our conversations always make me smile

and laugh and I'm so glad the book world brought us together. May we have many journeys ahead.

Autumn, thank you for not only being my Lauren Trent, but for the friendship we have.

My readers group is a great fun place where I get to hangout with my readers. I love seeing your feedback when I post something new.

The book community is amazing. I've made so many wonderful friends through my short journey.

My family and friends, you all know how much you mean to me.

Thank you readers for taking a chance on Moving On. I really do hope you enjoy Lauren Trent's story.

Contents

Prologue

"MUMMY."

His voice grabs my attention. I stop what I'm doing, turning to face him. "What's wrong?" I ask, as my eyes dart between Luke, my five-year-old son, and my best friend, Abbie, who has offered to watch my kids so I can surprise their dad at work.

"Will you be home in time for dinner?"

"Of course I will, Luke. And can I tell you a secret? Daddy will be home nice and early tonight. We'll all sit down and have dinner together," I tell him, ruffling his hair. David has been home later every night for the last few weeks; something about a big contract for work. "Now, promise me you'll be a good boy for Auntie Abbie."

"I promise, and I'll look after Kate too."

God, he makes my heart swell with the amount of love he has for his baby sister. Luke has been great since she was born, considering he wasn't that happy about me having a baby. All through my pregnancy he kept telling me he didn't want a baby. But the minute I laid Kate in his arms, he fell in love with her. He fusses over her all the time, and always has to check on her when she cries to make sure she is, in fact, okay.

"You do that. I'll be home soon."

"Go. Now, before I change my mind," Abbie says, holding Kate in her arms. "And by the way, you look fantastic."

With her words, I smile and kiss the three of them, before turning and walking out of the house and toward my car with some confidence that has been missing from me for the past few weeks. Maybe even months.

I'm not going to lie and say this time around having a baby has been a piece of cake; it hasn't. It's been hard. The end of my pregnancy was a nightmare. I seemed to suffer all the usual pregnancy problems and more this time around, unlike with Luke. My pregnancy with him was easy. Kate has been a demanding baby from day one, leaving me so exhausted at times that even getting dressed some mornings has been a struggle. I never expected to feel like this, so drained the second time around, especially when the first time was so easy and straightforward.

Whoever says being a parent is easy is talking crap. That statement is bullshit. It's by far the hardest job I've had, but it's also the most rewarding. All those long sleepless nights, teething, dirty nappies, can all be forgotten about in a heartbeat with a simple cute smile. No, I wouldn't change any of it, not even for a minute.

Twenty minutes later, I've parked my car next to David's BMW in front of our new offices. We only moved our business into these offices a month before I gave birth to our daughter. It's late Friday afternoon, and I already know most of the staff will either be finishing off or will have already left for the weekend.

We run a graphic design business, and David doesn't know it yet, but I intend to ease myself back into work over the next few weeks. I need to re-focus on the business because David looks so run down with running it all himself. I've been so busy with the kids, I couldn't even tell you how the business is doing at the moment, and David doesn't tell me much, other than it's busy. We've both worked hard the last few years, building up our reputation and our client base. Our children will always be my priority, but I need to get back to doing something for me. I miss work and my colleagues.

I take my security pass from my handbag, swiping it, and letting myself into the building. I pause inside and check my reflection in the mirrored glass wall to my left. Happy with my appearance, I start walking. The walk through the corridor to where our joint office is located is long and quiet; there seems to be no-one else in the building.

Opening the office door, I hear a low moan. I lift my eyes slowly and freeze in horror. Not the scene I was expected to be greeted with.

What the holy fuck?

I would recognise that long, dyed blonde hair anywhere.

Pain grips me, like a knife slicing through me layer by layer.

My eyes stay fixed on the scene in front of me; I'm unable to look away. The man I love, the father of my children, is having sex on my desk with my fucking sister . . . my little sister.

How could they?

David has her bent over the desk—my desk—taking her from behind. Her low moans get louder and I can't stand the fucking pain within my chest. It hurts so damn much. They are both so lost in the moment that neither has noticed they have company. The smell of sex makes me feel sick, yet I still can't look away.

This has to be a dream. I close my eyes, hoping and praying that I'm wrong, that my imagination is playing tricks with me.

But, no, as I re-open my eyes, the vision is still very much the same, my sister's moans getting louder with each thrust he makes.

Stacey throws her head back and David grabs hold of her long dyed blonde hair, wrapping it around his fingers. "I need more," she cries out.

He pulls on her hair. "Like that?" he asks through gritted teeth. His free hand grips onto her hip as he pulls back and rams into her harder.

"Yes," she cries. "More. Oh, dear God. Yes. I'm so close." Her high-pitched tone tells me exactly how close she is. My body shakes as I watch my sister and my man rip my heart in two.

Over and over he rams into her, and she comes, screaming his name as though she's done it a million times before. "Fuck, David . . ."

"Stacey, stay still, I'm nearly there." He grunts, thrusting wildly.

I take a deep breath, and with the little strength I have, I step into the room. Both their heads swing around and David stops thrusting. His eyes are wild and confused.

"Oh, don't let me stop you. I was enjoying the show." I spit the words at them.

David looks at Stacey and then back at me, his dick still inside her.

"Well, feel free to carry on," I say, this time with no emotion on display.

"Lauren, it's not what it looks like."

Good God. He hasn't just said that, has he?

"Really? You're not fucking my sister on my desk? Well, maybe you'd like to explain because that's what it sure as hell looked like to me. And from the way she called your name, it's not the first time you've fucked her." He moves, his dick slips out, and he starts walking toward me. "Don't come a step closer."

My eyes fall down his body, and now I take notice. He didn't even have the decency to wear a fucking condom. This just gets better by the minute. Stacey stands, fully naked, not even embarrassed that she's been caught in the act, and takes his hand in hers. I know she and I don't exactly get on, we've never been close, but this is a new low even for her. "She knows now. We've nothing to hide."

Fucking hell. Have I just heard her correctly? Nothing to hide. She might need to go into hiding because, right now, I want to kill both of them, and as my anger builds, that's a strong fucking possibility.

"Lauren, let's talk about this." David's pleading voice cuts through the air.

"No. There's no talking to be done. I have nothing to say to you."

I have nothing to say to either of them for their betrayal. Turning, I look away. Cheating on me is bad enough, but with my sister. There are no words in the world that can solve this.

Keeping my head high, I hold back my tears because I refuse to let either of them see me cry. I walk away without a second glance back. Neither of them will see the pain they have caused me. I make it into my car and frantically attempt to put it into gear. Pausing, I take a deep breath and try again. First gear, first time. Thank fuck. I pull away quickly, needing to put distance between me and everything that just happened.

My tears now fall. I hate them both.

I drive around desperately in what seems like circles before pulling over. I take my phone from my bag and call Abbie.

"Hey, babe. Was he surprised?"

"You could say that. He and Stacey were both surprised I interrupted their fucking session," I say bitterly through my tears.

"Lauren, where are you?" Her question is rushed.

"I'll be back home soon. Oh, shit. The kids. Luke can't see me like this." I stop talking and try to wipe away my tears.

"Don't worry about the kids. I'll call Mum and ask her to take them overnight for you. She'll love having them and I will stay here with you."

"Thank you. Text when they're gone and I'll come home." I end our call and my tears continue to fall for the pain their actions have caused, and for the pain I'm sure will follow. Poor Luke. I promised him Daddy would be home early tonight. He's too young to understand this. At least I know where David's been and who he's been with every night he told me he was working late.

Yeah, some big contract!

I thought he loved me as much as I love him. Obviously, I was wrong.

Seven years. Seven years we've been together and this is how it ends. Because for me, there's no going back.

What the hell do I do now? For me and the kids?

One

Eight months later

"LAUREN, ARE YOU OKAY?" ABBIE'S voice cuts through the icy air that surrounds me. It shouldn't feel cold, but it does to me. The sun has been shining all day and the temperature has been in the low twenties. I lift my head and she's staring at me, concern etched around her eyes and worry lines across her head.

"Yes, I'm fine. Glad this is finally over and he's out of my life now."

"You're allowed to be upset," she says, handing me a glass filled with white wine. "It's only natural."

I'm not upset. Relieved, yes, but not upset. Today has been a long, hard day, and this glass of wine is welcomed with warmth.

After eight long months of him arguing about the business and the house we shared, everything is finally settled. I'm glad we weren't married because that would've brought a whole host of problems to deal with.

He had to buy me out of both the business and the house. Then today, there was the uncertainty of the funds not being cleared in time. But I finally got the call from my bank manager late this afternoon to say the money was cleared and to arrange a meeting to go in and sort out things. I know this isn't part of his job; then again, I'm no average client. Grant is my uncle—my mother's brother. He took on the job of looking out for Stacey and me after Mum died. Not that I needed much looking after. I was already with David when she died. Grant just made sure we were okay.

Mum died a few years ago after a long and brave battle with cancer. My dad wasn't around; he and Mum had split up when I was in my early teens. Dad stayed on in our family home on the outskirts of London, and Mum moved back up north to Scotland to be closer to her family. Dad and I drifted apart. I was lucky if I saw him once a year.

Dad's contact has increased these last few months. He calls, checking up, making sure the kids and I are okay. He's always asking if we want to go and visit him. He knows David was cheating on me, but I didn't know how to tell him it was with Stacey. Our relationship isn't that strong, but it's getting there. He's been trying to repair the damage to his relationships with both me and Stacey. I didn't want to be the one to upset everything, even though I know I'm not to blame for this whole mess.

I blamed myself for a long time. Asked myself constantly what Stacey has that I don't. I've always felt she was prettier, taller, skinnier, but in reality, she's not better than me and the whole thing with David has proved that beyond doubt. I would never have betrayed her the way she has me, but then again, I have a conscience; something my sister sadly lacks.

I don't know whether to be happy or angry with my dad for now showing an interest in my life, especially when he wasn't around when I needed him the most; when my mum died.

I'll go with the former. Life is too short to be angry with him. He made his choices and he's the one who has to live with them.

I'm also past the stage of being angry toward Stacey and David for what they did to me. Having said that, I don't want to be around either of them any time soon. My sister did the unthinkable to me and there will never be any sort of relationship between us. And as for David, what he's doing now to the kids is hurting Luke. Kate doesn't know any better, but Luke questions me all the time, asking where his daddy is. That breaks my heart.

"My time for being upset and angry was after I found them together. Now, I don't feel anything for either of them. But I do feel my kids are missing out because their so-called father has decided he wants nothing to do with them."

"I think he's going through some sort of midlife crisis."

"He might be, but it doesn't make a blind bit of difference to me. But to Luke, it's making all the difference. He's still too young and thinks he's done something wrong to upset his dad."

"Lauren, he'll get there eventually, and the only person to help him through all this will be you," Abbie says. "David is the one missing out when it comes to the kids. You have to remember that. Now, Mum has said she and Dad are happy to have the kids overnight on Saturday so you and I can hit the town."

God, I don't know where I would be without Abbie's parents lately. Yes, Grant looked out for us and the kids and I moved in with him and my Aunt Liz when David made it clear he didn't want us in the house. But Sandra and Les have been like parents to me since Mum died. And to the kids, they're family. Luke calls them Papa Les and Nana Sandra. I know they think the world of my kids; they're always spoiling them.

"I'm not sure about going out," I say, with very little enthusiasm. Abbie has been talking about a night out for weeks, and I have put her off every time. Always something else to do, another excuse, like moving house. We only moved into our new family home a few weeks ago. Grant and Liz were more than happy for us to stay with them, but we needed our own place. I needed to stand on my own two feet.

I had only ever stayed with David. I'm still unsure what went wrong with our relationship. He went from a loving family man to . . . well, I don't know what he changed to because I thought things were good between us. God, how wrong was I?

I do know that wasn't the first time he had been with Stacey. He openly admitted to me that he had been seeing her the whole time I was pregnant. Nothing like kicking someone when they're already down. For a long time, I felt worthless.

"We're going out on Saturday, and I'm not taking no for an answer. All you do is look after the kids and work. You need some time for you. After all, you're still young and very much single."

Shit. I've run out of valid excuses not to go.

"I might be single, but in all honesty, no guy is going to be interested in anything more than a one-night stand when he realises I'm a twenty-nine-year-old mother with two kids," I say, taking a sip of my wine.

"Says who? You, my friend, have a lot to offer the right man."

"Hmm, well I don't think so. Anyway, I'm off men."

"You say that now, but I know the right one will fall your way sooner or later. Sooner if you stop working long hours here at home."

She does have a point, but I'm not about to tell her that. All I do is work from home and look after the kids. I started working for myself, doing work for a few clients. A lot of my clients came to me after they found out about David and me. My workload has increased on a weekly basis and has kept me busy and given me an income. Not that I was short of a bob or two. I had my inheritance that I had to use, first in the early days when I had no money coming in, then when I paid the deposit for our new home.

David has cut all ties with the kids and point blank refuses to provide for them, which I'm fine with now because I've proved to myself that I can more than provide everything they need. Yes, it's been hard, especially when I was coming to terms with everything that had happened, but I know I'm over the worst of it. This will be his loss at the end of the day. I did try and get him to see and spend time with Luke, but he refused each time, saying he was too busy. But he was never too busy to take Stacey away for dirty weekends or romantic nights out. More than one person told me when they were spotted out and about together.

"Lauren, are you happy?"

I turn to face Abbie. "Yes, I'm happy. I have my family who have all been there for me throughout this. I have work, this house, and my precious kids. What else do I need?"

She smiles at my answer. It's true. Abbie and I have always been really close. We're more than just best friends. Our mothers used to joke we were more like sisters than just friends. It's strange, because I used to wish Stacey and I were like this, but that was sadly never to be.

"Glad to hear it. Now, do you want me to stay over?"

"Does that mean this glass of wine will lead to another and another?"

"Yes. I don't have work tomorrow and that means I can give you a hand with the kids in the morning, or through the night if they get up," she says, topping up my glass.

"Well, then stay, but you might regret saying that when Kate decides to get up at six a.m."

"When it comes to your kids, there's nothing I will ever regret." I can hear the echo of sadness in her voice and see the pain she feels as she takes a deep breath.

Abbie can't have kids. She was in a car crash in her late teens. I remember the hurt look on her face after the doctors explained the extent of her injuries and how it would affect her life. At the time she was young, but she did grasp the seriousness of her injuries.

When I realised I was pregnant with Luke, I put off telling her because I was scared of how she would react. Yes, she cried when I finally told her, but she was overjoyed for me. I know when she finally meets the right man, she would consider adoption; we've spoken about it.

I think this is the reason her parents spoil my two.

"Well, how about I make us something to eat to soak up some of the alcohol? I do have to walk Luke to school in the morning."

"Phone for a pizza. Neither of us is cooking, and I can walk Luke. I've missed him tonight."

"He was exhausted when I picked him up today. They're having some sort of health week in school, trying out new activities. He told me a few other dads have been in, helping with the sports classes. I could hear the pang of disappointment when he spoke."

"Lauren, things will get easier for him. He's a tough kid and he has the best person I know in his life. You. Through all this crap, not once have you said a bad word about David. That says a lot about you as a person. Me, I don't think I would be so restrained. But you always put the kids' feelings before yourself."

"I do try, but sometimes it has hurt," I say, as Abbie moves closer to me on the couch. She wraps her arm around me and raises her glass.

"A toast! To my beautiful best friend, who is an amazing mum to my two gorgeous godchildren. Things are improving day by day for you. And those two sleeping soundly upstairs . . . you have nobody to thank but yourself for them. Always remember that."

"I will, and thank you for being my rock these last few months."

"I'm always here for you, just as I know you're always here when I need you. Now, enough mushy stuff. Let's drink."

Two

"SANDRA, ARE YOU SURE ABOUT having them?" I ask nervously, because they've only ever stayed overnight once before. The night I found out about David and my sister, and then I was in no fit state to look after myself, never mind them. Yes, Sandra and Les look after the kids for me and they love spending time with them, but I'm anxious when I'm not with them. Secretly, part of me wants Sandra to change her mind. It would make it easier for me because, bloody hell, I'm so nervous about going out.

"Yes, of course we are." She turns her attention to Luke. "You and Papa are going to set up the train set, aren't you?" My son nods his head with excitement. "And me and this little lady . . . well, I'm going to enjoy reading her stories and running around after her."

I laugh because even I know that since my daughter has discovered her feet, there's not a hope in hell of her sitting while Sandra reads to her unless she's really tired, and even then she will still fight against it. I can't believe it's almost my baby's birthday. One year old. Where has the time gone? It flies past so quickly.

"Go out and enjoy yourself. Don't worry about these two because you know they will be fine. Tomorrow, you will come for dinner with Abbie before taking them home."

"Okay," I say, because I know I don't really have much say in the matter. "Luke, come and give me a kiss. I'm going now." He wanders back over to me, and I pick him up and give him a kiss. "Now, be a good boy for Nana and Papa."

"I will. Now, will you promise to have fun with Auntie Abbie?"

"Yes, I promise. I love you."

His face lights up, shining brightly in front of me. He has had some insecurities since David left, so I always go out of my way to let him know he means the world to me. He has the most gorgeous smile that can instantly make me feel happy whenever I feel down.

"I love you too."

I put him down and he runs off to find Les. I give Kate a kiss and leave before I change my mind.

I glance in the full-length mirror in my bedroom and I'm suddenly more nervous than I was before. The palms of my hands are clammy. This isn't a good idea. The bedroom door opens. Abbie is standing in the doorway, mouth open and wide-eyed.

"Is it too much?" I finally ask when she just stands there staring at me.

"Too much?" She walks closer to me and stands behind me, her reflection in the mirror in front of me. "No way. It's just a long time since I saw you looking so fucking sexy. Jesus Christ. You, my beautiful, sexy friend, are going to turn heads tonight."

She's right; it is a long time since I put effort into my appearance. I think, over the years, I've lost pieces of me, and now it's time to claim it all back. Piece by piece. But I'm still unsure of my outfit choice. The dress is a bit more revealing than anything I've worn before.

"I think I'll change."

"You will not. The purple suits you. It shows off your sparkling green eyes, and I love that you've left your hair down." She runs her fingers through my dark hair, giving it a shake. "There. Perfect. Now, if you have finished titivating yourself, we need to go. I have a cab waiting outside."

"Yes, I'm ready." I slip my feet into ridiculous black high heels, grab my bag, and follow her outside to the waiting cab.

Abbie and I are busy talking and laughing, something so normal, yet almost alien to me. In this moment, I feel like the old me. The one that got lost along the way. And for tonight, I'm going to try and not worry about the kids and enjoy myself.

The warm air and the outside noise filters through the open cab windows. I had forgotten what it was like to be heading out on a Saturday night, everyone all dressed up to the nines and excited about the weekend.

"So, where are we going?" I ask Abbie, because she has been very secretive up to now about tonight.

"We are going to a club where we can have dinner in the restaurant first. A few drinks, and if that doesn't tire you out, we can go dancing in their nightclub."

I smile. "The club does sound appealing."

"Yippee!" she squeals, causing the taxi driver to laugh and shake his head. He must be used to this at the weekend; giggling and excited girls, although I'm sure it's from younger girls than us. The cab finally stops outside a plush venue. It's not one I've been in, but I have heard it's got a great reputation.

We pay the driver and thank him for putting up with us. He reminds us to phone the same company for returning home. He sounds like Uncle Grant and Les. Les said the other day that if we had trouble getting a cab to call him and he would come and get us. But I couldn't call him; he's doing enough with looking after the kids with Sandra.

We enter the building and are greeted by a young woman at the front desk. Abbie tells her we have a reservation and gives her name. A very young, good-looking guy appears and takes us to our table in the restaurant. He walks in front of us and we both check out his arse—and what a fine, rounded arse it is.

We both burst out in a fit of giggles and the poor guy turns, looking more than a little flustered. He hands us the menu when we sit down at our table, and we order drinks. "A bottle of prosecco," Abbie says.

"Are we celebrating?" I ask as the young waiter leaves our table.

"Of course we are. You are finally free from that arsehole, and you're out of the house for a change. And you don't have to worry about the kids. So yes, I think it calls for a celebration. Now, read the bloody menu because I'm starving."

We sit quietly reading, but there's far too much choice; I have no idea what to have. The waiter comes back to our table with the prosecco. Abbie and I stop reading and watch as he opens our wine. I think we make him nervous, although he does manage to talk to us at the same time.

"Ladies, a celebration?" he asks, pouring the wine.

"You could say that," Abbie tells him, smiling at me. "My friend here has finally cut loose from a complete waste of space."

"Abbie!" My skin tingles, and I repeatedly swallow, embarrassed at her telling a complete stranger my business.

"What? I'm only saying it how I see it."

"Well, congratulations," he says. "I'm sure his loss will be someone else's gain." He winks at me. Abbie shakes her head and laughs. She's thinking the same as me. He's only a bloody boy. "Have you both decided what to have?"

"No," Abbie says. "What do you recommend?"

"I can recommend everything on the menu; we have excellent chefs. But how about tonight's special? Braised venison with red wine served with a sweet mashed potato and vegetables."

"That sounds good to me," I say.

"Make that two."

"Would you like anything to start?"

"No. I want to keep room for a dessert," Abbie says, flashing him a huge smile. He shifts from one foot to the other. Yes, she's making him nervous, and me.

"Okay, I'll go and place your order. If you need anything, anything at all, just let me know. I'm Jack."

"Thanks, Jack." Abbie all but purrs his name. He leaves our table, grinning, and Abbie's eyes stay firmly on his arse as he walks out of sight.

"Bloody hell . . ."

"What? I'm only looking. There's no harm in that. You and I both know he's far too young for either of us," Abbie states matter-of-factly. She says that as though I'm interested in him. I shake my head and take a drink.

It feels good being out as we sit chatting and drinking. Out of the house, away from the kids and my laptop, which I do seem to spend too much time on lately. Tonight, for the first time in months, I feel totally relaxed. All the stress from the last eight months has been lifted.

Jack was right; the venison was to die for. When he clears our table, we order desserts, and of course, tell him how delicious our main course was. Abbie also orders cocktails for us. Why do I think tonight could get messy? Why? Because my very dear friend seems to be on a mission to get me drunk. And as it is, I can already feel the effects of the alcohol flowing through my bloodstream.

The restaurant is busy and has a great atmosphere, along with some really good-looking and efficient staff. The background music is modern with a beat to it and is already putting me in the mood for dancing, and that's something I've not done in such a long time.

"Here we go ladies." Jack puts down two glasses in front of us. "Between the Sheets."

"Abbie! Really?"

"Nothing to do with me. I told Jack to surprise us, and that he has."

"These come compliments of the management," he says almost shyly, looking toward the bar area. I follow his gaze. A well-suited man behind the bar is staring at our table. No, he's staring at me, and I can't do anything but stare back. Totally mesmerised.

On a scale of one to ten, I would say he's an eight, even from here, but if I get the chance to see him up close I might need to change my rating. He gives a whole new meaning to tall, dark, and most definitely handsome.

My eyes linger on his lips, and even from this distance, I can see the slight quirk to one side as his eyes focus on me. My body feels warm and I'm sure he will be able to see the flush on my face. I struggle to draw in a steady breath. Time stops as we stare at each other across the crowded room. Goosebumps spread across my skin.

"Ahem." Abbie coughs, drawing my attention back to her. "I'm glad to see you remember I'm here with you."

I shake my head and notice Jack has already left our table. "Of course I remember."

"Didn't seem like that to me. A certain someone was getting all hot and bothered under an intense gaze. I thought you were off men?"

"I am off men, but that doesn't mean I can't look and appreciate a fine-looking man when I see one."

"And dear God, he is one fine specimen of a man to look at." I look back over at the bar; he's busy talking to Jack. They both look in our direction. Mr Tall, Dark and Handsome smiles, and I quickly look away. "Well it's obvious he has your interest and you have his," she says, smirking. "Now, get drinking. Between the Sheets. Does that mean he wants to get between the sheets with you?"

"Bloody hell, Abbie! Do you have no shame?"

"The question should be does Mr Sexy have no shame? And I already know the answer to that question."

I shake my head, picking up the glass and taking a long drink. I don't look across the room but I do feel eyes burning into me. My need to drink and dance is strong. And that means I can leave the restaurant.

"Abbie, drink up."

Three

THE MUSIC IS POUNDING AND my feet are tapping underneath the table in the club. Jack showed us upstairs and ensured we both had seats, which was nice of him, although he did bring over more cocktails from the management. I think it's all a bit weird and creepy. Abbie thinks we should be grateful. I did think when we came upstairs that would be the last we saw of Jack, but no, he's been here constantly.

I take a moment to listen to the words of the song playing, closing my eyes as the beat flows around me, pulling me in.

We haven't been in the club long when squealing draws our attention.

"OH.MY.GOD!" Ashley screeches, walking towards us with her friend, Stephanie. Ashley works with Abbie; she's actually a really nice girl, although she can be extremely loud. "Lauren, it's so good to see you. You look fantastic. How are . . ."

Abbie looks at me with concern. I don't know why she's so concerned; we've dealt with David. I just don't want to hear his name in every single conversation someone has with me.

I cut in. "Don't say it."

"Okay, I won't, but you do look great. I hope the kids are doing well."

"They're fine," I say, grateful that she hasn't pressed further about David.

"What can I get you all to drink?" Jack asks, as Ashley and Stephanie sit down with us.

"Cocktails, ladies?" Abbie asks. A chorus of, 'hell yes,' surrounds our table. Jack walks away, smiling, looking more relaxed than he did earlier in the evening when Abbie and I arrived.

The noise has increased, as I expected with Ashley. The thing about her is there are never any long periods of awkward silence, and at this moment, I'm more than grateful for that. I smile; I'm glad Abbie talked me into coming out tonight. Jack brings over our drinks and tries to get away from our table as quickly as he can. Poor boy; Ashley embarrassed him. She pulled him down so he ended up sitting on her lap while she whispered in his ear. I don't even want to imagine what she said to him.

A figure moving across the room catches my eyes. Mr Handsome from the restaurant, and I have a clearer view of him than I did downstairs.

He looks pretty damn hot.

His dark hair is swept back off his face, and it's long enough for me to run my fingers through. Shit! I've had too much drink; it's making me have silly thoughts about strange men. He's stopped by someone on the dance floor. My gaze lingers on him, unable to look away. His eyes scan the room until they meet mine with intensity. From here, he looks so uninterested in the conversation he's having in the middle of the dance floor.

I watch him walk away from whoever it was that had stopped him. The man shakes his head and shouts after him, but he doesn't turn back. He walks with purpose towards our table, eyes still on me.

Shit.

Abbie nudges me with her elbow; she's obviously seen him. "Well . . . looks like someone has made an impression," she whispers.

"Cut it out," I say, without turning to face her. She sniggers. God, I feel so bloody warm.

"Evening, ladies," he says in a thick Glasgow accent. Bloody hell, he sounds as sexy as he looks. I do love a Scottish accent on a man; it has a certain appeal to me. Maybe that's because when I was growing up, all the men or boys I knew had an English accent like mine. "How was your meal?" he asks.

"It was enjoyable."

His bright green eyes burn through me and silence descends on our table. Now, with him standing only mere feet away from me, I can truly appreciate the man. Yes, my rating has gone up that little bit higher. He's tall, and I can imagine his suit is covering a perfect body. These thoughts shouldn't be in my head. He smirks. Bloody hell, he has everything going on for him and more, and he knows it.

"We aim to please. And the cocktails?" His eyes flick to the almost empty glass on the table in front of me. The corners of his mouth turn, not into a full grin, but into a smirk that tells me he knows the effect he's having on me. I'm sure anyone looking at me can tell the thoughts going through my head. My eyes are focused on his lips. Lips I wouldn't mind tasting.

I can't answer him.

"Cocktails are going down a treat," Abbie tells him, looking at me, puzzled. I can only shrug my shoulders.

"I'm glad. I hope you all enjoy tonight because, for me, it's suddenly got very interesting," he says, before walking away confidently, unlike me, whose body has turned into a pool of mush. My eyes follow him until he's out of sight. I let out a long breath and my body relaxes. "What the hell was all that about? Bloody hell, Lauren. You have some explaining to do." I hear the words, not knowing who has said them. Lifting my eyes, I find I have three people staring at me.

"What?"

"That was intense," Ashley states.

"It was not," I try to say with confidence, but even I can hear the waver in my voice.

"Lauren, don't you dare try to tell us he didn't have an effect on you. Christ, at least we all know those feelings are mutual between you. His gaze hardly left you. He wants you and only you. I've already said he's trying to tell you something with those cocktails. Between the Sheets, honey. That's where he wants you, and personally, I think you should go and have some fun," Abbie tells me, bringing gasps from not just me, but our friends too.

"Abbie, stop. Your imagination is in overdrive tonight. Now, who wants to dance with me?"

I need the distraction. Ashley squeals, and I take that as a yes and grab her hand, dragging her onto the dancefloor. Abbie tries to get my attention but I zone out. I don't want to hear whatever she has to say because I'm sure she's only going to talk about Mr Tall, Dark and oh-so-Handsome.

I try and lose myself to the beat of the music like Ashley, but I sense someone watching me. I know it's not Abbie because she is in my line of sight. I don't need to search the crowded room to know who's watching me. I have the same feeling buzzing through me as I did earlier every time he looked at me. Hairs stand up on the back of my neck and I shiver.

Ashley and I stay on the dance floor for two songs before returning to our table at the same time Jack arrives with more cocktails.

"Who ordered these?" I sigh heavily and he smiles weakly. The management again. "Jack, could I trouble you for a bottle of water?"

"Of course."

"Someone has certainly made an impression on the management," Ashley says sarcastically.

"What do you want me to do?" I shout louder than I should. My three friends look directly at me. "I want to go and tell Mr I'm So Fucking Handsome to shove his drinks up his arse."

"I bet he'd let you," Stephanie says, and we all burst out laughing.

"No, but seriously, I feel more than a little tipsy. All these cocktails and the wine from earlier are going straight to my head," I say, as Jack approaches our table with a bottle of water, which he hands to me. "Thank you. Jack, can you do me a favour? Please tell the management no more cocktails."'

"Understood, although I'm not sure my boss will be happy. My shift is almost finished. I hope you ladies enjoy the rest of your night," he says.

"Thank you." Abbie tries to hand him a tip but he refuses to accept it, something about it being against company policy.

I sit down, taking a drink of water. Dancing and drinking alcohol is thirsty work, or maybe it's because I'm so out of practice. We sit chatting; it's been a while since I saw Ashley and Stephanie, and it's good to be around normal conversations. Both girls are a few years younger than Abbie and me, so their conversations are a welcome change to me, as I listen to them moan about the lack of talent. It really is amusing listening to them.

It's not long before Abbie grabs me and pulls me onto the dance floor. Again, as I dance, I sense him watching me. I quickly scan the area to each side of me, but I don't have to look far to find him. He's standing just to my right, a short distance from the dance floor. He's with the same guy I saw him talking to earlier.

They look similar; maybe they're brothers or cousins.

I turn back to Abbie, who smiles. "What?"

"You're attracted to him." She shouts in my ear so I can hear above the noise of the music. What can I say to that? I can't deny it, so I shrug my shoulders and continue dancing. Now isn't the time or place to discuss my attraction to Mr Handsome. And boy,

I'm bloody attracted to him. Sex appeal oozes from him.

I move in time to the beat of the music as the vibrations flow quickly through my body, drawing me in. My eyes close briefly and I can feel the music flowing through my veins.

Goosebumps spread across my skin and I feel the hairs on the back of my neck stand to attention.

Someone is behind me, getting closer. Warm hands slip around my waist. I freeze. Opening my eyes, I look to Abbie for a hint of who it is. The look on her face answers my unspoken question.

The sexy man from earlier. She smiles and leaves the dance floor, leaving me alone with him, a complete stranger. Some bloody friend she is!

Oh, no. I'm done for. I can't be this close to him.

My breathing quickens and my temperature rises as his body inches closer to mine. I should pull away but I can't. My own body is holding me hostage to him. I try to channel my thoughts, but all is lost when he turns me in his arms and we're now face-to-face.

"I've watched you, totally mesmerised by you, since you first walked through the doors of the restaurant earlier tonight. Every single thought that has entered my mind tonight has been about you in my bed."

"Between the sheets," I whisper.

His lips curve to the side as he smirks. "Between the sheets is where I want you. I can't deny that." His hands grab onto my hips as his body sways from side to side.

My thoughts are in turmoil. No man has ever openly told me he wants me, and his statement alone excites me. I shouldn't let it, and I most definitely shouldn't consider it, but I would be lying to myself if I said that thought hadn't already crossed my mind. It doesn't take long before my body moves against him in time with the music. He pulls me closer until our bodies are touching, my breasts pressed up against his firm chest. His hands find their way to my arse. Our bodies move together. I raise my hands and slide them up the front of his open suit jacket to feel him. All I feel is the firmness of the muscles under his shirt, and all I want to do is slowly unbutton it so I can see and appreciate the body underneath it.

Lauren Trent, what the hell are you playing at? When did you become so brazen?

It has to be the alcohol.

He lowers his face to mine and my breath catches in the back of my throat. I feel warmth as his mouth hovers there, centimetres away from mine. *Please, God damn it, just kiss me.* I slide a hand up and around the back of his neck, giving him all the invitation he needs.

He takes it.

His lips touch mine, soft and warm, and oh-so-perfect. It takes a moment before my lips move with his. My eyes close as his tongue flicks slowly against my bottom lip. I moan as his tongue sweeps inside. With our bodies still dancing, I'm lost to the unexpected sensations sweeping through my veins.

His growing erection is obvious, showing me he's attracted to me. This kiss is strong and demanding, and I feel the energy buzzing through my bloodstream. Warm hands fondle my arse and I can feel my dress slowly inch up.

Oh, shit.

"We need to stop," he says, breaking contact. "We need to leave because I want more than a quick fumble in my office, and that's where I'll end up dragging you. I want to take my time and enjoy every single inch of your sexy body. Come on. We'll get your bag and I'll leave my number and address for your friend so she doesn't worry about you taking off with a complete stranger."

"But that's what you are. I don't even know your name."

"My friends call me Matt."

"Well, in that case, I presume I'll be calling you Mathew because we aren't friends," I say, with a hint of sarcasm. *Oh, Lauren.*

You're either brave or totally stupid.

"I should hope we're not friends. Friends don't do what we're about to do." He takes my hand in his and we walk back to the table. Abbie stands, hands on her hips, staring at Matt. He leans forward and speaks to her then she smiles before turning to me and giving me a hug. Really! She's meant to be my friend. The sensible one. She's meant to talk me out of doing stupid things.

"This is one way to get David well and truly out of your system. Call me in the morning because I want every last detail."

In the morning? In the morning, I know I'm going to regret whatever happens between me and Matt; of that, there's no question. But for now, with alcohol flowing through my veins, I have the confidence to do this.

Four

THE DRIVE HERE ACROSS TOWN was almost unbearable. Twenty long minutes; every minute passed by slowly, the tension between us building as silence filled his very flash car. I never noticed the make, only that it smelled brand spanking new, as though it was just out of a showroom. Every time I stole a glance in his direction, he was looking at me. It makes me wonder how the hell we managed to get here in one piece.

He steps to the side, letting me into his apartment, and closes the door behind me. I look around; it all looks very new and expensive and not very personal. This is all new to me. What does he expect me to do? Nerves are getting the better of me. What the hell am I doing here? I shouldn't be doing this.

I stand, frozen to the spot, unable to take a step further. I was stupid to think I could go ahead and have a one night stand. His footsteps walk slowly across the floor. I feel his body brush against me before he stands in front of me with his eyes on me. Intense. He runs his gaze over my body and back up to my face. He reaches forward and takes my bag from my hand, placing it down on the sideboard in his grand hallway.

His presence is commanding; his eyes darken, his lips smirking slightly. If I focus on his lips, my nerves might settle. But, no, my nerves don't settle as I watch his lips part a little further. Matt takes my face in his hands, tilting it upwards until my eyes are in line with his.

Heat flares within his eyes and I take a small step closer to him without thinking. There's a sexual pull between us. I wish there wasn't because it would make walking away easier.

He lowers his face to mine. His lips crash against mine with fervour. I wrap my arms around his neck, pulling him close, but still allowing him to control our kiss. He comes across as a man who commands and takes control of everything in his life, and right now, it's me he wants to control.

Maybe I can do this. Allow him control over my body. It's one night only, after all. No expectations.

His hands slide down my back as our kiss intensifies, cupping my arse once again, pulling me closer until our bodies are pressed tightly against the other's. I can feel the muscles of his chest through his shirt. A shirt I need to remove. Slowly, I move my hands from his neck and allow them to travel to his chest, feeling first-hand the firmness I already know is beneath the shirt. I run my hands down, stopping at the waistband of his suit trousers. I pull his shirt free and start to undo the buttons.

His lips leave mine and I miss the connection. As I reach the top button, I look at him; he's watching me and waiting . . . waiting to see what I'm going to do next. He shrugs his jacket and shirt off, and my eyes drop from his face. This man before me works out, a lot. My fingers trace patterns against his skin as they work their way down towards his toned abs. I can just see the hint of a perfect V that leads my eyes lower. I lower my hand and he moans when it brushes against his hard erection.

Matt grabs my dress with urgency, pulling at the hem until it's bunched around my waist. His lips press against mine lightly before his hands slide back to my arse. He takes hold of my thighs and lifts me.

My legs wrap around his waist and he carries me effortlessly through the apartment and straight into the bedroom. His gaze stays on me the entire time. He finally stops beside the enormous bed at the far side of the room and puts me down, all too gently for my liking. His erection rubs against me and I have to stop a moan from escaping. He pulls my dress that is bunched around my waist, and I lift my arms until the dress is free from my skin. It slips from his hands and I watch as it falls in slow motion to the floor.

Turning my attention back to the man before me, goosebumps spread across my skin as his eyes linger on my now heavy chest. It aches for his touch. My whole body is on fire, waiting. His tongue flicks along his bottom lip and now it's my turn to watch and wait. He exhales slowly, and before I know it, his hands thread roughly through my hair and his lips descend on mine once again.

Everything about this kiss screams hot and hurried. There's no Mr Patient. This is demanding. His tongue sweeps desperately inside my mouth, flicking against mine as he tastes and teases.

My hands move around to his back, trying to pull him closer so our skin is touching, but he's a man who wants to stay in control; he holds back. Although, from the glaze in his eyes, I can tell it's taking every ounce of self-control he has.

He releases my hair and pulls back, breaking our kiss. His hands lower on my back until he comes into contact with my bra. Quickly, he unhooks the clasp of my bra and lowers the straps down my arms, letting it fall to the bed and freeing my heavy, tender breasts.

He smiles as his eyes leave my face and travel a little down my body. He cups each breast, and I close my eyes and groan from his warm touch on my skin. My nipples harden instantly when soft fingers brush over them, sending a charge of electricity through my body.

Warm hands guide me, lowering me onto the bed. My head

falls back on the sheets. *Between the sheets is where he wants me.*

"So beautiful." The words leave him in a whisper as he stands before me, eyes running over my almost naked body. "I want to taste you," he says, hooking his fingers inside my knickers. Slowly, teasingly, he pulls them down my legs, removing them and my shoes. His words send chills down my spine, turning me on, exciting me. A very dangerous combination. I want everything he has to offer for one night only.

I gasp when he spreads my legs and lowers his face. My eyes close. Any doubts that were creeping into my mind are now long gone. With one long lick, he runs his tongue from back to front. The fire within me ignites and I know there's going to be no way to stop it until it explodes.

He groans.

He works his tongue back and forth, over and over, slipping it between my folds, flicking the tip of it against me as he moves. Small movements of extra pressure add to my building need. I can no longer fight it; my hips move with each teasing, sensual stroke of his tongue.

Pressure is mounting. I reach my hands down and thread them through his hair, holding him in place, ensuring he finishes the job he's started and sees me across the finish line.

He's driving me crazy and I don't care. Heat flares through me. My body is tight with tension and need. The need to come. He rubs his thumb against my clit. My legs tighten. My body trembles as my orgasm rips through me, flames exploding. I moan loudly.

My legs fall limply to the side and I feel him move between them. The sound of a zipper has me opening my eyes, and I watch as he removes his trousers and boxers in one go, freeing his erection. *Holy crap.*

What the hell am I supposed to do with that? I know what I want to do; taste. I watch with jealousy as he takes it in his hand and slowly slides his hand up and down his length. Pre-cum shines on the end and I lick my lips. He shakes his head and pushes me further up the bed.

He smirks and rolls on a condom. Thank fuck one of us has the ability to think straight because my senses seem to have left me. He crawls up the bed, bringing my ankles with him. *What the hell*? My legs are bent and my feet are now firmly on the bed either side of his hips. His body rests on his arms which are now resting on the bed by my shoulders.

My eyes widen as his dick nudges against me before quickly pushing inside me. I inhale sharply. It's not sore. Shit, that's a lie. Of course it's uncomfortable; I've not had sex since I was four months pregnant with Kate.

"You okay?" he asks, watching me.

I nod. He moves slowly before stilling. He's buried deep inside me, filling me completely. My body is adjusting to the intrusion. He's still watching me; I don't know what he's looking for. A sign, perhaps, that I don't want this. Well, he won't get that from me. Not now.

I reach out my hands, taking hold of his neck and pulling him closer until our skin is touching. I want this, but maybe Abbie is right. Maybe I need this more than I want it.

"I wanted to take my time with you, but now I have you here, I don't think I can. I'm going to fuck you hard then I might let you rest before I have you again. Understood?"

I gasp, and looking into his eyes, I don't doubt for one minute the sincerity behind his words. "Yes," I breathe.

The pace he sets is relentless, pounding over and over, each thrust harder than the last. Closing my eyes, I let my senses takeover. With each thrust deep inside me, I feel a rush of heat, evidence of my building pleasure. Every movement teases me.

His lips come crashing down on mine, and I feel totally and utterly helpless to him. He moves his hands and cups my face as desire builds. This kiss could very well be the death of me. His lips are deliciously wet and soft; the type of lips I could kiss all night long.

My last thought has no place in my head.

Matt pulls his lips away from mine. I open my eyes and his gaze settles on me. He's watching. He flexes his hips and desire rushes through me. The pace slows which I don't want. I need it harder and faster as he pushes me over the edge. He moves his hands from my face, slowly tracing his fingers down my exposed skin until he grabs my shoulders, holding me firmly in place.

I'm helpless to my building pleasure.

A series of moans escape me as he continues thrusting and changing the pace yet again. He moves faster, harder and deeper, and it's only a matter of time. Every muscle in my body tightens. My body trembles. An explosion of heat quickly spreads through my veins.

I cry out as my orgasm takes hold and rips through me violently. I bury my face in his neck as he continues to thrust against me. His moans of pleasure mixed with my now muffled moans fill the room as I feel his own release take hold.

I lift my head and look into his eyes, and his mouth drops to mine. This kiss isn't demanding, it's soft and gentle.

"I want you to join me in the shower then I want you between those sheets, not on top of them."

Shit. A one night stand is one thing, but I can't stay here the rest of the night. "Let me get my breath back and I'll join you."

He kisses me once more before leaving the bed and walking away. It would be wrong to stay, even though part of me wants to. When I hear the shower running, I move quickly, gather my clothes, and put them on. Slipping on my shoes, I leave his bedroom without looking back. I grab my bag on the way out of the front door.

My heart is pounding as I enter a waiting taxi. For the first time in months, I feel so fucking alive, and for that, I have Matt to thank. He's the type of man I could easily fall for, but he's the type of man I shouldn't see again. He's only interested in one thing, and tonight, he got it.

Nothing more than a one night stand.

five

"GET THAT KETTLE ON," ABBIE shouts from my hallway. She has a key to let herself in; it makes it easier when she calls around, especially if I'm busy with the kids. Although, today, as I sit feeling sorry for myself, I can't use the kids as an excuse. I get my arse up and off the couch, where I've been sitting since coming home and having a shower. So far, I've not slept since I came home. Every time I've closed my eyes, he's been there, staring at me with those wild green eyes.

"Tea or coffee?" I shout out.

"Not so bloody loud. Some of us had a lot more to drink than others," she says, entering the kitchen. She looks fresh out of the shower but I take comfort in the fact that she looks as bad as I feel.

"Hangover?"

"Like you wouldn't believe. And coffee, please, with plenty of sugar. Then you can tell me all the details about Mr Sexy."

"I'll make our coffees then I need to get comfy on the couch again. You're not the only one feeling delicate. Then I'll tell you everything. Well, almost everything." She smiles. "Have you heard from your mum?"

"No, but I already know you've been in touch to see how the kids are."

She knows me well. "Yes, they're fine. I was told not to dare go over until it's time for dinner."

"That's Mum for you."

I turn the television down as we settle on the couch. I grab the cover and wrap it around me because, for whatever reason, I can't get heat in me. That may have something to do with coming home in the middle of the night wearing only my dress.

"Talk," she says, taking a sip of her coffee. "Was he as good as he looked?"

"Nothing like going straight for the kill."

"I bet his dick was fucking huge." I try to keep a straight face, but my lips are twitching and I can already feel my face redden at her blunt words. "You, my friend, are blushing. Your bright red face answers my question. That big? Now spill, and don't leave anything out."

We sit cosy on the couch and I tell her all about my night with the handsome stranger. She sits quietly as I give her all the juicy details she has been waiting not-so-patiently for since last night when I walked out of the club on his arm.

"Okay, I have a question. Why the hell did you leave? He made it clear he wanted you to stay and I can only imagine how much more fun you could've had with him."

"Even I know you don't spend the full night with a one night stand. Yes, he made me feel so alive, but I'm not naïve enough to think there could be anything else between us. It was a fun night."

"Right, okay. On a scale of one to ten, where would Mr Sexy be?"

"That's not fair. I gave him an eight at the club. Maybe a nine. Although, I have no doubts if I had stayed the rest of the night, it would've been a perfect ten."

"Fucking hell, Lauren. And you walked away from him. You, my beautiful friend, need your head examined."

"I might, because all I've thought about since I came home

is him."

"Well, it couldn't have been all him because you have checked on the kids."

"Yes, and now it's time to put him behind me and concentrate on my kids and providing for them," I say, taking a deep breath. Yes, last night awakened my senses, but the reality is, I'm a single parent and I want to do my best for my babies. Because they both deserve that from me.

"We have a few hours before we need to be at Mum's, so put a movie on, and if I fall asleep, wake me up in plenty of time," Abbie says, pulling the covers up and over her at the other end of the couch. I put on a movie but I close my eyes and I know neither of us will be watching it.

We open the door to Sandra's house and Luke comes rushing towards us, so full of energy. He jumps straight up into my arms and I give him a sloppy kiss. God, I've missed him. I've missed them both, and now my night out with Matt fills my mind. Guilt floods through me. I wish I could go back and change the events of the night. *What the hell was I playing at?* I'm meant to be responsible. I shouldn't be out on the town sleeping with random men.

"Mummy, Nana says I can stay over anytime because I was such a good boy," he says with enthusiasm.

"Is that right?"

"Yes, it is, but I'm not sure about Kate. She has been a pain." Abbie and I look at each other and try not to laugh at his description of his sister. I know what he means. Since she found her feet, she's into everything, and she never gives her brother a minute's peace. Luke didn't walk until after his first birthday.

"Now, Luke," says Sandra, as we enter the living room. "Kate hasn't been that bad. Of course she can come and stay again too."

Luke pulls a face. He was obviously wanting a night here without Kate. At the mention of her name, Kate comes toddling into the room, holding Les' hand. Her tiny green eyes light up when she sees me. She lets go of Les' hand and walks to me. I bend with Luke still in my arms and I give them both a cuddle together when she throws her arms around my neck.

No better feeling in the world. Feeling wanted and loved by my two gorgeous kids. Even on my darkest of days, they can always make me smile, although I'm pretty sure there have been days when I've wanted to pull my hair out.

"Have my babies both been good?"

"Lauren, the kids are always good, and we are more than happy to have them anytime," Sandra tells me.

I smile and stand with both of them still in my arms then walk the short distance to the couch. "Luke, can you go and help Papa set the table for dinner?" He jumps down and runs to Les and they leave the room.

"Kate looks a bit grumpy," I say, taking in her appearance. Her cheeks are rosy red.

"She's tired. She was restless during the night. I've given her something for her gums; they seem to be annoying her, although it hasn't affected her appetite."

I laugh because, for such a small girl, she does love her food. I have no idea where she puts it. Kate snuggles in, her eyes looking heavy. I see a night at home snuggled up with my babies after we leave here. And given how I feel at the moment, that more than appeals to me. Luke likes to cuddle in with me a lot more now since his dad is gone, while Kate only cuddles when she's not feeling one-hundred percent.

"So, you two, how was your night?" Sandra asks.

Abbie and I exchange glances and I'm sure Sandra has picked up on it.

"It was great to be out," I finally say. "But I won't be making a habit of it."

"Don't say that. You still need time for you away from the kids," Sandra tells me.

"See?" Abbie's voice cuts through the air. "I can start planning our next night out together."

"There's no rush." I'm in no hurry for a repeat of last night.

I sigh heavily and it doesn't go un-noticed by my friend. Who am I kidding? Only myself, it would seem. I would love a repeat performance with Matt given half the chance.

Sandra leaves the room, and I sit and stroke Kate's face. She's very quiet. Abbie and I talk about work. I have a lot on this week for a few clients, so she offers to come over a few nights to entertain the kids. I usually get some work done when Luke is at school and Kate goes for a nap, but I'm increasingly finding myself working long after I get the kids tucked up in bed for the night.

"Mummy! Auntie Abbie! Dinner is ready," Luke calls out, running into the room. My boy never stops bloody running. Everywhere he goes, he runs. I'm forever telling him to slow down before he has an accident.

"Okay, we're coming." I stand, keeping Kate in my arms.

I love a Sunday roast, and it has to be said, Abbie's parents are amazing cooks. Dinner is gorgeous as always, but I feel bad because Kate is exhausted and I want to take her and Luke straight home. I offer to help with the dishes before I leave, but Les tells me not to be so daft and to take them both home.

Sandra gets Kate ready for bed because she thinks she will fall asleep in the car on the way home. Looking at Kate, I'm sure she's right, and as I look at Luke, he might not be far behind her as he stands yawning. Abbie offers to come home with me to give me a hand with them if they fall asleep in the car. I tell her no, that I'll manage, and Luke tells us all there's no way he will fall asleep in the car like Kate.

"Now, you be a good boy for Mummy and help when you get to the house," Sandra tells him, strapping him into his car seat.

"I promise, but I'm always good, Nana."

"I know you are, poppet. Papa and I might come and pick you up one day from school. Would you like that?"

"Yes," he says, with a smile full of love.

"Lauren, will that be okay? I know you have a lot of work on this week. I could take Kate for a few hours before then collect Luke, and give them their tea before bringing them home."

"Please, Mummy? Please?" Luke pleads with me, his eyes big and sad, and I struggle saying no to the look on his precious face right now.

"Sandra, that would be great. Thank you."

"No need to thank me. You know how Les and I feel about the three of you. You are part of our family," she says, with a sad smile. "Now get home and get these two into bed. We'll see you all soon."

I say goodbye and start the engine, and straight away, Luke starts chatting. I find myself grinning as I listen to the excitement in his voice as he tells me everything he's done since I dropped him off yesterday. God, I can't imagine my life without my kids. My thoughts turn to sadness as I think of Abbie. I watched her over the years as she accepted these two, and she is brilliant with them. She and her parents have so much love to give.

Six

"LUKE, COULD YOU PLEASE HURRY up?" I shout up the stairs. He's dragging his heels this morning, and today, I could do without it. "If you don't hurry up you will be late for school," I add. "Oh, sweetie. Mummy needs to sort lunch for Luke," I say to my crying daughter.

"Coming!" he calls.

I'm exhausted. Kate has been restless the whole night. No sooner than I got them both into bed, she woke up screaming in pain. Nothing I did or gave her seemed to help with the pain of teething. It's at times like last night, being up all night, that I miss having someone here to help me with the kids. It can be tiring. Not that David did much with either of them; he left that to me, always saying I was much better with the kids than he was.

Kate still cries, but I've had to put her down to sort out Luke's packed lunch. She's sitting on the floor, tears running down her face, feeling sorry for herself, and in turn, making me feel guilty. I promise I'll make it up to her. I hate seeing her in so much pain. When we drop Luke off at school, I'm going to the chemist to see if they have something else that can help her, then I'm all Kate's until three o'clock when we need to pick Luke back up. Hopefully, she will settle and we can both grab a couple of hours' sleep.

"I'm ready, Mum. Oh no, Kate. Don't cry. It's okay, Mummy will take care of you."

I turn with his lunch bag in my hands and watch as she stands. He holds his arms out to her. She walks straight into him and he gives her a big cuddle. She holds onto him for dear life, still sobbing. God, these two are going to have me crying in a minute.

"Come on. Let's get you to school and then you, little lady, can get some sleep when we come home," I say, picking her up. She rests her head on my shoulder.

"Will she be okay?" Luke asks with concern.

"Yes, she will. She just has some teeth coming in at the back of her mouth, and it's sore, but I'll go and get her some more medicine and that will help her."

"Okay." My answer seems to settle his concern and we leave the house with plenty of time to make it to school before the bell rings.

Kate isn't herself at all today. The whole time we were out she cried. No, I'll rephrase that. She screamed and screamed. There was a lovely elderly lady in the chemist who tried to tell me about an old remedy that I should try, something about cold vegetables. But it was almost impossible to have a conversation and hear what she was telling me above the noise Kate was making.

We are now home and I've grabbed a cover from my bed. I'm going to see if she will settle, cuddling in on the couch with me, and hopefully finally fall asleep. I'm hoping the medicine I've just given her will help. I had planned to do some work for a client today, but Kate comes first. And, if I'm truthful, I'm probably too tired to concentrate on anything today, so a wee day cuddled up with Kate is just what I need.

My phone buzzes; a text from Abbie:

How is my niece today? X

Me: Not so good. I've been up all night with her and now we are lying on the couch and I'm hoping we can both get some sleep.

Abbie: Do you want me or mum to come over later?

Me: I'm not sure. You are at work.

Abbie: Yes I am but I can come to yours as soon as I finish and anyway, we need to talk. I have a proposal for you. I'll give mum a call and see if she can pick up Luke at 3 pm. Go and rest and I'll see you tonight. X

Me: Okay x

I wonder what she wants to talk about. Kate wriggles in my arms and yawns. Her small eyes are heavy and I hope it's only a matter of time before she closes them. She is shattered and she's not the only one. I hold onto her tightly as she snuggles in.

She settles quickly, her steady breathing letting me know she is finally sleeping. I close my eyes and allow myself to drift off to sleep, knowing if she wakes up, I will feel her body wriggle against me.

Visions of Matt fill my dreams.

My phone ringing pulls me from my dreams. I fumble with the covers, trying to find it before the noise wakes Kate.

"Hello," I say, not recognising the number on the screen in front of me.

"Hello. Is this Lauren Trent?" a deep male voice asks.

"Yes. Can I help you?"

"I believe you can. Mr and Mrs Wright recommended you to me."

"Ah, yes, a lovely couple. What can I do for you, Mr . . . ?"

"Sorry, it's Mr Anderson. I'm looking to rebrand my whole

business." The name sounds oddly familiar. I'm sure the Wrights have spoken about him. "I was wondering when you would be free for a meeting. I've seen the work you've done for the Wrights and I've no doubt you're the best person for the job."

"I'm afraid it would have to be next week."

"Oh, shit. Sorry, is there no way we could meet sooner?"

I suppose I could arrange an evening meeting with him here, and ask Abbie to mind the kids, although I don't usually meet new clients at home. I'm sure it would be much easier meeting him somewhere else, but I like to be here for the kids at night. "I could do an evening this week but it would have to be at my home."

"Would tomorrow be okay with you? I'm keen to start on this project. Sooner rather than later. I've been putting it off for long enough."

"Tomorrow it is then." I'm just giving him my address when Kate wakes up crying. "Ssh. Ssh, baby girl," I say, stroking the side of her face.

"Someone doesn't sound very happy," he says, in an almost soothing voice. Memories of my night with a tall, handsome stranger flood my mind.

"No. She's not well."

"I won't keep you and I look forward to meeting with you tomorrow night."

We end the call and I know I will be thanking Mr and Mrs Wright in the near future because they are some of my clients that came with me when David and I went our separate ways; they've put a lot of work my way over recent months. I should give them a call and check out Mr Anderson, hear what they have to say.

"Well, baby girl, you look better and don't sound so grumpy," I say, as Kate stretches her arms out. I look at the time on my phone; it's almost one p.m. We've both managed to get a couple of hours' sleep, so I should make us some lunch. Hopefully, she will eat something.

I quickly change Kate's nappy before going into the kitchen. She does seem more content and rested as she toddles along beside me. Lifting her, I put her in the high chair so she can watch me. I also give her a drink.

As I wait on some soup heating, I pause and take a moment, staring at my beautiful baby girl. Her dark hair sits in a wavy mess on top of her head; it looks as though I might get a bobble in it. She lifts her head and looks at me; her green eyes sparkle as she smiles. She is perfect.

David is a lot of things, but he has given me two beautiful children, and I will always be grateful to have them in my life.

I take a phone call from Sandra. She tells me Abbie has been in touch and that she will collect Luke from school, then help with the kids until Abbie gets here after work. I've always been close to Abbie's parents, but since Mum died, they have been lifesavers to me. Yes, Grant and Liz have done their bit too, but they both lead very busy lives. Sandra is always there when I need her help or advice. Sometimes I feel as though they give me so much and I don't have much to offer them in return.

The next two hours fly by with Kate, and the medicine does seem to be helping her. She's definitely much more her normal, cheery self. We've spent our time playing on the floor with some toys, and cuddling in together on the couch. A nice relaxing afternoon.

"Mummy! Kate! I'm home," Luke calls out. I hear him running through the hallway. He rushes into the sitting room. "Is Kate okay?"

"Yes, she's fine," I tell him. Sandra comes into the room, smiling, carrying a large bag along with Luke's school things. "Hi, Sandra. Why is Nana carrying your things? Luke, what have I told you?"

"That I have to carry it myself. Sorry, Mum. Sorry, Nana." His shoulders sag as he walks back to Sandra and takes his school and lunch bags from her.

"You both look comfy. Is she any better?"

"She seems to be, but I might have her in with me tonight so I can keep an eye on her. Have you been shopping?" I ask, looking at the bag she has.

"This." She lifts the bag and shakes her head slightly. "No, but I have brought over some food for the freezer and a lasagne for dinner."

"Sandra, you didn't have to do that."

"Nonsense. I have to ensure you're all eating, including Abbie. I have some for Abbie to take away with her. I swear that girl only ever eats here or when we have you all over for dinner." Sandra has a point. Abbie's kitchen is in showroom condition because she doesn't use it. We both burst out laughing, obviously thinking the same thing.

"Well, Kate, are you coming to see Nana and we can help Luke with his homework, and let Mummy go and do some work?" Kate giggles as Sandra lifts her arms up into the air. "Now, you, my dear girl, can go into your office and see what you get done. I'll see to these two for a couple of hours."

I stand and give her a kiss on the cheek and she ushers me away with a warm, motherly smile.

It's amazing what I can accomplish in a few hours. I worked on some new ideas for one client, and spoke to another client who wanted to finalise the work I had done for her. She was so pleased with the final outcome. I even managed to call Mr Wright and he confirmed that Mr Anderson is a friend and business associate of his. He understood my reservations about having a new client at home, but he told me I had nothing to worry about, that Mr Anderson is very professional when it comes to business.

"Mum said you were in here."

I almost jump out of my chair as the office door creeps open. "Shit, Abbie. You bloody scared me."

"Sorry. You busy?"

"What do you think? Although, I've got a fair bit done since Mum basically sent me in here."

"Well, come and have dinner. It's ready."

We walk through to the kitchen, and it smells heavenly. Kate is in her high chair. She grins and babbles when she sees me. Luke is sitting down and Sandra is just finishing serving dinner; lasagne, garlic bread, and fresh salad.

"Well, you two, sit down and tuck in."

"What is Dad doing if you're having dinner here?"

"Abbie, love, your dad is more than capable of fending for himself." Sandra turns her attention to Luke, who has decided to start feeding Kate a tomato. "No, Luke. Give her this instead," she tells him, handing over a slice of garlic bread.

Chat around the table is light, and Luke tells us all about his day at school, what work he did, and who he played with. It's always Liam. The two of them have become really good friends. I love hearing about his day because he is always excited about it. Kate is very vocal and makes such a mess with her food. I swear there is some sauce in her hair.

"Okay, you two need to talk. I will get these two bathed because a certain someone needs it." Sandra picks up a very dirty Kate, takes Luke's hand, and leaves the kitchen.

I frown, looking at Abbie, whose expression gives nothing away. Why do I get the feeling she's up to something?

"Okay, what's going on?" I ask, as we start to clear the dishes on the table.

"I have a proposition for you and I want you to take your time and give it some serious consideration. Please?"

"Okay."

"How about you and me going into business together?"

I laugh because it's the funniest thing I've heard all day. Abbie has a great job within her dad's company doing marketing. She has loads of perks, including getting time off at a moment's notice. I can't understand why she would want to give all that up to go into business with me. "Lauren, I'm being serious."

"Sorry, but you have a great job, and do I look as though I have time to run a business?"

"You have to hear me out." I nod and sit down. The dishes can wait ten minutes. "You are amazing at what you do. You already have a good client base, and with a little bit of extra work, you could easily build on that. Graphic design and marketing go hand in hand. There is so much more we could do together as a business. Let's face it, you send clients to me. The idea came from Dad. He's even offered to help us with everything from funding to premises. He wants us both to have security."

She sits down opposite me and I'm speechless. "There's a lot for me to think about, especially with the kids. I'm already spending too much time working."

"Yes, and as you've just said, you're putting in longer hours. Wouldn't it be nice to work during the day and come home at night, spend time with the kids, and not have to worry about getting work done for clients because you would've already done it?"

"But I have Kate during the day."

"Yes, I know that, but we're a family. Mum and Dad want us to do this and we all know Mum is looking for an excuse to spend more time with Luke and Kate." I smile, feeling myself getting emotional at her words. "Think about it. There's no rush. I think it would give us both something to focus on. Some direction in our lives."

"Of course I'll think about it. Now, while we're on the subject of work, can you come here tomorrow night? I have a client coming at seven p.m."

"Yes, I'll be here. The kids will love Auntie Abbie tucking them into bed."

"Abbie." I say her name as she stands. "We might not be blood relatives, but if I had to choose a sister, I would choose you. And as for Mum and Dad . . . I don't know where I would be without all of you."

"Babe. I feel the same. We all love you and those two munchkins upstairs. Now, let's get this kitchen tided and then I'll try and talk Mum into going home so you can get an early night."

She must be kidding. There's no way I'm going to sleep after this discussion.

Seven

I WAS RIGHT. I GOT very little sleep and it wasn't because of Kate, although she did sleep in my bed with me, and for someone so small, she sure takes up a lot of space. No, there were two reasons I couldn't sleep. Firstly, Abbie gave me a lot to think about with her proposal. Part of me wants to at least give it a go and see what happens, but another part of me reflects on how things turned out with David and me and the business. Not that Abbie and I would ever fall out, but the whole business situation with David has cast doubts in the back of my mind.

The strange thing is, I know Abbie and I working together makes good business sense. Graphics and marketing *do* go together, and I have no doubts that the business wouldn't interfere with our relationship.

But would going into business now be the right thing for me and the kids? They are my top priority. Their arsehole of a sperm donor has chosen to walk away from them; they need stability, and the only person this can come from is me. I would want to talk to Sandra and Les before I made any sort of a decision that could affect our future, even though Sandra was quick to tell me last night that she is more than happy to have the kids on a daily basis.

We would all need to sit around the table and plan it properly if we went ahead with it. But it does have a certain appeal to me.

The second reason I couldn't sleep was Matt. I've not been able to get him out of my mind. Or rather, how he made me feel. If I close my eyes, I can still see him, every last inch of him.

Bloody hell.

I don't want to be thinking about Matt as I stand at the school gates, waiting for the bell to ring, and Luke to come bounding out full of energy. Sandra has Kate this afternoon. She was going to the park for a bit so I can spend some time with Luke. Today his homework can wait until later when we're home. I'm going to take him out for something to eat as a treat. We don't normally eat junk food, but if he wants a burger or a pizza then today we will.

The school run was awful a few months ago; I hated it. Some of the other mums would stand whispering at the side of me, never acknowledging I was there. I knew they were talking about me. *'There's that poor woman whose man fucked off with her sister.'* Now, it's not so bad, and I try to ignore it when people stare. Luke's friend Liam's parents, Patrick and Emma, started talking to me. They both made doing the school run a little less painful. Emma is lovely. I'm sure they've heard the gossip but not once has it ever been discussed between us, and for that, I'm grateful.

Today, though, there's no-one I recognise, but that doesn't bother me. I just want to spend some time with my boy. The bell rings and kids run free, so full of energy. It's a few minutes before I spot him. He sees me and waves before turning and saying goodbye to his friends.

"I thought Nana might get me today. Do you not need to work?" he asks, taking my hand.

"Nope, I'm all yours. Where would you like to go for something to eat?"

"Where's Kate?"

I knew he would ask. "She's with Nana, so you and I can do something together before she comes home. So I thought an early dinner."

"Okay, can we have anything at all?"

"Whatever you want," I tell him, as we walk back toward the car. In the car, he finally decides on pizza; I can cope with that. As I drive, he tells me all about his day. This is one thing I try to keep the same every day. I always ask how his day was. He tells me about a boy in his class who got into trouble for pushing a girl who fell over in a puddle. We talk about his work and his teacher, who he adores.

The one thing about my darling son is, he can talk for bloody Scotland, but I love that about him. He's confident and that's a great quality to have.

When we're in the restaurant, we order a large pizza between us, knowing that if we don't eat it, we can take it home.

"Mummy, I want to join a football team," he says, and then takes a large gulp of his juice.

"Do you? Who plays football?"

"Liam." Of course it would be Liam. "He started last week and loves it but his dad takes him." I watch as the smile that was there only seconds ago turns to a deep frown.

"Why don't I speak to Liam's mum or dad at school tomorrow, find out the details, and I can take you."

"But I know you don't like football."

God bless him, he's right, I don't, but I wouldn't let it stop me from taking him.

"I'll take you if you want to go. I'm not sure about standing on the sidelines in the rain to watch you play," I say, laughing.

"You could always sit in the car with Kate."

This boy of mine has an answer for everything.

A waitress approaches us with our pizza. "Yes, I could. Now, I think we should tuck into this." I turn and say thank you before she leaves our table.

Abbie's car is in the drive and Sandra's is parked out on the street when we arrive home. I park mine in the drive and Luke runs from the car and into the house. My phone rings and it's my dad. I stop at the front door.

"Hey you," I say. It's funny, but I still sometimes feel reluctant to call him *Dad*. Silly, I know, considering things are much better between us.

"How's my girl and my grandkids?"

"We're all good."

"You sure?" I can hear the tone in his question. He's always calling to make sure I'm okay.

"Yes, I'm just home. Luke and I went for pizza. I'm just going to see how Kate has behaved for Sandra."

"That's great. Okay, I'm going to be in Glasgow tomorrow for work. How about we meet up for an early dinner? With the kids, and of course, Abbie is more than welcome. I'm missing you."

"Yes, of course we'll be there. Just drop me a text letting me know where and when. Look, I need to go and organise the kids. I have a new client coming to meet me tonight."

"That's fine, sweetheart. I'll see you all tomorrow."

We end the call and I go inside. Everyone is in the sitting room. Abbie is lying on the floor with Kate crawling and climbing all over her, giggling away. I laugh. Kate stops, her tiny bright green eyes lock with mine, and she smiles. She climbs off Abbie and toddles straight into my arms, kissing me. Small moments like this might not seem like much to others, but to me, it's the world.

I don't claim to be the greatest mum in the world, but there is nothing I wouldn't do for either of them.

Sandra only stays long enough to tell me how Kate has been today, and that she gave her dinner. She also asked if I had given much thought to Abbie's proposal. I told her yes, that I've not thought about much else. But I also told her I would want us all to sit down and discuss how it could work for me. We've decided to wait until after Kate's birthday celebrations at the weekend, which Sandra said she is more than happy to help with.

God, I love her.

Abbie and I play with the kids for a while, and before I know it, it's almost seven p.m. Nearly time for my meeting with Mr Anderson. We make a start on tidying up the toys on the floor when there's a knock on the front door.

"I'll get it," Abbie says, standing and leaving the room.

"Will you help Auntie Abbie get Kate ready for bed? And when I've finished my meeting, I will come up and tuck you both in, if you're still awake."

"Lauren," Abbie calls. "Lauren, you might want to hurry up."

There's an edge to her voice. I wonder what's wrong. She knows I'm on my way and that I wouldn't intentionally leave her standing with a client for long.

"Mummy, you don't need to ask."

When the hell did my baby boy get so grown up? He's changed so much lately. I pick up Kate, walk out into the hallway, and freeze.

"Mummy, will you remember about football?" Taking a deep, pained breath, I close my eyes for a split second. God, how I wish I could go back to the weekend and change everything that happened.

I open my eyes, staring straight ahead in shock. Not who I was expecting to see standing in the hallway of my house. I now understand why Abbie was calling my name. Bloody hell. This is awkward, but he does look hotter than I remember.

"Mummy?"

"Sorry." I turn to my son. "Yes, I'll remember and speak to Liam's parents about football. Now, go and be a good boy for Auntie Abbie."

"Come on, precious," Abbie says, taking Kate from my hands and winking at me. "Bath time for you two. We'll let Mummy work." She avoids eye contact with me and I'm not surprised. Shit. I don't know what to say.

"Lauren." Matt's voice is formal as he holds out his hand to me. "I don't think we got around to proper introductions," he says with a smirk.

"Mr Anderson," I say, shaking his hand; it's warm in mine.

"I think we can lose the formalities, don't you? After all, I'm sure I've seen parts of your body I'm certain other clients haven't." This is going to be torturous. He's not going to make this easy for me. I stare at our joined hands, praying that he lets go. "Now, we have a few things to sort out, don't you think? First, why the FUCK did you run out on me? No, maybe on second thought, don't answer that."

"Let's go into my office and we can talk about what you want me to do."

"There's lots I want you to do, but now, it seems so inappropriate. Are both kids yours?" he asks, finally letting go of my now very sweaty hand.

"Yes." I lead the way into my office. He looks around before sitting down. "Can I get you anything to drink?"

"No." He pauses and draws in a deep breath, and for a moment, I think he's going to say something about Saturday night. "I should tell you what I'm thinking about doing for the restaurant and club."

"Rebranding, you said on the phone." Why the hell didn't I pick up on his voice last night?

"Yes, that's right." There's a long pause and it looks as though he's feeling as uncomfortable as me. "I now understand why you left in such a fucking hurry. To get home to your family, and I presume, husband. Don't worry, I won't utter a fucking word. Your secret is safe with me."

So much for Mr Anderson being professional when it comes to business. I swipe my hand across my desk, sending papers flying across the room. "What the FUCK? You really have a low opinion of me. Who the hell do you think you are? There is no husband, boyfriend, or partner on the scene. Not that it's any of your business. You are only in my home because you wanted to do business with me." The bloody cheek of him. Every muscle in my body quivers as my heartbeat pounds in my chest. "I think you need to leave," I say, moving from my seat and walking to the door.

"Miss Trent, I'm sorry. I shouldn't have said that. I presumed wrongly."

"No kidding. But I think it would be for the best. I don't think I'll be able to work with someone who speaks to me the way you have." I huff, still standing by the door, my hand clenched around the door handle.

"Can we start again?" he asks, his voice now calm and softer than the angry tone of moments ago. "I do want to work with you, regardless of what went on between us. According to the Wrights, you are the best they've worked with."

"The Wrights are good clients. They came with me when I left the business I co-owned." Crap! Why the hell did I say that? I didn't mean to say it. I walk back to my desk and sit down. His eyes are on me and he's frowning. He opens his mouth but nothing comes out.

"Why would you leave your business?" he finally asks.

"I don't think that's any of your concern," I answer dryly.

"I think it is. I need to know who I'm going to be working alongside. I don't think there would be a good enough reason for me to walk away from a business. So, yes, I would like to know." His tone is even as he speaks.

"How about walking into your office and finding your partner fucking your sister? Would that do it?" I snap, and stare at my hands that are clasped together, my knuckles whitening with the pressure.

"Fuck, Lauren. I'm sorry. Yes, that would be reason enough. I do hope you got something out of the business?"

Fuck. Is there anything about me he doesn't want to know?

"Yes, I did. Now, can we move onto work? My personal life isn't up for discussion."

"Yes, of course. You've been in the club and restaurant," he says, smirking and wide-eyed. Oh boy! Haven't I just, and look where it ended up. In his bed. I'm sure my face flushes with the reminder. He lets out a low laugh as he studies me. Yes, he knows my chain of thoughts.

Could this be any more fucking embarrassing?

We spend the next hour and a half talking about what he's hoping to achieve. New branding is top of his list; everything from the sign above the front door to the menus in the restaurant. He also wants to spend a lot of money on a big marketing campaign, and this is where I think of Abbie. I tell him that Abbie is in marketing, and as far as I'm concerned, she is one of the best in the area. He says he'll think about that, but wants to know his brand is solid going forward.

To me, that makes perfect business sense.

We are just wrapping up when there's a knock on the door, and Abbie sticks her head in. "I'm going to head home. Kate is sleeping and Luke says he wants you to tuck him in before he goes to sleep."

"Thanks for tonight. We're just finished." I look at Matt and he nods in agreement. "I'll text you as soon as I hear from Dad about where we're meeting him."

"Okay. How long is he in town for?"

"He travels home tomorrow night."

"Well, I'll see you and the kids tomorrow then. Matt, I'll see you around."

"I'm sure you will," he says before she leaves. "I'd better go and let you see to your son."

"Yes, and when he's settled, I'll make a start on your work."

"There's no rush. Your family comes first. As long as we can work together and I see progress, I'll be happy." We both stand at the same time and I walk him to the front door. He stops and takes a pen from his inside pocket and scribbles on a business card. "The business number, but also my mobile. Feel free to call me anytime."

"Okay."

He takes my hand, lifting it to his mouth, and places a warm soft kiss in the centre, leaving my hand tingling all over. "Thank you, Lauren."

I watch as he walks away to his very expensive car. The car, only a few nights ago, I was in.

Eight

OF ALL THE BLOODY RESTAURANTS in Glasgow city centre, Dad had to pick this one to meet us in. Matt's. Part of me doesn't want to see him, but there's a part of me that is desperate to see him again. Although, I'm sure from his point of view, we will only be seeing each other in a professional capacity. Let's face it, a successful businessman isn't going to be interested in me now he knows about my kids, if he was ever interested in the first place.

It's time to face facts. Saturday night was a one night stand.

"We're here again." Abbie sounds very dramatic as she speaks. She has quizzed me several times on what Matt and I spoke about. I tried to convince her it was strictly professional, but she doesn't believe me.

"Luke, come and take my hand, please. We don't want you getting lost. It's very busy." I have Kate in my arms and she won't keep still. All she wants is to be put down so she can walk. I wish I'd brought her buggy with me.

"Have you spoken to him today?"

"No, but I have been busy working on a few designs for him," I say as we enter. I give my name to the woman who greets us at the door. Her eyes linger on me for longer than they should before she smiles and shows us to our table, where my dad is already sitting. Why would she do that? Maybe it's because she was here on Saturday night when I left with her boss. That would explain it.

"Can I get you a high chair?"

"Yes, thank you." I turn to face my dad. "Hope we haven't kept you waiting long."

"No, sweetheart," he says, standing and giving me a kiss on the cheek. He takes Kate from my arms. "Look at you, gorgeous girl. You've got so big. And as for you." He turns his attention to Luke. "You look very handsome. How's school? I want you to tell me all about it."

Dad sits down, still with Kate in his arms, and Luke sits in the seat beside him. I can't help but smile as my son launches into telling him all about his friends and school. Abbie and I take a seat, and I find myself staring into space.

Abbie nudges me. "Are you okay?"

"Yes, it's just strange seeing the kids with him."

She nods. I don't have to tell her any more; she knows me better than most. She knows all about my relationship with the man who now sits before me, happy and relaxed with my kids. Abbie was the first friend I made when we came to Scotland to stay. Everyone else at school made fun of my accent. She accepted me as I was and we've been inseparable since the very first day we met.

A waiter comes over and asks us what we'd like to drink. "Mum, can I have juice?" Luke asks.

"Yes, but only one."

"So, sweetheart, how have you been?" Dad asks, putting Kate in the high chair.

"I've been good." His eyes hold my gaze and he frowns, not truly believing my answer. "Really, I have."

"Abbie?" Dad looks at her, seeking her reassurance, which I know she will give him. If she was worried about me at all, she would tell him.

"Adam, honestly. They are all great and she has me and my parents to keep an eye on her, and then there's these two. They keep her busy."

That's all true. I don't have time to be anything other than okay.

We all sit chatting and reading through the menu. Dad tells me he has Kate's birthday present in a bag under the table. Bloody hell, the bag is enormous. What the hell has he got her? He also tells me there is something for Luke. He doesn't have to do this; shower the kids with gifts when he sees them. Luke is more than happy to spend time with his grandad. Dad tells me there is something in the bag for me too. I shake my head.

I read out what's on the menu for Luke, but he doesn't seem all that impressed with it, and I'll be honest, there's not a great kids choice. Something I will mention to Matt when I see him. I already know I'll order soup for Kate, although I'm sure she will want to feed herself. That's not happening; she makes too much mess.

Shivers run down my spine and my heartbeat starts racing as I sense someone watching me. I try not to, but I find myself scanning the restaurant, searching for him. My eyes stop at the far end of the bar.

Matt is standing there, a few customers in front of him, but he's looking in our direction. I smile before turning away. The waiter comes back to our table and asks if we're ready to order.

"Can you come back? We're still waiting on one more," Dad says, looking toward the door.

"Who are we waiting for?" I close my eyes and rub my forehead. It has to be Stacey. Why didn't I think about this?

"Your sister."

"Please tell me this is a joke," Abbie says with her voice raised. Luke stops talking.

"No, it's not. Of course I'd want to see both of my daughters when I'm in town." Dad looks between me and Abbie, puzzled by her outburst.

"Abbie, he doesn't know. I haven't told him," I say, lowering my voice because I'm aware that Luke's attention is on me.

"What am I missing? What is it you haven't told me?"

I don't know if I can do this. I didn't tell him because I didn't want him stuck in the middle of something. He's not here in Scotland often.

"Lauren, tell me."

I try to lower my voice yet again, and Abbie starts talking to Luke to distract him. "The day I went to the office, it was Stacey. David had been having an affair with Stacey, and they are still very much together."

"No! She wouldn't." He looks at me and glances to Abbie. She nods, confirming it's true. "Why didn't you tell me?"

"Because I didn't want you feeling as though you had to take sides. I thought it would be easier on everyone if you didn't know." Movement at the side of me catches my eye. I turn to see Matt standing at our table. Has he overheard our conversation? He offers me a sad smile and places his hand softly on my shoulder. That will be my answer then. Yes.

"Lauren, it's good to see you."

"Mr Anderson." Dad looks between Matt and me, trying to work out who he is. "Dad, this is Mr Anderson. He's a new client."

"Mr Trent," Matt says, holding his hand out to my dad. "Your daughter came highly recommended to me. You must be very proud of her. I'm looking forward to working on the rebranding of this place." Always the professional.

"Yes, I'm very proud and I'm sure you will be happy with the final designs."

"No fucking way!" Abbie shouts, startling Luke and Kate. Luke jumps and frowns.

"Abbie!" I scold her, but her eyes are focused behind me. Without turning, I know Stacey has just entered the restaurant.

Why the hell could she not just cancel like she's done many times before when Dad's been visiting? Surely she would've known I would be here with the kids. Am I ready to spend time in her company? I don't think I am. I don't want to be here. The desire to run out is strong, but I won't.

"Daddy!"

My heart sinks. David is here. There's an empty feeling in the pit of my stomach. Luke's eyes light up and he jumps from his seat and runs toward him. *Please let this be okay*. Luke hasn't seen his dad in seven months, so of course my son is going to be excited.

"Adam, this isn't good. David hasn't had any contact with the kids in seven months," Abbie tells Dad. I finally stand, turning around, and I'm met with Matt's eyes. Something passes between us. I draw in a deep breath and slowly follow Luke, because deep down, I have the most horrible feeling that this meeting isn't going to end well for my son.

"Daddy!" David's eyes dart around the room and I know he's looking for his quickest escape. *Bloody coward*. Luke stands in front of David and Stacey. It looks to me as though she is holding his hand tightly, not wanting to let go. She looks very smug with herself. Neither of them acknowledge Luke. "I need to leave," David tells Stacey, who looks bemused by the whole situation. She's fucking loving this. I can't believe she would deliberately hurt my children. David turns his back on Luke and slowly steps away.

Luke starts crying, uncontrollable sobs.

"You bastard." The words are out of my mouth before I realise what I'm saying as I pick Luke up, wrapping my arms tightly around him and protecting him. "How can you do this to Luke? I hope you feel good about this!" I scream at him. Luke buries his face in my neck and I feel his tears roll down his face. David turns but avoids looking at me.

Matt moves quickly, placing his hand on David's shoulder, stopping him. "What the fuck is wrong with you?" Matt hisses through gritted teeth. "You're not a man. A real man would never turn his back on his child, leaving his son crying."

David shrugs his shoulders. I turn to check on Kate, and Abbie is entertaining her. Dad is now standing beside me, looking somewhat bewildered. Has he heard what Matt said to David? I think the whole restaurant heard. Dad is the first to admit he fucked up, but I'm sure it still hurts him.

"Hi, Dad," Stacey says, smiling. I don't know what the fuck she has to smile about. If it wasn't for Luke in my arms, I'm sure I would've slapped the smile from her face.

"Don't *Dad* me. I'm disgusted with you."

"But . . ."

"Save it. I've lost all respect for you after this little stunt tonight. Nothing you can say is going to make this situation better. If you had any sense and thought back to your own childhood without me, you would be encouraging David to see his kids. Because he might be infatuated with you now, but he will resent you years down the line when he realises he's missed out on so much. Luke is far too young to understand. He's going to go through life, like you both did, thinking he's done something wrong. And he doesn't deserve this."

"There's no-one to blame but Lauren. It's not my fault she couldn't keep her man happy."

I cringe at the words. Matt catches my eye. He opens his mouth and I shake my head slightly, but he notices. He closes his mouth.

"You are one spiteful little girl."

"Dad, stop. She can say what she wants. I don't need to listen to the crap she spouts from that vicious mouth. I'm going to take the kids home."

"No, Lauren. Stacey is the one leaving."

"It's okay. I'm going. It was nice to catch up." She turns on her heel and walks toward the door, where David is waiting on her.

Did Stacey plan this? Is my sister really that spiteful? Yes, on both counts. I hate that she has hurt Luke. That they've both hurt him.

"Lauren, go and sit down with your family. Stay and have dinner, please," Matt says softly, his hand against my back. Luke lifts his head, still crying.

"I don't know."

"Sweetheart, please. I want to spend a bit of time with you."

Luke's body shakes against mine. I can't get over the fact that David refused to acknowledge him. A little boy who has spent his short childhood worshipping his daddy.

"Okay," I reluctantly say. Dad holds out his arms and takes Luke from me. "Are you okay?" Luke nods and I wipe his tears away.

"Babe, are you okay?" Abbie asks, handing me a drink.

"Yeah. I just hate that he's hurt Luke again."

"As I've told you before, Luke will be fine because of you, no-one else. David will have to face up to what he's done sooner or later. One day, this will haunt him, but at the moment, he's too infatuated with her, for whatever reason. And believe me, she is nothing special. Sorry, Adam. I know she's your daughter."

"Abbie is right, sweetheart. This will haunt him," Dad says.

I offer him a slight smile. Dad asks Luke about football and now my son flows into a full conversation about joining a local team with his friend Liam.

"Lauren."

I turn around to face Matt. "Sorry, Matt."

"Don't apologise. Will you be okay?"

"Yes. I'm tougher than I look."

He shoots me a knowing look. "I don't doubt it." God, I wonder what is going through his mind. On second thoughts, I don't want to know. "I'll get a waiter to take your order, and this is on me."

"No," I say.

"Lauren, this isn't up for debate." His voice is stern and his eyes are narrowed. He turns, leaving the table, and my eyes follow him as he walks back toward the bar. I shouldn't, but I allow my eyes to linger on him longer than I should. The words he spoke to David were true. He didn't have to say them, but the anger in his voice was a bit intimidating. He didn't have to say anything, so why did he?

Dad manages to keep Luke entertained with talk of football. He tells him he would love to take him to a game. We'll see about that. Dad tells Luke he should try lots of sports to see what he likes. The rest of our time passes quickly and uneventfully, which I'm grateful for.

Matt was very attentive to us for the rest of the evening, although now that we're leaving, he's nowhere to be found.

"Sweetheart, I'm sorry for tonight. Will you all be okay?" Dad asks as we stand outside the restaurant. He has Kate in his arms, and it has to be said, he looks lost.

"Yes, we'll be fine."

"I wish I could be here at the weekend for this one's birthday. I'm going to try and get up more often, and maybe next time I could come up and spend the weekend with you and the kids?"

"We'd like that."

"Or maybe you could all come and stay with me during the summer holidays."

"We'll see what happens about the business." We spoke about Abbie's proposition, and he was very encouraging and offered to help in any way he could.

He gives Kate a kiss and hands her back to me before picking up Luke. "Remember and look after your mum and sister for me, sport, and I'll see you soon."

"I will." Dad gives him a kiss and I can see he's struggling to let us go. All our emotions are still running high. There's no doubt what happened earlier is the reason behind it.

He puts Luke down and Abbie takes his hand. Dad wraps his arms around me and Kate, and I think I might cry. "I'm so sorry, sweetheart. For everything. I never stopped loving you or Stacey. If I had been around, she might not have ended up so bitter and twisted."

"The way Stacey is isn't your fault. I've turned out okay."

"You've turned out more than okay. I love you so much. I'll speak to you in a few days."

"I love you too." I lift my head and see his tears. That's the first time since I was a little girl that I've told him I love him. I suddenly realise I do mean those three little words.

Nine

I FLOP DOWN ON MY sofa, relieved that I've finally managed to get Luke settled. Kate settled straight away, she was exhausted, but not Luke. I had a mountain of questions from my upset son, who had finally cried himself to sleep in my arms. The kids aren't the only ones tired by the turn of events tonight; I'm shattered. I know I should give in and go to bed, but I'm so wound up. It might be a school night, but I think I more than deserve the large glass of wine I've poured myself.

What a night it's been.

The bloody nerve of Stacey. I swear she has more balls than any man I've ever known. What she did to Luke tonight was unforgivable. She deliberately set out to hurt someone tonight—I'm sure that someone was me—but to do that to her own nephew . . . I have no words for her.

I'm grateful to my dad for getting Luke settled so quickly at the restaurant with talk of football. Dad looked furious with both David and Stacey. I should've told him before tonight what had been going on.

And as for Matt, he had a look of thunder on his face as he confronted David. I still can't believe he approached David.

Now I have thoughts of Matt firmly in my mind. I close my

eyes and all I see is him. My thoughts are of Saturday night, and not just the time we spent at his apartment. No, my thoughts start with the very first time our eyes met. There was something irresistible about him. Something about the way he looked at me made me feel wanted and desired. Then there was the dance floor . . .

I mentally chastise myself for these thoughts. I open my eyes and shake my head.

As I take a drink, my phone rings. It won't be Abbie; I've already spoken to her since I got home. She was worried about me and the kids. I reassured her more than once that we would be fine. I pick up my phone and see Matt's name on the caller ID.

"Hey," I say trying to sound cheerier than I feel, and wondering why he's calling me.

"Lauren, I wanted to catch you before you left then something came up. Then I wanted to call but thought you would be busy with the kids." He's rambling.

"Yeah, it took me a while to get Luke settled into his bed. I've just sat down with a glass of wine that I think I deserve." Now it's me that's rambling.

"Yes, I think you do. How is Luke?"

"He's fine. He must take after me. I'm just hoping this doesn't set him back." Why I tell him this, I don't know. This feels like a very strange conversation. I wonder if there's a point to it.

"Lauren, I'm on my way to yours. I need to see you. I promise I won't stay long. I just need to know you're okay."

"I'm fine. I was planning on finishing this drink and going to bed."

"I'll be there in ten minutes and I won't keep you, I promise."

"Okay." I close my eyes when he ends the call, sinking further into the sofa with a sigh. I hope this isn't work related because I don't want to think about work. Especially not tonight. But now I've heard his voice, work is the last thing on my mind. I shouldn't feel this attraction that I do for him. Although, I don't think it's work that's bringing him to my door tonight. He sounded genuinely concerned about me and the kids. There was a certain edgy tension to his voice.

When he was standing inside my hallway last night, I should've used what little common sense I have left and told him I couldn't work for him. What the hell was I thinking? It's going to be so bloody hard for me to remain professional around him considering how intimate we've been.

I'm going to have to keep my emotions in check.

I allow myself to sit with thoughts of Matt Anderson firmly in my mind when there's a knock at the front door. Setting my glass down, I stand, giving myself a quick glance over, and I'm relieved I haven't yet changed from my clothes.

"Hey," I say, opening the door and standing to the side, allowing him to enter.

He stops abruptly, turns to face me, and places his hands on my shoulders, pulling me toward him as he hugs me. This feels strange. Slightly weird, but nice. "How are you? And I mean truthfully."

"What is it you want to hear?" I pull from his grip. "Why are you so bloody concerned?" I snap.

"Lauren . . . I could tell you were upset earlier."

"Come on through." I sigh deeply before leading the way into the sitting room. "Yes, I was hurt, but not for myself. I was angry for the way he treated Luke. My son didn't deserve that from his so-called father. Please sit down. Can I get you anything?"

I sit down on the couch and take a drink from my wine.

"No, thank you." His eyes roam the room, stopping at the sideboard where I have loads of pictures of the kids. "Lauren, you do know you're better off without him?"

"I am, but Luke's not. I know only too well what it's like not having my dad around for a good chunk of my childhood. When my parents split up, we moved up here and Dad stayed in London, and we drifted apart. So, yes. I know I'm better off, but I wish he wanted to be in the kids' lives."

"I'm sorry."

"You don't have to be sorry. But thank you for stepping in and saying what you said to David."

"I just don't understand how he could be so unaffected by his own son. Fucking hell, the way he turned away from him made me so angry. Can I ask a question?" I nod. "How long were you together?"

"Seven years. We had the kids, a nice house, and the business together. It obviously wasn't enough for him. Or rather I . . ." I stop myself saying it. Stacey has already said it tonight. I shake my head.

"So, I can only presume finding the two of them together was a shock."

"Yes. Kate was only four months old. It's her birthday on Sunday. She doesn't know David. He wasn't around much after she was born. At least now I know why. He was too busy fucking my sister. I don't know why I'm telling you this."

"Because I'm easy to talk to. I'm a good guy. Lauren, I have to say this . . . at the weekend, when I got out of the shower and you'd gone, I repeatedly asked myself what I had done wrong. I wanted to wake up in the morning with you in my arms, and for me, that's not something I do."

I can't do this. Not tonight. My head feels as though it could explode at any moment. What the hell is wrong with me? His words hit me hard, but the truth is, he's been in my thoughts since I walked out of his apartment and left him in the shower.

I take another gulp of my wine. "What do you want me to say to that? We both knew what it was."

"Yes, you're right, but that was before I had you in my bed. Lauren, I wanted you . . ."

"Matt, please. Do I look like someone who can deal with this tonight? You don't seem like a man who would be short of women wanting to jump into bed with you."

"Lauren, I could be . . ."

"Offended? I don't think so. You don't come across as someone who could be easily offended." I'm trying to sound confident, but I'm sure my voice sounds weak. Matt sits opposite me, his gaze a mixture of hurt and intense as he stares at me. My eyes stay on him and I'm sure he's trying to read my mind.

Nervous. He makes me feel so bloody nervous. My feet are firmly on the ground but are itching to move. This is ridiculous. I'm in my home, I shouldn't be feeling nervous.

A slow smile plays on his lips, and he knows. He must sense how I feel around him. He looks so damn relaxed, and here I am, my entire body a mass of adrenaline and unexplained emotions. I look away first, breaking our connection, and I swear I hear him snigger. *Cocky bastard.*

I wish he hadn't popped by tonight. It's nice to know he was thinking about me, but this . . . this won't do our working relationship any good, and that's what I need to remember.

I need to stay professional.

At all times.

I look up to find his eyes still on me. This is so confusing.

"Matt, I'm tired. It's been a long day."

"Sorry. I'm keeping you back. Can we meet up tomorrow? You could come to the restaurant and we can discuss ideas."

"I can be there anytime from nine-thirty until two-thirty. After that is out of the question." I know Sandra is happy to have the kids, but I love being able to pick Luke up from school myself.

"Yes, I understand," he says with a soft smile. "So how about we say ten o'clock?"

"That works for me."

"Perfect. I look forward to spending the day with you." He

stands with a grin that has me feeling both uncomfortable and excited. My eyes set on his slightly parted lips, and I remember every last touch they placed on my skin. Every mouth-watering kiss we shared, I can still feel. And here and now, this isn't something I should be thinking about.

I'm going to spend tomorrow with Matt Anderson and it's going to be torture. Damn this man that stands before me, looking so fucking pleased with himself.

I walk out into the hallway, Matt following close behind, and I'm met with a very sleepy Luke coming down the stairs. He rubs his eyes and looks at Matt.

"What's wrong, buddy?"

"I couldn't sleep, Mum. I hate my dad."

"Luke, we don't hate anyone," I say, lowering myself to his level. Matt stands at the side and I wish he would leave because . . . oh, I don't know why.

"You should hate him, Mum."

"I don't hate him. I feel sorry for him because he's chosen not to spend time with you or Kate. That makes me sad because you both bring me so much happiness."

Luke smiles and launches himself into my arms, his head against my chest. My gaze lands on Matt, his eyes narrowed in concern, and if it wasn't for him standing there, I'm certain I would be crying now.

"Lauren, I'll go."

Finally.

Luke tilts his head, hearing Matt's voice. "You were here last night and tonight when we were having dinner. Are you a friend of my mum's?"

"Yes. Your mum is going to do some work for me."

"Everyone says Mum's work is the best."

"I'm sure it is. Lauren, I'll see you tomorrow, and Luke, goodnight."

"Yes, I'll see you then, and thanks for coming around." He leaves and I don't allow my eyes to linger as he walks away, closing the front door behind him. My attention is on my son. "How about I lock up and quickly tidy my mess, then we can go to bed? I can read you a story or you can cuddle in with me."

"Mum, I'm nearly six. I'll sleep in my own bed." Yes, my baby boy has grown up so quickly. "Unless you need a cuddle?"

"Mums always need cuddles."

Ten

WHY IS IT WHEN YOU need to be somewhere in a hurry, the traffic is at a complete standstill? The motorway is gridlocked. I'm hoping there's roadworks up ahead and not an accident.

This morning was going so well. I dropped off Kate with Sandra then went on to school with Luke. He went away happy because I spoke to Liam's mum about football since he's been talking about it non-stop. Turns out it's on tonight in the school. I promised him I would take him.

Emma said I need to take him tonight to fill out forms, and if he decides he likes it, we will share drop off and pick-ups between us. She's happy to do the pick-up and let me get Kate settled. I thought that was really nice of her. Liam is her youngest out of three.

I look at the time; it's five to ten, and there's no way I'm going to be in Glasgow's city centre in five minutes. I need to call Matt.

"Morning," he says, answering on the first ring and sounding much cheerier than me.

"Matt, I'm stuck in traffic. I'm not sure when I'll get to you."

"That's fine. As long as I know you're on your way, I'm happy. We have a lot to discuss."

"I'm hoping it won't be too long until the traffic starts moving."

"If you want, I can stay on the phone and keep you company. I'm up for whispering in your ear. I think I'd enjoy that."

Is he flirting with me?

"I'm going to hang up now." I hear him laugh before I end our call. God, I hope he's not going to spend the day flirting with me because I'm not getting paid for that. I try to clear my mind because I have a feeling I'm going to need my wits about me today.

The traffic takes another fifteen minutes before it starts moving, then another fifteen for me to get into Glasgow. I was right—roadworks.

I'm standing on the pavement outside his restaurant and club. With a quick look at my reflection in the window, I smile, take a deep breath, and open the door. He's standing at the bar, talking on his phone, his back to me. I pause inside the doorway and take him in. He looks sexy and in control. In control of his empire.

The door bangs behind me and startles me. At the same time, Matt spins around to face me, a grin on his face. His eyes dance over my body, taking in my appearance, which I spent more time on than usual. "I need this stock within the next hour. If you can't do that we won't be doing business again." He ends his call abruptly, putting the phone in his inside jacket pocket, and stalks toward me. "Nice of you to join me, Miss Trent. You look edible." And there it is; his cocky smile that slowly curls at the corners of his mouth. A smile that wasn't evident last night, but one I remember well from Saturday.

His mouth. That has touched my body over and over. These thoughts need to disappear because if they don't, I'm going to be done for. Who am I kidding? I'm already done for and heading on a collision course for disaster if he keeps this up.

"Mr Anderson." My voice is calm and steady, even though my pulse is racing.

He takes my hand, lifting it to his mouth, and kisses it. Seconds tick away slowly as he keeps my hand in his, watching and waiting to see how I'm going to react.

"Where do you want me?" As the question leaves me, I already know I shouldn't have asked it. His smile has grown wider and his eyebrows are raised. *Please*. Is this how it's going to be all day?

"Oh, let's see. Are you sure you want to hear my answer?"

"No, I don't think I do." I pull my hand from his, much to his amusement. "I'll be sitting over there." I point to a table in the corner. "And I take one sugar and milk in my tea. Thank you." My face remains straight until I turn and walk away from him. I hear him inhale deeply before his footsteps cross the floor.

Two can play at his game. Whatever game it is he's chosen to play.

I clear one of the bigger tables and start taking papers and my laptop from my case. Well, I'm going to need plenty of room to work. Firing up my laptop, I open the files I need for today. I do have a few ideas of my own, but I always listen to what the client wants. And as for Mr Anderson, he comes across as the type of man who knows exactly what he wants and how to get it.

Of that, I have no doubts.

"Tea," he says, placing two cups down on the table.

"What, no offer of a chocolate biscuit or even a cake?" I say sarcastically.

"I didn't have you down for a chocolate lover."

"You don't know me very well, then, do you?"

"No, I don't, but I do plan on rectifying that. Although, there are certain parts of your body I know very well."

In this moment, I'm thankful that the room is dimly lit, although I'm sure it does nothing to hide my reddened face.

"Has anyone ever told you that you are exasperating?"

"No." I find his answer hard to believe.

"Well, why do I have the feeling I might tell you that on more than one occasion today? Now, we have a lot of work to get through before I leave, so if you don't mind?"

"I don't mind at all, but we will be stopping for lunch."

"I won't. I intend to work through."

He doesn't tease or say any smart mouth comment, which is just as well, because I'm more than ready to stand my ground with him. Instead, we sit down and I ask more questions about the restaurant and the nightclub.

It has to be said, we do fall into easy work-related conversations, and his ideas almost match mine. This job could be one of the easiest to work on for me. He wants to have a more upmarket image to attract the right clientele. At the moment, the image of the restaurant and club, to me, sends off mixed messages, and in business, that's never a good idea.

It's not as difficult being around him as I thought it would be, considering not just last night, but our steamy, sexy encounter at the weekend. *Between the sheets*. I hate to admit it, but I do think that is how I will remember him. All because of a bloody drink. A drink I plan on staying well clear of in the future.

The saying, 'time flies when you're having fun,' springs to mind. It always does when I get so wrapped up in my work. I love my job, but having a client who is open to all my ideas and suggestions is the icing on the cake.

"Lauren, we need to eat. I can't have you here working and not feed you." I lift my head from the laptop, glance around the room, and notice it's almost full with customers.

"I'm happy to eat while I continue working."

"Lauren! Save what you're working on and have lunch with me. Please?" I want to say no, but as I look at him, I know I'm going to agree.

"Fine. You've twisted my arm."

He orders food for us both while I finish off the last piece I'm working on before I hit save. The conversation has flowed with ease between us because it's all been work related. But now, I feel nervous as to what we will talk about. I don't think we have much in common unless Saturday night counts. Now, that's not a topic I plan on discussing. There won't be a repeat performance, even though the thought has entered my mind on more than one occasion since I left his apartment in the wee small hours.

"Here we go," he says. "Two burgers, chips, and salad."

"Thank you," I say, taking a plate from him. "This looks great."

"Well, then tuck in."

I intend to, because now we've stopped working, I've realised I am hungry. There's an awkward silence hanging in the air between us now; something that hasn't been there all morning. His phone rings several times, and each time he looks at the number and silences it.

"If you need to take that call, feel free."

"It's my sister. I'll call her back later on. She'll only be wanting me to do something for her. What are your plans for the rest of the day when you leave me?"

"Pick up Luke, then Kate, make dinner, then it's back out because Luke is starting some football training thing in the school tonight. Then when we get home, it will be bedtime for both of them and I can do a bit more work."

"You don't look over-enthused at the idea of football."

"I'm not a football lover, but Luke is."

"I also get the impression you might work too hard."

"Yes, I suppose I do, but I spend as much time with the kids as I possibly can. I tend to do a lot of my work at night."

"What about time for just you?"

"I'm a single mum with two kids; there's not much time for me. Saturday night was my first night out in God knows how long. Probably before I was pregnant with Kate."

"Well, I'm honoured to have been able to spend time with you then and now, even though we are working." I don't know what to say in reply. His words leave me feeling embarrassed. "So, no hot dates with other sexy men on the cards?"

"You think you're sexy?" I ask, already dreading where this conversation will end up.

"I know I'm sexy, but you also know it."

"Mr Anderson, you really would try the patience of a bloody saint."

"Well, it's a good thing I know you're not a saint then," he says, with a smirk full of unspoken promises. "I think you and I should go on a date."

"I don't think so. My kids are my top priority."

"You need to get out more, enjoy yourself. Let your hair down."

"I did that on Saturday night and look where it got me."

"Yes, in my bed. But not between my sheets where I wanted you to be."

"Matt . . ."

"Lauren, you already know I was disappointed you left. I won't hide that fact. And to say I was surprised to see you the other night is an understatement. So, yes, I think I might be selfish but I do want to take you out on a date, and I'm not taking no for an answer."

"I'll have to think about it. The idea of mixing business and pleasure doesn't exactly thrill me."

"Sweetheart, I think it's a bit late for that." I shake my head in annoyance, because he's right, it is too late for worrying about that. I've already broken rules that I made to myself.

Eleven

"MUM, CAN YOU HURRY UP?" Luke calls after me as I unstrap Kate from her car seat. He's been impatient since I collected him from here at three o'clock. I swear I've never seen Luke so excited about anything before, especially coming back to school. Locking the car, I keep Kate in my arms, even though she wants to walk.

"Mum!"

"Luke, stop and wait there, please." He stops and waits at the doors, sighing heavily. I hope he's only like this because it's his first night. A few boys run up to him; they all seem glad to see him. I'm glad he's made friends in school, especially under the circumstances of the last few months. He does seem to be coping well, although where he's concerned, I won't take my eye off the ball.

"Lauren, you made it," Emma says, as I enter the school gym hall. I put Kate down and let her toddle about.

"Yes, although this one would've been back here as soon as we finished dinner. He's really excited."

"Liam has been the same today, and I put that down to Luke joining tonight. The two boys get along really well. Do you realise we stay on the same street?"

"No, I didn't, but then I've been so busy since I moved in. I've not really met any of my neighbours yet, but I'm sure the boys would love to play together."

"Yes. I'll give you my number and if you need anything, anything at all, please call. Even if it's only half an hour of peace and quiet."

"Thanks." I'm not sure if I will take her up on that, but it's very kind of her to offer.

"Mum!" I look up to see Kate trying to kick a ball.

"Let me. You go and sign his forms," Emma says. I do just that. The coach I speak to seems really nice and assures me Luke will love it. He tells what time to come back and I leave with Emma. I did call over to Luke to let him know I was leaving but he was too busy with his friends.

"So, Lauren, do you work from home?"

"Yes, I do now. Although my friend wants me to go into business with her."

"Oh, that sounds interesting. We should grab a coffee one morning," Emma says, as we stand in the school car park.

"Yeah, I'd like that. So how close do we stay together?"

"You're number four and we're round the corner on the same side as you. We're twenty-six."

"So walking distance for the boys?"

"Yes. There are a lot of kids in the street. Tomorrow, after school, I'll get Liam to introduce Luke to the other kids. They all play at the park great together, which usually includes playing football. Patrick has been known to go out and have a kick about with them all. Our other boys are usually out playing and tend to keep an eye on Liam."

"I'm sure he'd love that. Not sure I will, though. I'm so anxious when it comes to the kids."

"You wouldn't be a good parent if you weren't anxious about your kids. Look, I better go. I want to go to the shops first before they finish training."

"Okay, see you later."

When I get home, I decide it would be best to get Kate bathed and ready for bed. I need to pick up Luke at eight o'clock and I usually have her in her bed for then.

Kate splashes water everywhere and giggles whenever I try to tell her off. Bath time isn't usually this messy or noisy with her. Then again, she changes so much on an almost daily basis. I have a feeling this one is going to be more mischievous than her brother.

I finally get her out of the bath and put her pyjamas on. We still have thirty minutes before I need to collect Luke, so we go downstairs and I let her play with some of her toys on the living room floor.

I've not spoken to Abbie today and I'm surprised there have been no texts or calls. I grab my phone and dial her number as I sit watching Kate playing away happily.

"I was going to call you later tonight," she says.

"Oh, and why is that?"

"Because I know Luke has football and then you would be trying to get the kids into bed after that. And I hate to interrupt you while you're doing that. So, why are you calling?"

"Luke is still at football and I've just finished getting madam bathed and ready for bed. I pick Luke up soon. It turns out his friend Liam stays just a little further up the street."

"That's great. He already has a friend and you know his parents. I've spoken to them a few times. They seem like nice people. So this move has worked out for the best."

"Yes, I think it has. I've been thinking about your proposal, and as long as I can sort out the kids, I think we should go for it. I mean really see if it can happen."

"Really?" she squeals.

"Yes. As I said to your mum, we have a lot to discuss, but I do want to give it a go. In all fairness, what have we got to lose? Not a lot. Although, I don't want Les being out of pocket and

I'm more than happy to put my own money into the business."

"Oh my God. Oh my God. Have I told you how much I love you lately?"

"No, but I'm sure you're going to."

"Lauren. This is brilliant." I agree with her and we spend another few minutes talking. I tell her all about my meeting with Matt but leave out the part about him asking me out on a date.

My drive over to the school is filled with all sorts of thoughts; the kids growing up surrounded by their friends, the possibility of a new business venture. It's all very exciting. A new chapter for us all.

I must call Grant in the morning to see what time he has free this week to meet with me. It would be good to hear his opinion on this. He might have ideas to help. I've spoken to him a few times since I moved but I'm missing him and Liz.

I park the car in the car park, take Kate from her seat, and look around for Emma's car, but I don't see it. I'm a few minutes early, so I'm sure she'll be here soon enough. Kate settles in my arms and doesn't put up a fight to get down to walk. She's too tired. I'm hoping she won't be the only one and I get Luke settled quickly tonight.

But as I enter the school gym and look at my very flushed son, I don't think I will. He still looks as though he could run around kicking a football all night long. There's already a few parents waiting, and I stand just inside the door. Luke sees me, waves, and carries on playing and listening to his coach.

The door opens behind me, I turn around, hoping it's Emma. But it's not. And it's not someone I thought I was going to see again until later in the week. I try to hide the small fact that his presence has surprised me, but I'm certain my body gives me away.

Matt.

He stands there staring at me with a smile on his face. Now this is *freaky*. What the hell is he doing here? I swear he's following me. Does he have kids? Is he married? Christ, I never asked. He slowly moves toward me. There's a fluttering in my stomach; the same feeling I've felt every time I see him.

"Hi. Fancy seeing you again." I narrow my eyes and turn away from him. "You look great." His unexpected words take me completely by surprise. I know I don't look as good as I did earlier today for our meeting.

"What are you doing here?" I ask, without looking in his direction.

"The call from my sister today. She wanted to see if I was around tonight in case she was going to be late."

Okay, so it's not his kid he's here to pick up.

The coach blows a whistle and all the boys stop what they're doing. He speaks to them for a few minutes before letting them go.

"Uncle Matt." It's Liam who runs over, with Luke beside him. Matt bends, picks him up, and spins him around. "Why are you here? Where's my mum?"

"She's still at the shops and your dad is picking up your brothers, so I'm afraid you're left with me."

"So, you're Emma's brother?" I ask, already knowing the answer. This is getting weird.

"Yes."

"Mummy, did you see I scored a goal?"

"Yes, I did. You did great! So, do you like football training?"

"Yes! I can't wait until next week."

I tell Luke he has to walk beside me and not run off because my arms are full with Kate, who has now fallen asleep. We walk outside with Matt. The boys are talking excitedly about the training. Matt's car is parked right beside mine. Did he know I was going to be here tonight?

I think he did. I know I told him I was taking Luke to training. What are the chances of him turning up here?

"So, Lauren, you know my sister?"

"Yes, it would appear so. I've known her and Patrick since last year when the boys started school, only to say hello to at the school gate."

"They are good people and will be great neighbours for you."

I'm a bit lost for words. What the hell do I say to him? I stop beside my car and move Kate's position so I can get into my jacket pocket for my car keys to open the damn door, but I can't reach it. I just want to get home quickly. I've already spent too much time around Matt today and I don't believe he's good for my health.

"Here, let me. Liam don't move." He gently takes Kate from my arms. I take the key from my pocket. I open the door and take my sleeping daughter from him and secure her in the car seat. "Lauren, have you given any thought to my question today?"

"No, I haven't. I do have other things on my mind besides you." I know I sound snappy but I can't help it.

"Well, it's good to know you are thinking about me." I shake my head, say goodbye to Liam, and tell Luke to get in the car. Matt stands by his car, watching me. "Lauren, I'll call you tomorrow."

I don't answer him, I just get in my car and drive home.

Twelve

IT'S FOUR A.M. AND I'VE tossed and turned the whole night so far. I know I'm not going to get any sleep now. Every single time I close my eyes, I see him. Matt Anderson. Even my thoughts of him send my heart rate soaring. I can't deny there's a spark between us, an instant attraction, but I can't allow this thing between us to simmer away. I have my kids to think about.

But I also can't deny my night with him made me feel alive.

Every delicate touch is engraved into the depths of my memory, where they will stay for all time. I would be mad to consider going on a date with him. He's the type of man who would break my heart in two. But as I lie here in my bed in the quiet of the night, I'm considering his offer of a date because I do believe him when he says he won't take no for an answer.

Could I just have some fun with him? After all, I'm sure that's all he's looking for. I don't think I could; that's where the problem is. Then there is the small matter that his sister stays beside me, and his nephew and Luke are best friends. If we did go out on a date it could make for an interesting situation. And I don't want anyone feeling awkward because of it.

But I do want to see him again, away from work and the kids.

I close my eyes and I can feel his body against mine on the

dance floor of the nightclub. The look in his eyes. Our very first kiss of that night awakened every last part of my body and had me longing with desire for him.

He's a man I shouldn't be thinking about, yet I'm unable to shake these thoughts of him from my mind.

Opening my eyes, I reach for my phone and stare at it for a long few moments before typing out a text.

If you still want to, I'll go on a date with you.

I hit send before I have to chance to change my mind and hit delete. There. I've done it, and I'm probably going to live to regret it. Although, I'm sure if I turned him down, I would regret that decision too. It's a lose-lose situation for me.

I stretch out in my bed and yawn. The phone beeps.

Matt: Now I have something to look forward to. It's also nice to know at this time of the morning you're thinking about me.

What the hell do I say to that?

Matt: What I want to know is, am I the reason you can't sleep or is it one of the kids?

Me: You are the reason for my sleepless night.

Matt: Phone me then.

Deep down, I know it's a bad idea. I shouldn't do it. But it still doesn't stop me pressing call on my phone.

"Hey you," he says, his voice sounding smooth.

"Hi."

"Do you want to tell me what's keeping you awake? What's worrying you?"

"I'm not too sure. You. Me."

"Lauren, I can't deny I want to get to know you better. There is something pulling us together. I know you feel it too."

"I don't know what to say."

"You don't have to say anything, although you should tell me when we can go on our date."

"Let me speak with Abbie or her parents to see who can watch the kids for me and when. Abbie's mum, Sandra, has done a lot for me and the kids lately when I've been working. I don't want her to think I'm taking advantage."

"Of course. I do understand. Did Luke settle after football?"

"Oh God, no. It was nine-thirty before I even got him into his bed. He was so excited and happy about it. He's also desperate to get out and play with Liam. I've promised him he can. It's just been hard trying to find my own routine since we moved in here."

"I'm sure you'll get there. Everything takes time. I'm sure Emma will become a frequent visitor and I know she will help you if she can."

We spend another twenty minutes talking about the designs I'm working on before soft crying interrupts our conversation. Kate. I abruptly end the call and go to her. She's sitting up in her cot, crying. I pick her up and she snuggles straight into me. I take her into my bed, hold her in my arms, and she falls straight back to sleep.

I pick up my phone and type out a text.

Sorry, I had to see to Kate. She is now fast asleep in my bed beside me.

Matt: Lucky Kate.

I almost laugh at his response.

"You are a dark horse," Emma says, walking toward me. "You and Matt."

"Oh."

"Don't *oh* me. So, you were the woman who left him alone on Saturday night?"

I quickly look around to see if anyone else can hear our

conversation. Luke left my side, giving me a kiss the minute he saw Liam in the playground. Both boys ran off to play with some friends.

"Emma, I don't know what to say to you."

"Your face tells me all I need to know. Bloody hell, you knocked the stuffing out of him. I've never known my brother to be so taken with someone. And now you're working for him."

"In my defence, that came as a huge surprise to me."

"My brother and I are close, but I have a feeling I'm going to be seeing a lot more of him if these last two days are anything to go by. I'm sure he will be dropping by a lot more now he knows where you stay." I can feel myself blush. I'm not sure how I feel about her knowing about Saturday night. "Lauren! What's wrong?"

"God, where do I start?" I pick up Kate who has been toddling beside me. "Saturday night was so out of character for me. It's not something I make a habit of."

"I know that. You do know you're allowed to have fun?"

"Yes, but my kids . . ."

"Lauren, I've not said a thing to you about what happened with David, but I've stood on the sidelines and listened to what others had to say about you, as you well know. Those closest to you aren't going to judge you for wanting to have some fun. And for those that want something to gossip about, let them talk. What are you doing this morning?"

"Not a lot. Hoping this one goes for a sleep at some point so I can as well."

"Did she have you up all night?"

"No, but I haven't slept. I'm feeling pretty exhausted now."

"In that case, why don't you come for a coffee at mine and we can talk about my brother?" Something about the way she says it has me thinking there is more than meets the eye with Mathew Anderson.

"Okay."

"Perfect. See you both at mine shortly."

Up until last night, I did think Emma and I could become friends, but with Matt being her brother, I'm not sure it's a good idea. I have a fairly good idea of the type of man he is and I'm certain that is what Emma is going to confirm. Should I tell her I've agreed to a date with him? What has he told his sister about me? Shit, I don't think I want to know.

"Here, let me take Kate," Emma says, as she opens her front door. Kate isn't strange with anyone and that worries me. She'll happily go to anyone who wants to show her attention. "Come on through."

I follow her to the kitchen and sit down at the table. Her home is lovely and fresh; very welcoming. She puts Kate down on the floor, and Kate starts to wander around, having a right old nosey.

"Do you want tea or coffee?"

"Make it coffee." I keep a close eye on Kate; I don't want her getting in Emma's way as she makes our hot drinks.

"Can she have a plain biscuit?"

"Yeah," I answer, as she puts our drinks on the table.

"Well, gorgeous girl, this is for you," she says, handing Kate a biscuit. If we're lucky, that will keep her occupied for a few minutes. "Now, Lauren. My brother."

"What can I say? I'm doing some re-branding work for the restaurant and club."

"That's not what I meant and you know it. So, is it just Matt you're dealing with or have you met Danny as well?"

"Who's Danny?"

"He's my brother too."

"Not met him, although I'm sure I saw him on Saturday night, talking to Matt."

"I'll be completely honest with you. In my opinion, Matt is very much a jack the lad, but you seem to have him falling over himself. I've never seen him like this before."

"We're going on a date." The words are out of my mouth before I can stop them.

"What the hell?" Kate decides now is as good a time as any to interrupt. "Oh, Kate. You don't give your mum a break do you?" Emma says, picking her up, sitting her on her knee, and giving her another biscuit. "A date? What have you done to my brother?"

"He asked yesterday. I told him I would think about it, sent a message, and we ended up on the phone talking during the night."

"Back up. Are we sure we're talking about the same brother?"

"Well, unless you're going to tell me it wasn't Matt that picked up Liam . . . ?"

"No, that was Matt. *Bloody hell*. Now it's me that's lost for words. Can I ask a question?"

"Of course."

"Does David help out with the kids? Tell me to mind my own business if you like, but you always have them. So I was surprised when Matt told me last night that it was you he was with on Saturday."

"Not half as surprised as me. And no. David hasn't bothered with either of them since we separated. Even the other night, my dad was in town and wanted to meet up. Stacey, my sister, decided to bring David with her and he completely blanked Luke. Matt was there and he had words with David."

"Back up."

I tell her all about the incident in the restaurant and how Matt spoke with David. She stares at me, although every now and then her gaze turns to Kate. "So, who helps you?"

"My friend Abbie and her parents."

"Ah, I thought it was your mum I had seen at the school a few times."

"No, but Sandra seems to have taken over that role for me and the kids."

We fall into a much easier conversation when we stop talking about Matt. Although, Emma does say if I can't get anyone to watch the kids for me, she'll have them. I'm in no hurry to go on this date. Or am I?

Thirteen

"YES, UNCLE GRANT. WHY DON'T you come over for dinner tonight? It would be nice to see you."

"Will you stop with the *uncle,* and yes, I want to see you all. I've missed you since you moved out."

"Okay then. You can give me a hand with the kids and I'm sure Luke will tell you all about his football."

"Sounds good. When does school finish up?"

"Two weeks on Friday." These summer holidays might be the death of me. Seven long weeks. I plan on maybe taking the kids away for a week or so, just to break it up for Luke. Also, I could do with a change of scenery. It might do me some good.

"Okay, I'll talk to you tonight. Liz and I would like to take the kids away for a few days to give you a proper break."

"But . . ."

"Lauren, honey, this won't be up for debate. If your mum was here, she would do this for you and so much more. It would please us both. Love you." He hangs up and I shake my head before getting out of my car. Grant and Liz never had kids of their own and they dote on my two, but I'm not sure how I would cope without them for a few days. I unstrap Kate from her seat, and as we have a good ten minutes before school finishes, I let her walk. The only downside to Kate walking outside is it's torture on my back having to bend so she can walk with my hand in hers. Although, she is much more independent than Luke was at this age. She wants to do everything by herself.

When we're safely in the school playground, I let go of her hands, allowing her some freedom. As she strolls around, I follow closely behind her. It still amazes me that she is on her feet and walking around. Thinking back, Luke seemed to take forever before he was on his feet, and then it took him a long time before he was confident.

"Lauren." His voice sends shockwaves all through my core, and the hairs on the back of my neck stand. I didn't expect to see him. He must be here to collect Liam. Although, other than last night, I've never seen him here at the school before. He's someone I would've remembered. "I thought it was you."

Checking to make sure Kate is okay, I turn slowly to face him. I check him out; he's wearing jeans and a dark red T-shirt. He looks great, whereas I know I look like shit.

"Hey," I say when my gaze meets his. There's a slow lip-curling smile on his lips, but it quickly changes to a frown. "What?"

"You look tired."

"Thanks." I turn away from him just in time to see Kate fall over, and she cries. I move quickly to pick her up, but not quick enough. Matt scoops her into his arms. She looks tiny as he tries to comfort her.

"What the hell?" Emma's voice distracts me from Matt. "What's wrong with Kate?" she asks with concern, looking between me and Matt, who is now rubbing her back.

"She fell."

"And why does my brother have her?" she whispers, standing beside me, her eyes still on Matt, who hasn't yet acknowledged her.

"That's anyone's guess." I watch, mesmerised, as he finally settles her and she stops crying. Emma and I exchange questioning glances. Kate doesn't have a mark on her from the fall, which I know will be the first of many. "He looks relaxed," I say, lowering my own voice.

"Yes, but this isn't Matt. What have you done to my brother?"

"Emma, I can hear you." I smirk, and Emma shakes her head. Kate cuddles into him, settling her head on his chest. "It would seem she likes me."

"Hmph."

"Don't huff, Emma. It's not a good look on you. And I think Kate likes me as much as her mum does."

"Jumping the gun a bit there, don't you think?" I say, bringing a frown to Matt's face and a giggle from his sister. "Here, let me take her."

"Leave her. She's fine and happy where she is."

"Matt, what are you doing here?" Emma asks, and I'm a little curious as to the answer.

"I was passing and thought I would come visiting."

"Yeah, right. I know it's not me you've come to visit."

"Of course, coming to visit you and the boys does have its advantages. But it looks like I came along at the right time. Lauren, you need to sleep."

"Did you not get any sleep when you left my house?"

"No. This one has played all day, and now look at her. She's ready to fall asleep there."

"Why don't I take Luke and Kate to mine and you can sleep? I can help the boys with their homework and look after Kate."

"No, I'll be fine until I get them into their beds, and then I can go to my own bed. I also have my uncle coming over for dinner."

"Lauren, dinner can be sorted after you've rested. Emma will take the kids for you, even for an hour, and I'll be with her. But I'm driving your car home."

"But . . ." What is it with him? Does it really look to people on the outside that I can't cope with looking after my own kids? Not every day is as bad as today, and, yes I'm exhausted and I know I look like crap. But I still don't like being told what to do. Even if what he and Emma are suggesting makes sense.

"No. It's not up for discussion I'll get my car later on. I get the impression you don't take orders very well." His eyes narrow before he smirks. He's right, I don't take orders well, but then again, being on my own, I don't have to. "Just once do as you're told." I glance at Emma and she nods sympathetically.

The bell rings and it's a few minutes before I spot the boys. They're together, deep in conversation. "Mum, where's Kate?"

"Just there, with Liam's Uncle Matt."

I step aside so he can see. Liam calls out to Matt, who in return, urges him to be quiet. Kate has fallen asleep in his arms.

"Why do you have *my* sister?"

"Because she fell over and hurt herself," Matt tells him.

"Is she going to be okay?" Luke asks, turning to face me.

"Yes. She's tired. How would you like to go to Liam's when we get home? Kate is going too."

"Where are you going?"

"Luke, your mum is a bit tired," Emma says, crouching down to speak with him. "You can play and have your dinner at mine, and when Mum's had a rest, you will go home. Is that okay?"

Luke glances between Emma and Matt before turning to me. "I can look after you."

"Sport, I'm not sick, and you can play football with Liam."

"Okay then."

And there we go; the football has won it for me. I take his hand and we walk out of school towards the car park. Liam is busy talking about what they can do when they get home. I'm really pleased he has Liam as a friend. Everyone needs friends.

"Lauren, remember and give Matt a bag for Kate. And try and sleep."

"I will, and thank you for this."

"Don't be silly, and don't worry about the kids. They will be fine."

I open the car, and Luke climbs into his seat and straps himself before I check he's done it correctly. Matt gently hands me Kate and I secure her in her seat. She doesn't open her tiny eyelids. I hope I can sleep when I get home.

"Lauren? What do you normally do when you have a day like today when you're so exhausted?" Matt asks, as I climb into the passenger seat of my own car.

"Deal with it. That's all I can do. Or if I have a few days like this in a row, I get Sandra to look after them for me for a few hours."

"Let's get you home," he says, starting the engine.

The sound of silence fills the air around me. I panic then remember where the kids are, so I stretch, opening my eyes slowly and allow them to adjust to the brightness of my living room. With no kids rushing me, I allow myself the extra time to awaken fully. I never even managed to lie down. I fell asleep sitting up on the sofa.

"Shit!" A quick glance at the time tells me I need to move my arse. I jump from the sofa. Grant should be here soon.

Stopping, I pause. Something smells great and there's someone in the kitchen. I enter the kitchen and find Grant opening the oven.

"Sleeping beauty is finally awake. Are you okay?" he asks, his voice full of concern as he takes a pie from the oven. "I presume the pie and vegetables are for dinner?"

I frown. Where did the pie come from? Matt or Emma. It can only be from them. "Yes, that's for dinner, and sorry."

"I have to say, you still look tired. Where are the kids?" He cuts the pie and serves it along with the vegetables.

"A neighbour has them. Emma, she's Liam's mum."

"Ah, Luke's friend from school."

"Yes. She stays further along the street."

"Well, I'm pleased you're meeting new people. Liz is always saying you need to get out more." I smile at his words. "Now, do we have time to eat without interruptions?"

"I'm sure we do."

We sit down and tuck into the most amazing steak pie I've tasted in a long time. Something about it reminds me of my mum; she always cooked her own pies. Not once do I remember her buying one. I ask why Liz isn't here, but she's been out with a friend shopping all day and then going for dinner.

He asks with concern how I'm coping here on my own, and I tell him the truth. That at times it's really tough, but that I still wouldn't change any of it.

I tell him all about Abbie's business proposal. He listens with interest and tells me he thinks it's a fantastic idea because, as far as he's concerned, it was me who brought in the most work when David and I worked together. Although, he does tell me not to rush into anything.

I tell him what happened at the restaurant when I met my dad. Grant and my dad used to be the best of friends, but when my parents separated, their friendship ended, which is sad. He's not happy with Stacey. His words were, "She's one selfish bitch." I happen to agree with him on that. Grant tried to talk to Stacey when David and I first split up, but she wasn't interested in anything he had to say.

He asks about taking the kids away as soon as Luke finishes school. This conversation I didn't want to have, but as he speaks, I know he and Liz are excited about it. They've booked a lodge in the countryside. Luke would love it, I know he would, but I will miss them both like crazy. He's over the moon when I finally agree after a lot of persuasion. Maybe Abbie and I can plan something for next weekend.

"Dinner was perfect, even if I had to make it," he says jokingly, as he starts to clear the plates. The front door opens.

"Mum, where are you?"

"In the kitchen, sport, and we have a visitor," I call out. "That will be Emma, bringing the kids back." I stand up to help.

"Sit back down," he tells me. "I'm more than capable of loading a few dishes into the dishwasher. Then I'm going to spend some time with the kids."

Luke comes into the kitchen. "Uncle Grant!" He runs over and jumps into his arms. "I've missed you."

"I've missed you too." There's a long pause and Grant frowns. "Mathew." That's why he's frowning. Oh God, they know each other.

"Grant, how are you?" Matt asks, handing Kate to me.

"I'm fine, but why do you have my niece and nephew? What am I missing here?"

"My sister had them. I'm just bringing them home."

Matt doesn't stay, which pleases Grant and confuses me.

"What's wrong?" I ask him.

"I'm his bank manager. I didn't realise you knew the Andersons. He's good at what he does in terms of business, but he's not someone I would want you associated with. Now, his brother, Danny, is different. He's a one woman man." As opposed to Matt having a string of women. I sigh. He's not telling me something I hadn't already worked out for myself.

"And you're telling me this because . . . ?"

"Because I saw the look in both your eyes. Don't try and deny it, honey. It's obvious there is something more than him being a neighbour's brother."

"I'm doing the re-branding work at the restaurant and nightclub."

With a shake of his head, he comes and lifts Kate from me. "We'll go and play. Why don't you go and grab a shower? And have a think about what I've said."

"I will." As I say the words I'm not sure what it is I'm thinking about.

Fourteen

IT'S LATE SATURDAY AFTERNOON AND I'm sitting out in the garden, enjoying the sunshine. The house is decorated ready for Kate's birthday tomorrow and I've wrapped all her presents. I'm doing lunch for everyone; Abbie, Sandra, Les, Grant, and Liz. I also said to Emma to bring the boys down if she wanted, although I'm sure they would much rather play football.

I opened the bag earlier that Dad had given me for Kate, and as usual, he has not only got Kate too much, but Luke too. There was also an envelope in the bag with my name on it. I opened it to find five-hundred pounds, with a note saying to use this to treat the kids during the holidays. I did call him to say I couldn't accept it, which upset him. I don't want his money. I'm happy enough having a relationship with him. I finally agreed to use it for the kids, and maybe put it towards taking the two of them away for a holiday.

Luke is playing football at the park with Liam and some of the other boys in the street, including Liam's older brothers. I've called Emma a few times to check on him, and each time she tells me to stop worrying and that he's fine. Kate is sitting on a rug I've laid out, playing with some toys. She keeps pulling her hat off. I'm so glad I put plenty of sun cream on her today.

Matt and I have shared a few phone calls and lots of texts since yesterday. We haven't spoken about Grant, but what Grant said to me has been playing over and over in my mind.

Matt was keen for our date to be this weekend, but I talked him into going for dinner on Monday night. He understood when I told him it was Kate's birthday. Abbie said she would watch the kids

My phone buzzes. A text.

Emma: Just letting you know the boys are in the garden having a water fight.

Me: Okay. I hope Luke's behaving.

Emma: Of course he is. What are you doing?

Me: Sitting in the garden with Kate enjoying the sun.

Emma: Why don't you come up? Patrick is going to put the BBQ on. Bring Kate's pram and a bag and we could have a glass of wine.

Me: Maybe.

Emma: I'll see you here in ten minutes. TOPS.

God, she can be a bossy cow. I gather up the toys, much to Kate's disapproval, and boy does she make it known by screaming at me. Taking her hand, we go back inside and I get a few things together for her; nappies and a change of clothes. Oh, and a bottle of wine. I put her in her pram to walk the short distance to Emma's house.

The closer I get to Emma's house, the noisier it becomes. I swear every kid in the street must be in her back garden, playing. I wonder if any of the other neighbours will be here. I've not really met any of them yet, so it might be nice to meet them. I don't knock on the front door because I know it wouldn't be heard. Instead, I make my way around to the back garden.

It sounds like there are more kids than there actually are in the garden; Emma's three, Luke, and another two boys are playing at the back of the garden.

"So, you came," Patrick says, kissing me on the cheek. "Although you weren't getting much choice in the matter. She was getting ready to come and get you."

"Hey, you, enough," Emma says, slapping his arm.

"Ouch."

"Come on, beautiful girl. Let's get you out of there." She lifts Kate from her pram. "Who's a beautiful girl today?"

"Oh, thanks," I say, teasing.

"I wasn't talking to you, but you do look good." Her eyes scan my appearance and she smiles. I'm wearing shorts, flip flops, and a vest. Well, it is a gorgeous day, after all, and I was sitting out in the sun. "Your mummy looks scrummy."

"Oh, no. How much wine have you had already?"

"Hey, cheeky! Just a sip. I've just opened us a bottle." I stare at her and shake my head. "Come on. Let's find somewhere safe out of the way for us to sit with this little one."

Luke sees me, smiles, waves, and then goes back to playing with the boys. He looks as though he's having fun. I hope it's still nice tomorrow. There's something about a warm summer's day that makes me feel good.

Emma has a cover on the grass and puts Kate down. She sits down but I can already see her eyes scanning the garden to see what she can get up to.

"So, my brother. Have you seen him?"

"No."

"Not the answer I was expecting, although I do know he's busy at work."

"Yeah, I know. We've spoken."

"Have you now?"

"What?"

"Here you go, ladies." Patrick hands us a glass of wine each.

"What about Kate?"

"I'll go and get her some water."

"Give me her cup." I hand Patrick her cup and sit back and watch Emma with my baby. Emma loves her boys, but there's no doubt in my mind she would love a little girl. I turn my attention to the boys at the other end of the garden, having a water fight. That's one way of keeping cool today.

"I want the gossip, Lauren. Well, not all of it. Some things I'm better off not knowing about my brother."

I laugh nervously because there is no hope in hell that I'm going to sit and discuss my night with Matt.

"Ladies." I turn to face, I presume, Danny. Now that I see him up close, he does look like Matt, only a younger version.

"Talk of brothers and they always seem to pop up unexpectedly."

"What? Patrick invited me. I was at a loose end. Lauren." He holds his hand out to me, which I take. He bends and kisses it.

"Don't let Matt see you doing that." I turn back to Emma and frown. "I'm only saying it as I see it and he seems to be a bit possessive where you're concerned."

"And this little lady must be Kate," he says, taking her hand. Kate looks at him, smiles, and stands. "You look like your mummy, gorgeous girl."

"Danny . . ."

"Emma, give it a rest. Will we go and see what the boys are up to?" Kate walks away, holding his hand.

"Don't let her get wet," Emma shouts after him. He turns and shakes his head, laughing. "Bloody pain in the arse. Although, I know he will be careful with her."

"I'm sure he will, but he might not get her away from the boys. She will want to play with them."

"Good. He can look after her for a bit while we sit with our wine and enjoy the sunshine." That sounds good to me.

We sit talking about the school holidays, or what we're going to do with our kids for seven long weeks. I tell her about Grant and Liz taking my two away, and she insists I do something other than work. Emma has me well and truly sussed out. It's pleasant and relaxing sitting around in the garden, even with the noise of the kids.

"Food is ready," Patrick shouts. "Can one of you tell Danny and the kids?"

"I'll go," I say. "And rescue him. He's had Kate long enough."

"Okay. I'll go and sort out some soft drinks for the boys."

I walk down the garden and the boys are all still running around, minus the water guns, and there is Kate running after them, giggling away.

Danny lifts his head, noticing me. "She's not shy, is she?"

"No, she's not. Boys, food is ready," I call out to them. They all start shouting and running back up toward the house. Kate starts to follow them. "Not you, Little Miss," I say, scooping her up into my arms. She pulls a face that just makes her look cuter than she already is.

"Is she always so full of energy?"

I laugh. "Yes."

"God, you must be exhausted with her."

"She's worth it. They're both worth it."

We walk back up the garden, talking about the kids. Danny is really easy to be around and talk to. Patrick asks what I want for Kate to eat. I tell him I have her dinner and fruit in my bag. I sit and feed Kate whilst the others eat; I can grab something when she's finished. The boys all sit down on the rug, while we sit around the table. Conversation flows between the four of us.

"Here, let me. Go and have something to eat before the kids finish everything," Danny says taking the spoon I'm feeding Kate with.

"Is everyone in your family so damn bossy?" I ask with a laugh.

"Us? Bossy? Never," says Emma, with a smirk. "I'm sure you have Danny and me confused with someone else." They exchange glances and I sigh heavily, knowing there's nothing I can say. Danny takes Kate and she screams until he gives her a spoonful of food. I take a burger and some salad, and Patrick tops up the wine glasses on the table.

I can hear the boys talking about football training. About how much they are all looking forward to it. It's funny listening to them; their conversation sounds so serious. Patrick tells me that after the summer holidays, the boys' football team starts playing games on a Saturday morning. *Just what I was dreading*. He must sense my lack of enthusiasm for this because he offers to take Luke, although Emma says I have to attend the games. She says it can be fun, and even Danny tries to convince me.

"Lauren, you will love it. You need to go when he starts playing games because, from what I've seen, he's a good wee player. Knows a lot about the game itself. So go on, tell me you will go?" he pleads with me.

"And where is it she's going exactly?" I turn to see Matt. He stands by the patio doors and he looks pissed off as he looks between me and Danny. "Well? I'm waiting." The tone of his voice is controlled, yet deep, but the clenching of his fists suggests he's not feeling in control.

"What the hell is wrong with you?" Emma finally asks him, after staring at him for a few moments.

"Me? Nothing. I hadn't realised there was a private party going on. All nice and cosy looking."

Kate chooses now to cry. Danny has finished feeding her and she's not happy. He stands holding Kate against him, trying to console her, and rubbing her back. Matt stands watching, his eyes darting between Danny and me. What the hell is his problem?

"Green isn't a good colour on you," Emma snaps.

"What the fuck?" He stares at her, shaking his head.

"Matt, don't you dare try to deny it. There is nothing going on."

And finally, the penny drops with me.

"Danny, give her to me." He nods. I take her in my arms, turn my back to Matt, and try to comfort her, but it's not working. I ask Emma if I can take her inside so I can change her. Matt is impossible. When Emma said earlier that he was possessive as far as I was concerned, I thought she was just trying to be funny.

He can try and be possessive all he wants, but it's not going to happen. I'm not a fucking possession, and certainly won't be treated like one by a man who, technically, I'm not involved with. He keeps that attitude up and I won't be long in cancelling our date on Monday night.

Emma smiles weakly as I walk away with a crying Kate.

"Oh, baby girl, you're not happy. I think someone is tired."

"I think she is." I turn, finding Emma standing at the door. "Matt wanted to follow you inside. I told him to stay away until he reins in his temper. He's outside mouthing off at Danny."

"It will be the heat today. She's had sunscreen on and plenty of water but she's played outside most of the day. And as for Matt, I don't want to think about his performance outside. Christ, I was only talking to Danny."

"I know. It's actually really amusing."

"It's not. It's not as though we're an item or anything."

"Well, I don't think that's how Matt sees it." Kate has finally stopped crying. It's still early but I change her into her pyjamas because I do think today's heat is making her tired. Emma picks her up and she cuddles into her. "You coming back outside to have another drink? We can sit in the shade with this one and we'll both ignore my brother. Let the boys play."

"Is Luke okay?"

"Yes. Now, come on."

We go back outside and there's no-one sitting around the table. Everyone is playing football with the boys. I release my breath and move Kate's pram closer to the table. It's only been a matter of moments but she is already sound asleep in Emma's arms. I put her in the pram, checking her temperature. It's still warm so I don't put any covers on her.

"Here, I think you need this more than me," she says handing me a glass of wine. As I take a drink, I have to agree with her. My mounting frustration with Matt is playing heavily on my mind. I'm angry with myself for letting him get to me. I really need to calm myself down.

"I needed that," I say, putting the glass down. "What is it he wants from me?"

"You're asking the wrong person because I don't have the answers. As I've said, you're the first person I've seen him getting his boxers in a twist for." I find that statement amusing, but it doesn't help me. "You need to ask him."

"I'm going to cancel our date and probably stop working with him."

"Oh, hold on a minute, lady." There's a long pause as she takes a drink of her wine. "Firstly, I don't want Matt to come between us, no matter what happens with you two. Secondly, it shouldn't interfere with your work. You still need to earn a living. Deal with Danny. Thirdly, cancel the date if that's what you really want, but I don't think it is."

She has a point or three. "I don't know what the hell I want. I should concentrate on the kids, not myself."

"Stop there. You always put those two first. Always. But you need to think of yourself too. I'm not saying rush into a relationship, even with my brother, but you need to live a life as well."

"That's easier said than done. It's not as though David takes the kids, spends time with them. Unless I'm working, I have them."

She moves her chair closer to me and wraps her arm around me. I lean my head against her shoulder. "Lauren, if you're not careful, you will make yourself ill. Christ, I still need time away from my three and I have Patrick here to help me."

She's hit a sore point with me. I close my eyes because I want to forget that it's just me and the kids. Or me on my own when the kids are tucked up in bed at night. It's no wonder I've thrown myself into work these last few months.

"What's wrong?" Matt asks with an edge of concern.

I open my eyes, sitting back up straight, and smile. "Nothing, although I should take the kids home."

He narrows his eyes and frowns. "I think you will be one down tonight. Liam asked if Luke could stay over and Patrick said he could as long as it was okay with you."

"And what about me?" says Emma. Matt shrugs his shoulders. "Lauren, he can stay. I don't mind having him."

"I don't know," I say, already starting to feel anxious.

"He'll be fine. You know he will."

"Are you sure?"

"Yes, and I will bring him down early for Kate's birthday. I'm sure he'll want to be with you both in the morning and then I'll come down with the boys in the afternoon."

I sigh heavily. "In that case, I'm going to go home, put Kate into her bed and try to have a relaxing bath in peace."

"I can't tempt you to have another wine?"

"No."

Matt stares at me. "I'm coming to yours."

"What the hell?"

"It's not up for debate. If Kate wakes up crying, you won't get that relaxing bath. If I'm there, I can see to her. Don't worry; I'll only stay for as long as I'm welcome."

Emma and I exchange glances and I resign myself to the fact Matt is coming home with me.

fifteen

I CLOSE KATE'S ROOM DOOR behind me, the baby monitor in my hand, and stop dead, almost crashing into Matt as he walks out of my bedroom. "Hey, I hope you don't mind but I've run a bath for you while you were seeing to Kate." I want it to bother me that he feels comfortable in my house, but in all honesty, it doesn't. He seems troubled, a little distant, or maybe it's my own troubles I'm picking up on.

"Thanks." I look past him at my bedroom door and wonder what mess I left behind me when I was getting ready this morning. Shit, did I pick up my undies from the bathroom floor? Fuck, I can't remember. Matt turns his head to see what I'm looking at, and he sniggers. Christ, now I have a feeling my clothes are lying in a heap on the bathroom floor.

Brilliant.

"I'll take that." He takes the monitor from me with a smile. "Go and relax. I'll be downstairs with a glass of wine for you when you're finished."

I watch him walk downstairs; he doesn't look back. Not having Luke in the house is strange. At night, before he goes to bed, he can always be found following me around the house, talking, usually about football and Liam.

The scented aroma in my bathroom hits me straight away. It's subtle, yet distinctive. Lavender. *Thoughtful.* I test the water and I'm pleasantly surprised that it's perfect for me. I strip and climb in.

Heavenly. Leaning back, I rest my head against the edge of the bath and close my eyes. I can't remember the last time I had a bath. With the kids, all I get is a quick five minutes in the shower, and even that is nearly always interrupted.

My thoughts drift to Matt as I lie here, relaxing. Knowing he's downstairs, probably getting comfy on my sofa, is torture. Why the hell is he here? This past week, he's popped up everywhere. If I didn't know any better, I would think I had a stalker. But who in their right mind wants to stalk an almost thirty-year-old with two kids?

Everything about him has my nerve endings tingling. I want the bathroom door to slowly creep open. His husky voice would ask me to scoot forward, and he would climb into the bath behind me. One thing would lead to another and I would end up screaming his name. *Where the hell did that thought come from?* I open my eyes and concentrate on my breathing, which has rapidly got out of control.

Matt Anderson has taken me out of my comfort zone. My thoughts are all jumbled up. Whenever I'm around him, he makes me lose control, and for the past eight months, that's something I'm used to having—control.

I climb out of the bath because that's something I can control at the moment. Taking a fluffy white towel from the shelf, I stand and dry myself thoroughly. Opening the bathroom door, I peek into my room, just to make sure he's not there. He's not. I quickly put on short pyjamas and a vest and leave my bedroom.

I pause at the living room door, watching him. He doesn't turn, even though he must've heard me walking down the stairs. I allow my eyes to linger on the man who looks relaxed and comfortable sitting on my sofa in a room filled with pink and white balloons, shoes off, feet on the coffee table. He's a man of his word. There's a bottle of wine already opened with two glasses poured.

Taking a deep breath, I mentally tell myself to enter the room.

"Hope you don't mind," he says, turning his head away from the TV. He seems much more relaxed than he did earlier when he first arrived at his sister's. Fuck, I'm still not sure Emma was right about him being jealous, but then again, we are going on a date Monday night.

I stand, hovering, unsure of where to sit. Do I sit down on the sofa beside him? Or do I take the safe option and sit on the chair?

I'm not one for playing it safe these days it seems.

"How was that?"

"Relaxing." I flop down beside him. He smiles and hands me one of the glasses of wine. "We should talk about earlier."

"What can I say? I didn't like seeing you looking so happy with Danny."

I didn't expect him to be so fucking honest. I thought he would skirt around his feelings. Fuck. Fuck. And fuck again.

"Don't look so worried. I've spoken with Danny and he now understands."

"I'm glad someone does." I take a large gulp of wine. "Maybe you might care to explain to me what is going on because I seem to have been left out of the loop. Or maybe I just didn't get the memo."

"I deserved that."

"Yeah, I think you did. We haven't even been on our date yet, and you've laid claim to me."

"Lauren, I laid claim to you that night in my apartment. You are mine, we just need to iron out the finer details." He makes it sound like a damn business contract, waiting for me to sign on the dotted line. I don't think so.

"Hold on one minute, buddy." I pause. One, because I'm not too sure what to say to that, two, because the wine is going straight to my head, and three, his words are going straight to another part of my anatomy. "Matt, we have to work together . . ."

"I'm not going to sit here and listen to you rhyme off a whole load of reasons why we shouldn't get together. But you need to think of the reasons why we should be together."

"We don't really know each other and I have my kids."

"Lauren, stop looking for excuses. We're going out on Monday night and I know why you picked then, I'm not stupid. But even you have to admit there's something between us, and it's more than just a physical attraction. I want to see where this leads."

Why can't my life just be simple?

"Oh, fuck it."

"I'd like to fuck you but it will have to wait." Why the hell did he let those words pass his lips? He's tormenting me, or am I tormenting myself by denying myself his touch? I know how fucking good he feels against my body.

As I said—torture.

"Do you want me to go? Or are you happy for me to keep you company?"

"Stay." The word leaves me before I've thought about the meaning behind it. But it's simple; I do want him to stay, and with Luke not being here, it makes it easier.

"Lauren . . . ?" He shifts position, turning to face me. "That isn't what I meant, even though I would like nothing more than to wake up in the morning with you in my arms."

"I know, but I want you to stay."

It's official. I've totally lost the plot. So much for me putting my kids first. Here I am, going to put out again.

He lifts his hand, bringing it up and touching my face. I melt against him. Every single cell in my body is now alive, dancing from his touch. I need to be careful because something tells me if he breaks my heart in two, there will be nothing in the world strong enough to hold it back together. But it's not just me I need to think about. I've just agreed to see what happens between us, which means Matt will be in the kids' lives. They've been hurt and I don't want to see Luke get hurt again.

Neither of us can make promises to the other, but for the rest of the night, or as long as Kate stays sleeping, I'm going to make a promise to myself. A promise to enjoy every second we spend together.

"I want you. I want this tonight," I say softly.

"For tonight, you have me. Then tomorrow, we will find some common ground for us. I won't come between your time with the kids, but I do want to spend as much time with you as I can before spending time with the kids. I want them to get used to seeing me around before . . ."

I press my lips to his, silencing him. Yes, I'm sure he wants to work things out, but it needs to happen at my pace. I wrap my arms around his back and a sense of familiarity comes to me. His warm hands travel slowly across my shoulders, and the strap on my vest is lowered. His tongue slides along my bottom lip, seeking entry. I don't deny him because I would only be denying myself.

A low moan escapes his mouth as he breaks our kiss. I shiver from the loss of contact. He presses his forehead against mine, his eyes glazed and focused.

"This, between us. Tell me I'm not imagining it." His request hangs in the air around us. His eyes search mine, desperate for an answer.

My thoughts are now firmly of our first meeting, when our eyes met across the room. "No. It's not your imagination." The feelings he sparked then and now still send a shiver down my spine. This can't be normal. But I'm relieved we're both feeling the same thing, whatever it is.

I no longer want to be sitting here on the sofa with his arms around me. I want him in my bed. Memories of how alive he made me feel burn my mind. But I don't want memories. I need a reminder.

As if reading my mind, he tilts his head, lowering his lips to mine, at the same time lowering me on the sofa. His lips brush against mine slowly as he positions himself above me. Fuck, I'm done for. I can already feel a build-up of pressure as he grinds his hips against me. Heat soars through my body at a lightning pace.

He pulls back; I miss those lips. Hovering above, his hands on either side of me, he looks at me, waiting. For what though, I've no clue. I frown and he smiles. What a combination.

"You're going to make me beg?"

"I never thought of that, but now you mention it, I kind of like the idea of you begging me. Pleading with me."

"I won't do it." Or will I? To get what I want.

"Here's the thing; you don't have to beg me."

Thank God for that. But I'm not about to divulge that I would've begged and pleaded to get what I want.

Pressing a soft kiss to my lips, he sits back up and frowns. He stares at the baby monitor and I finally make the connection; my babbling daughter. Oh, Kate, you can sure pick your timing.

"Let's go and see if we can settle your baby." He stands and pulls me to my feet.

Sixteen

"IS SHE OKAY?" HE ASKS, as I walk into my bedroom. He stands in the middle of the room, minus his shirt, the belt loosened on his jeans, the top button undone. His naked torso looks so much better than I remember. So much better.

"Yes, she was only dreaming. Never even opened her eyes." I often wonder what she dreams about. It must've been a good dream for her not to wake up, but I stood at the side of her cot, gently stroking her face, soothing her until she was settled back into a deep sleep.

"I'm glad, because now I can have you all to myself," he says, grabbing my wrists roughly and pulling me until our bodies are touching. His lips are in touching distance of mine. "I'm about to give you a reminder of how good we are together. So, now, I'm hoping and praying that Kate sleeps long enough for this to happen. And this time you can't run from me."

"I don't want to run."

My words make him smile. There's a flutter in my belly that only he causes. The same flutter I feel every single time I see him. The effect he has on me is welcoming, yet it terrifies me too.

With his body pressed against me, he turns me around and starts walking, eyes never leaving mine. We come to a stop when the back of my legs hit my bed. I close my eyes and inhale deeply. A hint of citrus and sandalwood. He smells heavenly. Chuckling brings me back to my senses.

I open my eyes and he's smiling. A smile that melts my heart and renders me speechless.

My heart is hammering in my chest, anticipation running through my veins.

He places a hand under my chin. "You are perfect."

"I'm far from perfect," I whisper against his lips.

My lips part when he runs his thumb along them. "I never imagined anyone in the world was perfect, but you, Lauren, you most certainly are. Don't ever let anyone tell you any different. Now, we have unfinished business. Between the sheets is where I wanted you, if I remember correctly."

His gaze drops to my lips. He parts his and slowly they lower to mine.

This kiss is different. There's no rush. No sense of urgency. I could stand here and kiss him all night. His words go around and around in my mind, making me dizzy. *Between the sheets.* Well, I suppose I should make this happen.

Pulling his lips from mine, he takes a step back. I reach down, grab the bottom of my vest and slowly pull it up over my head, dropping it to the floor. His eyes are on me and I feel confident. I tuck my thumbs into the waistband of my shorts and smile before dropping them to the floor and stepping out of them. I stand before him completely naked and unashamed. His eyes light up, and for a moment, a split moment, he has me distracted by the smile on his face as his eyes roam my body.

"And you don't think you're perfect?" He takes a step toward me, closing the distance between us, eyes wide and brimming with desire. My breath catches in the back of my throat and shivers race up and down, leaving my skin buzzing.

My thoughts drift to our night together, his lips on mine, his naked body inches from me, his touch against my skin; a touch I'm now desperate for.

It barely registers when his lips touch mine. This kiss starts off slow and sweet. I throw my arms around him. He grabs my hair in one hand, and with the other, he grasps my hip.

My fingers dig into his shoulders as his lips work forcefully against mine. His grip on my hair tightens, holding me in place. Everything about him is intoxicating. My desire and need for him are building.

This is bad. He was only ever meant to be a one-night stand, yet here we are in my home. I've no restraint when it comes to him. I trail my fingers lightly away from his shoulders, down his muscular chest, allowing them to continue down his sculpted body until they rest on the waistband of his jeans.

His tongue slides inside my mouth, exploring and tasting. He lets go of my hair and I feel myself being lowered gently onto the bed. The bulge in his jeans presses against me. He needs to lose the jeans, now.

I brush my hand across it, pausing. His lips leave mine. His breath hisses against my neck and I groan.

"I can't believe I'm here with you. Having you around yet unable to touch has been unbearable. I remember the way your body felt against mine. You were made for me. Only me."

He takes one of my breasts in his hand and palms it lightly. My eyes close and my back arches into him. Small sparks ignite the burning need inside of me. Warm sensations sweep through me as I feel the heat of his breath against my nipple. The first touch of his tongue against my skin has me pressing my legs together, trying to relieve the building tension.

This feels heavenly.

No other man has ever made me feel so desired, and yet, here we are, and for a second time he has me experiencing new feelings.

Our conversation springs to mind. Can I allow myself to see

where this is heading? I want to but I have to put the kids first.

"Babe, you've gone all tense. Relax." I open my eyes and he's hovering above me, frown lines around his eyes as he watches me. "Don't think. Not tonight. Tonight is about us. Me and you. Or at least it is until Kate decides to wake up."

I can't help but smile. He's right; she could wake up at any time. I shouldn't be wasting our time together thinking.

"Okay then. As you were." I quickly lift my hand to cover my mouth and stop myself from laughing.

"As you wish." His lips twist in amusement as he stares at me, shaking his head.

His lips trail slowly around my neck. All the tension from a moment ago leaves my body. My eyes close again and all my thoughts are of here and now. *Only us*.

Soft lips caress my tingling skin. A wave of mist surrounds me, my judgement where he is concerned is clouded.

"Oh God," I moan, when his lips nip against my earlobe.

Fingers trace down my skin, stopping on my leg. He continues kissing me, his lips working their way back to mine. *I hope*. I shudder when his knuckles brush against my inner thighs. His lips meet mine and he wastes no time sliding his tongue inside, caressing mine. It's a slow movement and I groan when my legs are pushed apart. Christ, all I want to do is squeeze them together to relieve the building pleasure.

Our kiss deepens and I wrap my arms around him, threading my hands through his dark hair, tugging it slightly. The moan that escapes him does it. I open my eyes for the briefest of moments, and all I see when I look at him is desire and lust.

I draw in a deep breath that his mouth covers as he slides one finger, followed by another, into me. There's no way I'm going to last as he works his fingers in and out. His pace is steady but I'm greedy for more.

He stops kissing me and removes his fingers. I squirm. He

can't build me up like this and then . . . nothing.

I look at him. The room is almost dark now, except for a sliver of light shining through the window. I have no idea of time. Everything has been lost to Matt. He stops, stands, and stares. A slow smile twitches at the corners of his lips.

The light shines on him and I can totally appreciate the way his body moves as he kicks off his shoes before removing his jeans and underwear in one go. The view I have is pretty perfect.

"See something you like?" he asks with a smirk.

"Not sure yet. I think I need that reminder, *now*."

"Yeah, I'm sure you do." He picks up his jeans, taking a condom from his pocket. I watch as he opens the wrapper and rolls it on.

I still and hold my breath as he crawls up the bed, and I shiver when I feel him exactly where I want him. I move, attempting to get some friction where I need it most. His face is in line with mine, a sinful smirk on his lips. And dear God, this is so much more than before. Before we were two strangers, but this . . . this is something else. His muscular arms hold his weight at either side of my head.

"Matt!" I don't get to finish what I was about to say as he pushes into me with one long, hard push. "Ah!"

"Shit! You're not the only one needing this."

As I look into his eyes, I can see he needs this as much, if not more than I do. He's watching me intently. His movements are slow but they're having the desired effect.

"You, Lauren, are so fucking sexy," he almost growls as he moves in and out. "You are so much more than I remembered." There's that word again, *more*. "You feel this? It's only for you."

His words have me in a spin. The pace changes. Unable to focus on him, my eyes roll to the back of my head. I'm surrounded in a haze of fog.

Each thrust into me is harder than the one before, going that little bit deeper. My body is on fire. I'm so close.

Opening my eyes, I see he's worked up a bit of a sweat as it glistens on his skin. He is, after all, the one doing all the work.

My vision is blurring as the build-up starts. A sudden rush through my bloodstream and I'm lost. "Matt!"

I'm out of breath and panting. He moves his hands, grabbing hold of my shoulders as he moves with quick, deep thrusts, rocking back and forth. His face lowers and his lips meet mine. This time it feels urgent.

The kiss.

The thrusting.

Back and forth.

My need starts to build again.

His moans only add fuel to the fire. I come again quickly as I hear him fall apart. The weight of his body sags against me only for a moment before he moves. I close my eyes and don't bother opening them when I feel the bed shift beneath me. I should get cleaned up but I don't want to move.

In a few short minutes, he is back in bed beside me, curling up behind me, pulling the covers up and over our naked bodies.

"Now we are between the sheets," he whispers against me, kissing my neck.

I smile and snuggle closer to him. He wraps his arm around me. This feels comforting. If my daughter doesn't decide to get up anytime soon, I might, just might, get a good night's sleep. If I do, it's all because of the delicious man holding me close.

Seventeen

HIS ARMS ARE AROUND ME, and I smile as I open my eyes. It feels good having his arms around me. Someone that wants to spend time with me. I glance at my bedside clock. Seven a.m. This is a long lie-in for me. I jump and sit up. Kate is usually up before now.

"Lauren, she's fine."

I turn to face Matt. "Morning."

"Yes, it is a good morning," he says, pulling me back down in the bed and pressing his lips to mine. "You look rested."

"I feel it. And how do you know Kate is fine?"

"Because she woke up grumpy at five-thirty. I changed her and gave her some milk and she fell asleep in my arms. Not quite the same feeling as her mother falling asleep in them, but I've surprised myself."

"You changed her nappy?"

"Don't sound so surprised. You've seen my nephews, and believe it or not, I did change a nappy or two for them."

"A man of many talents then."

"You better believe it, and if you play your cards right, you might just find out what my other talents are."

"Mmm, I like the sound of that," I say, inching closer to him. I place my hand on his chest and allow my fingers to trace patterns on his skin as they slowly descend.

"You might like the sound of that, but I do love the direction you're travelling," he says, with amusement in his voice. I love his playful tone. "I think you and I are about to find out how much we enjoy waking up in each other's arms."

I think he might be right. I allow my hand to travel until I feel him, all of him, straining against his boxers. He must've put them on when he got up with Kate.

"I might make you my new form of morning exercise," he says softly. His voice sounds super sexy in the morning, penetrating deep to my core.

Quickly, he pushes me onto my back, positioning himself above me. Lips glide over mine and I want him. I throw my arms around his neck, pulling the weight of his body onto me. His mouth crashes against mine.

His hand moves downward and he pushes my legs apart. When his fingers hit that spot, I moan breathlessly into his mouth. He's barely touched me, yet I'm wet and ready for him again.

"Now, this is the type of cardio workout I could get used to," he says, sliding his finger deep inside me. My eyes close as I savour the building sensations that ripple through my body.

"Gaga. Gaga."

My eyes fly open. "Shit." Kate!

Matt kisses my nose. "I'll quickly wash up and get her for you. That will give you time to pull something on," he says, leaving the bed. My eyes follow him as he wanders into my bathroom. I sigh, listening to Kate babbling away, although I'm sure it will only be a matter of time before she gets upset. I climb out of bed and Matt leaves the bathroom.

"Do you mind if I grab a quick shower?" I ask.

"Go on. I'm sure Kate and I will be fine." His eyes roam my

body. A small smile at the corners of his mouth has me grinning inside.

"Thanks."

Dressed in jeans and a T-shirt, I wrap a towel around my wet hair and leave my bathroom. I stop in the doorway and watch Matt playing with Kate on my bed. She is giggling away and squirms as he tickles her. I can't help but smile. He looks so relaxed with her.

He lifts his head. "Oh, look. Mummy has decided to join us," he says, scooping Kate up in his arms. She's still giggling when she looks at me. Matt's eyes roam my body before he returns his attention to my baby.

"Someone is happy this morning. Happy birthday, my beautiful baby." She holds her hands out to me and I take her, giving her a kiss and a cuddle. She babbles away and I feel guilty that I wasn't the one to see to her when she first woke up. It's her day, after all. A day to spoil her.

"Is she always so good?" Matt asks.

"She has her moments, but yeah, she is a great-natured girl. Unless she's tired or unwell."

"Now, that I can understand. We're all guilty of being a little crabbit when we're sick. But if she's this happy, you must be doing something right."

My eyes fall on Kate as she continues to babble in my arms. I smile because he does make a point that I agree with. I don't think I'm doing too badly with my kids. Yes, it's hard, but it's bloody worth it.

"What are your plans for the day?" Matt asks.

"I'm doing lunch for everyone to celebrate, and I know Sandra and Les want to talk to me about them looking after the kids. Abbie is really keen on us going into business."

"That sounds interesting." He already knows about this; we've spoken about Abbie's proposal.

"I hope I can work out the kids with Sandra because I do agree with Abbie and me going into business. We're both great at what we do."

"I'm sure it will all work out for the best. And you know where I am for advice." I nod. "Now, as I'm a guest in your home, I think you need to feed me before I leave."

"I can make you something to eat but you don't have to leave." He looks confused. "You're more than welcome to stay for lunch with us. Emma is going to bring the boys down later."

He gets up from the bed and stands in front of me, his face close to mine. "Yes, I could stay," he says in a whisper, pressing his lips to mine. I shut my eyes, enjoying the feeling of his smooth lips against me. Kate giggles. I open my eyes and she's looking between us.

"Let's get you both some breakfast. I'll phone Emma to bring Luke down so he can open presents with this one."

"Breakfast sounds good." He takes Kate from me, and she's more than happy to be in his arms. "And you, young lady, well, we can watch Mummy in the kitchen." He flashes me *that* smile before walking away from me.

My heart skips a beat. I know I shouldn't be rushing into anything, but everything with Matt feels so right. A week, that's all I've known him. I need to slow things down for my own benefit.

I quickly towel dry my hair, brush it, and tie it back. With a glance in the mirror, I decide I look okay and make my way downstairs to the kitchen. Matt is sitting at the table with Kate still in his arms. I hope she doesn't expect to be in my arms for the rest of the day because it's not happening.

"Tea or coffee?"

"Make it coffee. I might need it to keep me alert today," he says smugly, eyes firmly on me. And I know what he means. I shake my head and turn, putting the kettle on. As I move around the kitchen, I don't have to turn around; I can feel his eyes on me. It's slightly unnerving. I make some toast and chop up an apple for Kate; that should keep her busy and quiet long enough for me to finish breakfast for Matt and me.

"Okay, Little Miss, time for your breakfast," I say, putting the food down. Matt straps her into her high chair. She looks up at me, fluttering her eyelashes, tilting her head to the side. God, she will always get what she wants if she does that all the time.

"You're too cute," I say, placing a kiss on the top of her head.

"There's only one person she takes the cuteness from." I don't engage in that conversation because I have bacon cooking under the grill. As I cook, I hear him talking to Kate. It saddens me because my thoughts now to turn to David, of all people. I've seen how comfortable Matt is with Kate and Luke, yet David, their own dad, can't be bothered with them. Now that I think about it, he was never relaxed with either of them.

It saddens me today. There's a part of me that would love nothing more than to see David walk through my front door to wish Kate a happy birthday, but deep down, I know it's not going to happen.

"What are you thinking about?" he asks softly, wrapping his arms around my waist and resting his head on my shoulder.

How the hell do I put this?

"I'm going to spit it out but I don't mean to offend you. I was thinking about David." He spins me around, his eyebrows raised, waiting for me to explain. "Not like that. I don't miss him or anything. It's just . . . I've seen you, a complete stranger to my kids, yet you've been more relaxed around them than he ever was."

"And . . . ?"

"It's just made me think, that's all. And especially today."

"It's his loss. Not the kids'."

"I know." I press my head to his chest while he gently strokes my back in comfort. "You'll have to let me go or I'm going to burn breakfast."

He lets me go after kissing me and he sets the table for us. A few minutes later, we're both tucking into toast and bacon, while Kate sits happily eating more toast. Kate ensures there is no lingering silence at the table.

"Are we still going on our date tomorrow night?" he asks.

"Yes."

"Tomorrow will be fun, and I'll be the perfect gentleman."

"Hmm."

"Hey, it's a date, and if you're lucky I might even kiss you when I bring you back home."

"Behave. Now, I should get this little lady dressed."

"You see to Kate and I'll tidy up."

"Are you trying to impress me?"

"No. I think I've impressed you already."

I stand, shaking my head. "You are impossible."

Emma's eyes dart between Matt, who is still wearing last night's clothes and has Kate in his arms, and me.

"How has Luke been?" I ask.

"He was fine. The boys all played great together. I swear they would have a football at their feet in their sleep if they could get away with it. From the look of you, my dear brother, you haven't been home."

"No, I haven't."

I close my eyes because I don't want to see what Emma thinks of me.

"I'll come to yours for a bit, spend some time with the boys, and grab a shower. Then I'll come back here for the celebrations," Matt says.

"Oh."

"Emma, close your mouth," he tells her. I take Kate from his arms and watch as he takes Emma's arms and guides her from my kitchen. I can't help but smirk, and I'm looking forward to seeing them both soon. Now to spend some quality time with my babies.

Eighteen

OUR MORNING TOGETHER HAS PASSED by so quickly. Luke has played with Kate and fussed over her. It's always great seeing him with her, but it means more today. Even when she's thrown a tantrum, he's been patient with her. He helped her with her presents and sang Happy Birthday to her. Kate's face has been a picture all morning.

I look at the time. I should make a start on organising food for everyone. After all, I did tell them I was making a late lunch.

"Luke, Mummy has to start cooking lunch for everyone. If I put Kate in her high chair, can you still play with her?"

"Of course." I don't know why his answer surprises me because he always helps out. I'm sure as he gets older that will change.

There's a knock at the front door. I pick up Kate, and Luke rushes to answer it. "Mummy, it's Liam's Uncle Matt." Of course, it is.

Matt is standing on my doorstep with a large pink gift bag in one hand and a pink unicorn in the other. I smile. "Come in."

"Is that a birthday present for Kate?" Luke asks.

"Yes. A little birdie told me it was a special birthday today."

"It is," Luke says enthusiastically. "She's one. She's not a baby anymore."

"No, but she still needs to be taken care of," I tell him.

We go into the kitchen and I strap Kate into her high chair. "You shouldn't have done this," I say, as Matt hands the unicorn to Kate.

"What? It's her birthday. I can't come to a party and not give the birthday girl a present. Now, can I help you?"

"You any good in the kitchen?"

"If you had stayed at mine last week, you would already know the answer to that," he whispers, leaning in close. I close my eyes and take a deep breath. "Yes. I can help you."

I open my eyes and look at the kids, who are both playing, and take another deep breath. "Matt, please. Today, I need you to behave. Whatever this is," I say, pointing between us, "has to stay between us. I don't want Luke picking up on it and asking questions. Not yet. He's been through enough already, and until we decide what we're doing, I don't want to . . ."

"It's fine," he says flatly. "I do understand, but it's going to take willpower, because even now, all I want to do is wrap my arms around you and feel you relax in my arms. Inhale your scent and just touch you."

"I'm sorry."

"Don't be. I'm not, but I am looking forward to our date tomorrow. Now, what are we cooking?"

"Chicken, rice, and some salads. I have burgers for the boys, although I'm sure all they'll want to do is play football."

"You could be onto something there, but I think Luke will spend the day with Kate," he says, smiling at my kids.

Luke keeps Kate entertained while Matt helps me. It has been noted that we work well together in the kitchen. I shouldn't be thinking about that but I can't help it. He doesn't get in my way and the work gets done in half the time, as he prepares several different salads. Matt looks at home in a kitchen. Or is it that he is just so relaxed that he would look at home anywhere?

Stirring the rice, I turn it off and put the lid on the pot. It's ready. I turn around and Matt is leaning against the worktop, staring. "What?"

"Nothing, I've just been admiring the view. Now, would you like to open Kate's present?" Shit. I completely forgot he had a bag in his hands when he came in.

"Sorry, and yes."

He picks the bag up and I walk over and sit down beside Kate, who is eating some banana. Matt puts the bag on the table. Luke stops talking to Kate and watches me. The first thing I take out is a beautiful pink dress and cardigan. "Sorry. I didn't have time to wrap it."

"It's pretty but she can't wear it playing in the garden with me," Luke says. We both laugh because he's right.

"It's beautiful."

"Open the rest."

There are more clothes and a box at the bottom of the bag. I lift my head; he's watching me. I take the box from the bag and open it. I throw my hand over my mouth. It's stunning. It's perfect. A beautiful gold charm bracelet with the initial K on it.

"Do you like it?"

"It's gorgeous, but you shouldn't have."

"It comes with extra links and can be extended the older she gets."

"That's very thoughtful, but it's too much."

"It's her birthday, and Luke will agree with me, it's a special birthday."

Luke eagerly nods his head.

"Lauren?" Emma's voice rings through from the front door. I had a feeling she would be here early.

"We're in the kitchen," I call out. "Matt, remember what I said? And Luke."

"Yes, Mum?"

"Remember and play with Kate as well as Liam and the boys."

"I will, and I'm sure she will play football as well."

No. I don't want my baby girl playing football. I shake my head from side to side and Kate laughs.

"Well, this all looks very cosy," Emma says, as she enters the kitchen, followed by the boys.

"Emma . . ." I can hear the warning in Matt's voice. She stops and kisses Kate, ignoring Matt.

"Happy Birthday, beautiful girl. Don't you look pretty today." She unstraps her from the highchair and picks her up, giving her a big cuddle. The boys and Luke start chatting and the noise level increases as they talk football. God, I have no idea how I'm going to cope with football.

"Now, this I like," says Emma, holding the unicorn. "Did Mummy get this for you?"

"No, it's from Matt," I say.

"So, that's where you went this morning?"

"I couldn't come here without a present, no matter what her mother says or thinks."

I shake my head at him and turn my attention to the boys. Liam has a football in his arms. "You can go outside with that."

"Yes, Mum." The boys go out into the garden and Matt follows. I carry on tidying up and sorting the food.

"Lauren?"

I turn around. Emma's eyes are narrowed, and she looks concerned.

"What?" I all but snap at her.

"Lauren, do you want me to speak to Matt?"

"Yes. No. I don't know."

"Oh, honey. Talk to me. He's my brother, and yes, I love him, but I'm your friend and I don't want anything to come between that."

"This is all moving too quick for me. He wants to see where this is going. I'm not ready for that. Yes, I like him, a lot, but that doesn't mean . . . Oh shit, I don't know what it means. I'm confused."

"I'll talk to him later."

I smile weakly at her. "Thank you."

"Now, do you need me to do anything?"

"Nope. All organised."

"Okay. Well, I'm going to keep this little one company until everyone else gets here and, no doubt, takes her from me."

I can hear the front door open. "We're in the kitchen," I call out.

"Where is my beautiful goddaughter?" Abbie, followed by her parents. "Hi," she says to Emma. "Let's see you, gorgeous girl." Emma hands Kate over and my baby giggles and kisses Abbie. I introduce Emma to Sandra and Les.

"How are you?" Sandra asks, giving me a kiss.

"I'm good."

She frowns. God, am I that easy to read?

"I'll take that answer for now, but I know there's something wrong. You can always talk to me."

"Thanks." Matt enters the kitchen, out of breath. Sandra's eyes dart between him and me.

"Sandra, this is Matt. He's Emma's brother, and a friend of mine."

He holds his hand out, which she accepts, but her eyes are still darting back and forth. "Nice to meet you."

"And you."

Emma quickly arranges drinks for everyone, as though sensing the awkwardness I feel in the room. The boys rush in looking for drinks and food, which I give them. I'm handing Luke his when Grant and Liz come into the kitchen.

"There's one of my girls and my boy," says Grant, giving me a hug.

"You made it."

"Yes. It's my fault we're late. Liz had been pestering me to hurry up but I was working on something."

"Grant, good to see you again." Grant shifts from one foot to the other and it's obvious he's not happy to see Matt again. He looks at Matt with venom in his eyes. I've never seen Grant look at anyone like that before. I can feel the blood drain from my face as I look between the men standing only feet away from me. Grant's body is tense and he looks around the kitchen. I'm the only one who seems to have picked up on the tension that radiates from Grant. I don't need this today.

"Uncle Grant," I say, my voice strained. "I don't know what's going on between you, but this is my daughter's day, and if you both can't be civil, then I will ask you both to leave." I stand and wait for either of them to acknowledge me.

"I'm sorry, sweetheart," says Grant, offering his hand to Matt. "It's good to see you. We should have lunch this week. There are things we need to discuss."

"That would be good."

I watch as both men turn. Grant goes straight to Liz, who now has Kate, and Matt stands with Emma, who has a scowl on her face. I shake my head, put a smile on my face, and promise myself to enjoy today and deal with Grant and Matt tomorrow.

As I finish tidying up the kitchen, it's safe to say my girl has been spoiled by everyone. Kate and Luke are in bed, fast asleep, and everyone has left. Grant and Matt managed to stay civil to each other when I was there, although I'm not sure I can say the same when I wasn't there.

It's been a great but exhausting weekend, and I'm more than ready to fall into my bed. My phone beeps as I walk up the stairs after switching everything off.

Matt: I can't wait until I pick you up tomorrow for our date.

Me: I'm looking forward to it too but I'm looking forward to going to sleep more.

Matt: Goodnight x

Nineteen

"LAUREN, ARE YOU READY?" ABBIE calls out. I can hear her coming up the staircase. "He'll be here soon."

I look at my appearance in the full-length mirror, wondering if I've made the right choice with this black dress. Matt did tell me to get dressed up, but I think this might be too much for a Monday night.

"Oh, wow. You look hot." I turn, skimming my hands down my dress, and nervously smile. Abbie has Kate in her arms. "What the hell are you nervous about?"

"I don't know."

"You have nothing to be nervous about. This is a guy who wants to spend time with you."

"That's what frightens me."

She shakes her head, hands firmly on her hips. "Lauren Trent, enough. Get it into your head, he bloody likes YOU. He's spent time, although only a short time, pursuing you, even if you don't realise it. You spent Saturday night with him in that very bed. Yesterday, he spent the day here for this one's birthday. Tonight is all about finding out more about each other. Talking. So whatever is going on in that head of yours, push it right to the back and go out with that sexy man and enjoy some good food and his company."

"I know what you're saying. He wants to see where this, whatever it is, goes. But I have the kids, and then there is what Grant said and how they were with each other yesterday. It's been going over and over in my head."

"Lauren, I'm sure Matt will be expecting you to ask what the problem is, especially after yesterday. In my opinion, you come out and ask. To me, that seems the easiest option."

Of course, she's right, but maybe I'm scared of what his answer might be. He could be a murderer or a drug dealer for all I know. Now I'm being silly. I've spent too much time watching dramas on TV.

"Now, get your smile on your face and get that sexy arse downstairs . . ." She doesn't finish because the door bell rings.

"I'll get it," shouts Luke from downstairs.

"Hurry up," Abbie says, walking out of my bedroom.

Another look in the mirror. 'You can do this Lauren,' I say to myself. With a smile, I grab my handbag and make my way downstairs. There's laughter coming from the living room. I pause at the doorway and take a deep breath before entering. He has his back to me but has Kate in his arms; she's giggling away, and Luke is bouncing up and down. God, I hope they both settle for Abbie when I leave.

Luke sees me first and stops. "Mummy." He rushes toward me and Matt turns. "You look really nice, Mum." I ruffle his hair and he shows me the biggest of smiles.

"Fuck." That's the only word that leaves Matt's gaping mouth. His eyes linger on my face before they roam my body. He's taking every last detail in, like I'm doing with him. His hair. His suit that fits perfectly. I smile because I have the pleasure of already knowing exactly how he looks under that suit.

"Mummy, Matt said a bad word."

"I heard."

"Sorry. I didn't think."

Abbie is standing near the window, smirking. I'm so glad she finds this amusing. He stalks toward me, Kate babbling in his arms, but his attention is on me.

"I didn't mean to swear but you took my breath away," he says in a whisper, leaning in and kissing my cheek.

Luke giggles. "Matt kissed Mummy."

Oh no. We need to get out of here because I'm not ready for the questions I'm sure my son will start asking.

"I think we should go," I say.

"You might be right."

"Okay, I'll take you," Abbie says, lifting Kate from Matt. "Now, you two go and have a fun night."

I kiss both kids and we leave quickly.

Matt stops walking as soon as I close the front door behind us. He steps in front of me, eyes smouldering. "I'm sorry I swore in front of the kids. That's something I'm going to have to learn not to do. But seriously, every time I see you it's like seeing you for the first time all over again. You look amazing tonight, but in my eyes, you always do."

I close my eyes and allow his words to float through my head. He's smooth . . . real smooth. I'll give him that. He takes my hand and we walk to his car. I don't turn around because I know Abbie is at the window, watching us. Ever the gentleman, he opens the passenger door and I enter as gracefully as I can before he closes the door.

The car smells just how I remember it; new. He slides effortlessly into the driver's seat, flashes me a smile, and starts the engine. It roars to life and we drive off. I try to relax but I can't. I've not been on a date in seven years, so for me, this is nerve-wracking.

"Lauren, relax. We're going to have fun." I turn my head and look at the impressive man in the driving seat. The grin on his face is infectious and I find myself smiling. "That's better. You have nothing to be nervous about. This will be the perfect date."

I'm sure he's right.

Matt starts talking about the kids and we fall into easy conversation. Conversation changes to family and friends. We've touched on this a little during recent talks, but this time I get to find out a little about his family. He is the oldest of three at thirty-five; Emma is thirty-two and Danny is twenty-seven. I learn that he lost his dad ten years ago; he died following a car crash.

He goes on to tell me that he is really close to his mum and that he can't wait for me to meet her. I think he's jumping the gun a bit, but I don't tell him that.

"We're here." I look out of the window to see we've stopped outside what looks like a very prestigious restaurant; there's a doorman waiting to open my car door. Now I'm glad I opted for this dress. Matt gets out and the doorman opens my door. Slowly, I get out and smooth down my dress.

"Beautiful," says Matt, who is now at my side. He hands his car key over and takes my hand.

We enter the restaurant and are greeted by a woman in a revealing dress, cleavage on show, who air kisses Matt. She's wearing far too much make-up; it's practically caked on her face. From the look of disappointment when her eyes cast over me, she knows the man beside me who still has my hand in his. She looks out of place here, although she wouldn't look out of place on a street corner. She looks cheap, unlike the restaurant we're in.

How well does she know him, or want to know him?

"It's been a few months, Matt." Her voice is soft but there's an edge to it. She fidgets with her hands. Her face is flushed and I'm sure if my eyes travelled down her body, she would be pressing her legs together. I can't help it. My eyes travel and confirm what I already knew.

"Yes, it has. My mother's birthday, I believe."

"Yes, it was. Your table is ready if you'd like to follow me."

She turns on her heels and we follow behind as she sashays her hips in front of us. I turn slightly to see his reaction to her, but his eyes are on me. He tightens his grip, rubs his thumb slowly on my hand, and smiles.

We are shown to an almost private table in the busy restaurant. "Your table, Matt. A bottle of our finest, as per usual?" she asks. Pangs of jealousy flit through my mind. Yes, it's clear this woman knows him very well, or at least wants me to think she knows him well.

"Lauren . . . ? I wont be drinking."

"I don't intend drinking a bottle on my own, but I will have a glass of wine with my meal."

"I'll go and leave you to read the menu," the woman says.

"Sorry."

"What is it you're sorry for?" I ask him.

"For . . . nothing. It doesn't matter." His gaping mouth closes and his eyes fall from me.

"I think it does, otherwise you wouldn't have mentioned anything. So, are you sorry for the way your friend ran her eyes over me, disapproving? Or are you sorry for you and Grant yesterday?" I sit back in the oversized velvet chair, cross my legs, and fold my arms. This wasn't how I saw this conversation going, but his friend has made me feel uncomfortable yet brave.

"Lauren, yes, I'm sorry for the way Martine has behaved. It was very unprofessional and I will ensure she knows that."

"So, who is she?"

"She is the manager here."

"Okay, but what is she to you?" There's a coldness to my question and I almost don't recognise my own voice.

He stares at me, thinking about his answer, and suddenly, I don't want to know. I push my chair back and stand. "This isn't a good idea."

"No, Lauren. Please. She's a friend and we used to be business partners."

I stop. "Oh, but she wants you."

"Yes, she does and always has, but she's never had me. Please stay." I sit down and he reaches across the table and takes my hand. "Lauren, I wanted tonight to be perfect. Now I'm wishing I hadn't come here, even though the food is, in my opinion, the best in Glasgow."

I sigh. "Well, let's read the menu."

We do but there is an uncomfortable atmosphere surrounding us, and I can't help feeling this is my fault. I shouldn't have asked. It's none of my business who she is. It's obvious to me he is a man with a past. A colourful past.

It's not Martine that comes back to take our order, and for that, I'm grateful. We order food and drinks, including a glass of red wine for me.

"Lauren, I suppose it's up to me to clear things up. What do you want to know?" Already I sense that this first date isn't going well, or as well as he had hoped for.

"Let's start with Grant. I wanted to know but was going to leave it until later on."

"I'm sure Grant has told you he is my bank manager."

"Yes, but that doesn't explain why he would warn me to stay away from you. And then there's the way you each were with the other yesterday."

He takes a deep breath, his eyes look lost, and suddenly, I feel cold. Why do I already know I'm not going to like what he tells me? "Because you are his niece and he loves you and will want to protect you. Grant and I move in much the same circles." The hairs on the back of my neck stand up on edge. "I'm proud of the restaurant and club and what I'm trying to achieve with it, but let's just say business hasn't always been easy for me."

"What do you mean?" A waiter appears, interrupting our conversation with our food, and it looks like a work of art on a plate. "Thank you," I say to him, before he scurries off. He obviously felt the tension between us. Poor guy.

"Shit, Lauren. This isn't easy to say . . ."

"I suggest you spit it out."

"Martine and I ran an escort agency."

I drop the cutlery and it crashes onto my plate. Suddenly, the restaurant falls silent, and I know if I turn around, everyone in my line of sight will be looking in our direction. Of all the things he could've told me, I never fucking expected that. "As in prostitution?"

"Yes." His eyes fall to the table and he can't look at me. That would explain why I thought she looked like a hooker.

What the hell? I can't do this. He finally lifts his head and he looks as disappointed as I feel. In the space of a week, he has turned my world upside down.

I need to escape. Escape from here. From him.

There's a deep need to protect myself once again. But this feels different from the last time I turned my back on a man. I push my chair back and look into his eyes, and he already knows I'm leaving.

"Lauren, please let me explain."

I shake my head and turn away from him. For me, this is the right thing to do. I have to think of my family and they will always come first. Eyes are on me as I walk away, leaving him behind. Martine attempts to speak to me, but I brush past her.

Outside, I flag down a taxi. I'm closing the door behind me when I hear him call after me. "Please drive." The cab starts moving and I allow myself to turn around to see him standing in the middle of the road.

Yes, this is the right thing to do, so why the hell do I feel so bad? My body sinks into the seat as my body shakes. My phone starts ringing, and it's Matt. I switch it off and close my eyes.

Twenty

"ABBIE, WE CAN TALK TOMORROW. I'm not feeling great."

She looks at me as though she's staring straight through me, to the depths of my soul. I don't want to talk, not tonight. What do I say to her? *Hey, that sexy man I've been spending time with is a . . .* I don't even know what I would say to my best friend.

"Why didn't Matt bring you home?" I should've known I would face an inquisition from her, but I'm not ready to reveal the details of tonight. Not yet.

"Abbie, I'm going to bed, and hopefully it's only a twenty-four-hour bug and I'll be fine tomorrow."

"You don't look good. Do you want me to stay over?"

"No. You go home."

"Okay, but I'll come around in the morning, and if you're still not feeling great, I'll take Luke to school and Kate to Mum's."

"Okay. Thank you." She kisses me before reluctantly leaving. Abbie isn't daft. She knows there's more to me feeling unwell and she knows I'll tell her when I'm ready.

I climb the stairs in a daze and look in on the kids; they're both fast asleep. I remove my dress as I enter the bedroom, and climb into bed, not bothering to put anything else on.

I close my eyes but he's all I see. Everything . . . I see it all. The way he looked at me when he first turned around and saw me earlier downstairs in my sitting room. He looked as happy as I felt. Then there was the look on his face when I stood and walked away from him. He looked hurt. But what did he expect me to do after that revelation? Did he think I would carry on having dinner and pretend he never mentioned it? Matt Anderson was and maybe still is nothing better than a fucking pimp, for all I know.

The question that runs on a loop in my mind is, did he just pimp out prostitutes for others' pleasure, or did he sell his own soul?

My stomach churns and I run to the bathroom, hand over my mouth. I slump on the bathroom floor and my tears fall.

No wonder Grant warned me off him, but what I can't understand is why he wouldn't just come out and tell me he ran an escort agency. If I had known that, it would've changed everything this week.

Everything has changed, except my night with him at his apartment. That can't be changed, and even if it could, I wouldn't want to. That one night awakened all my senses. Senses that had long been closed off. He made me feel alive and wanted, and for that, I will always be grateful.

Trust.

I don't think I'll ever trust another man again. Look where it's got me. Lost and alone.

My morning routine is done on auto-pilot; showering, getting dressed, waking up the kids. No thought goes into any of it.

"Mummy, are you sick?"

"Not really. I'm a bit tired," I say, putting down a bowl of breakfast cereal for Luke and handing Kate some toast.

"I hope Kate is good for you today."

"Me too. Me too, buddy."

Loud banging on the front door has me stopping in the middle of the kitchen floor. Surely he wouldn't come around here banging about when I have the kids here?

"Lauren, open this door." Abbie. My body relaxes and my feet start moving in the direction of the noise. "Why the hell have you not answered my calls?" she asks, stomping into the house when I open the door. She might have a key, but, well . . . she can't get in if I have the chain on.

"Good morning to you too."

"Don't *good morning* me. I've been worried sick about you." She stands in the hallway, huffing at me.

"Well, as you can see, I'm perfectly fine and there's no need to be worried."

"Yes, you might have painted a face on today, but I can still see that you've been crying. So, you better start explaining. What went so wrong with your date with Matt?"

I take a deep breath and try to sort out all the jumbled words, but it's no use. There's no way to pretty this up. "He ran an escort agency."

"Fucking hell." She gasps.

"Mum, Kate is throwing her milk about."

I move automatically and stop, watching my daughter, who is throwing her cup onto the floor and laughing when Luke picks it up. She's a little madam.

"Enough of that, lady." She turns, still laughing. I can't help but smile as I look at her. She's going to keep me on my toes today. There will be no time for me to dwell on the events of last night. That can only be a good thing. "Luke, you need to finish your breakfast and then brush your teeth. We will be leaving soon."

"Yes, Mum."

Abbie picks up Kate, brushing her clothes down to remove all the toast crumbs. "Lauren, are we going to talk about this?"

"What's to talk about? This is why Grant warned me off him.

I understand now."

"But it doesn't add up. Do you want me to come over after work tonight?"

"No. I'm fine, honestly. Tonight I'm all about the kids. Just me and them. No work."

She frowns, pulling her bottom lip into her mouth. "What about working for him?"

"That's not going to happen. Not now. He can find someone else." I grab my phone while Abbie has Kate and switch it on. I sigh dramatically when my phone lights up. Bloody hell. Six missed calls from Abbie, twenty-four from Matt, along with ten text messages. Well, he's bloody persistent.

"What's wrong?" I show her my phone. "Oh, looks like someone wants to talk," she says, watching me with wide eyes.

"Well, I'm in no mood or hurry to talk to him. Luke, can you hurry up? It's nice and I want to walk to school instead of taking the car." He puts the spoon down that he's been playing with the last few minutes and leaves the room.

"You will have to talk to him at some point."

"I don't have to do anything."

"Lauren . . ."

"Don't *Lauren* me. Haven't you got some place to be? Like work." I press my lips tightly together.

She gives Kate a kiss on her cheek. "It seems, my sweet girl, Mummy is about to lose her temper with me." She hands Kate to me. "Lauren, you can't brush this under the carpet. You do like him, a lot more than you're letting on. I'll go and you can have your night with just the kids, but tomorrow, you don't get to dismiss me. We will talk and I'll bring dinner because I will not allow you to wallow in your own self-pity. I love you. See you tomorrow." It's my turn to get a kiss on the cheek before she walks out of the kitchen, and moments later, I hear the front door closing behind her.

Well, that's me told.

"Mum, I'm ready," Luke calls out. I quickly put Kate's jacket on and put her in her pram. A walk will do me the world of good. Once I've dropped Luke at school, I might even go to the park. Yes, that's what I'll do. It will keep us out of the house. It looks as though it's going to be too nice to be stuck indoors.

I tuck my phone into the back pocket of my jeans and the three of us leave the house for the fifteen minute walk to school. We've done this walk a few times since moving, but not as often as I would've liked. Luke chats away; he's looking forward to football training tomorrow night. God, that's been the hot topic of conversation in the house since last week. He really loves it.

My phone buzzes more than once, but I resist the temptation to see who it is. If it's work-related, it can wait until tomorrow. Today, work is taking a back seat. And if it's Matt, I'm in no hurry to speak with him.

We stop at the school gates. Luke doesn't want me to go into the playground with him. He gives me and Kate a hug and a kiss before he runs off, no doubt to find Liam. Shit! I'm going to have to face Emma. I don't know if I'll be able to see her or talk to her.

I turn the pram around and bang straight into her. "Oh my God, I'm sorry."

"Don't worry, I'm fine, but more importantly, how did your date go and when is your next one?" I shrug, trying to play it cool and trying not to look at her. "Lauren, what's he done? I'll bloody kill him. I told you, he might be my brother but I don't want him to come between us or the boys."

I lift my head and see hurt in her eyes. "Do you have time for a walk? I'm going to the park with Kate. I need to clear my head."

"Fuck! That bad? And yes, I'm coming with you. I may as well know what he's done."

"Okay, you need to tell me."

I look at Kate who is sitting in her pram, watching everything we pass. When she hears a dog bark, she turns around, looking for it. She's not scared of the noise, more excited, and I know if she wasn't in her pram she would be running around, chasing after it.

"I met Martine last night at the restaurant."

"Oh!" She sighs heavily and doesn't even try to act surprised at my statement. Her eyes lower. There's a pained expression on her face and her body sags as heavily as the sigh that's just escaped her.

"Yes, *oh*. So our date was a non-starter. I should've listened to Grant. He did try to warn me off him."

"Matt's my brother and I love him, but I'm the first to admit he's made some wrong choices in his life. And being in business with Martine was the biggest and most costly mistake he's ever made. Yes, I know what was going on and I'm sure Danny does too, but it was a good few years ago and my mum doesn't know. I wouldn't dream of shattering her image of him. He's not proud of that part of his life."

"So why did he take me there?"

"He's a man. They don't tend to think." I laugh, because I know that's true. "Has he been in touch?"

"What do you think?" That's reminded me, I've not checked my phone. I pull it from my back pocket and there are another three missed calls from him. Emma looks on as I feel myself frowning.

"You have to hear him out. I'm sure he'll be completely honest with you. I could sit here and tell you why he ended up with an escort agency as a business, but I think you need to hear it from him. And when you do speak to my brother, come back to me if you want anything clarified."

"Why don't you just tell me?"

"Because it's not my story to tell. Now, you've met Martine . . . she desperately wants to dig her claws into him and have him all to herself. It doesn't matter what fancy clothes she puts on, she will always be a hooker in my eyes."

"Oh!" My mouth falls open, and there's a sudden coldness within me. Scrambled thoughts flit through my head about her wanting Matt; my first impression of her was correct. She was one of his hookers. "It looks as though she's done well for herself."

"Oh, she has, but that's down to Matt. She was the most expensive he had on his books. I don't want to think about what she did that threatened her money or a reputation."

No, me neither.

"Call him. It can't do any harm."

"I don't think I should. You know how it was with me and David. Part of me thinks I shouldn't get involved, just concentrate on the kids."

"Lauren, that's all very well, but there will come a point when you'll be lonely and the kids will be grown up. Moving on, doing their own thing. Then what?"

"I don't know."

Twenty-One

ELEVEN DAYS. THAT'S ALL IT'S been since I last saw Matt Anderson. For having only known him for just over a week, thoughts of him have lingered within me, at the back of my mind. Thoughts I wish I didn't have.

I've refused to answer his many calls and text messages; what is there to talk about? Emma told me she had to stop him on more than one occasion from coming to my house. She's made it clear that Matt is upset. Well, here's the surprise; he's not the only one.

I've thrown myself into work and the kids, although not the designs for Matt's business because I don't need a man like him in any part of my life. He supplied prostitutes.

There's nothing pretty about running an escort agency. It bloody disgusts me.

Emma and Abbie have urged me to pick up my phone and call him, but I can't. God, I've wanted to so many times, but for my kids, I haven't. Emma asked me if I wanted to know the reason he ended up with an escort agency as a business, but it really doesn't make a difference to me, so I told her no. But there is a part of me that does want to know.

I've spent the last eleven days looking over my shoulder, waiting for him to appear when I've been doing the school run.

Today, everything is an effort; from getting out of bed, doing the school run, and making sure I have everything packed for the kids going away this afternoon. I'm really not looking forward to a full weekend without them. I would go as far as saying I'm dreading not being with them. Luke is looking forward to it. Grant has promised him they can go fishing.

Abbie and Emma have said we should go out tomorrow night. They say it will take my mind off the kids, but I'm not so sure. Look what happened on my last Saturday night out. I ended up in bed with Emma's brother.

I feel as though my two friends are ganging up on me, both of them wanting me to speak to Matt and then not taking no for an answer about tomorrow. They've also both been here checking on me, making sure I'm okay, not feeling sorry for myself. And I've not, not really. Okay, I have, but I shouldn't be feeling this down. After all, it's been my choice to avoid Matt.

Sandra has had Kate this morning because, as she says, she will miss her this weekend.

I walk down the stairs carrying the suitcase and leave it at the front door. Sandra is bringing Kate home soon, then it will be time to collect Luke from school. Then Grant and Liz are coming to pick the kids up at two, and I know I'm going to be so lost.

I enter the kitchen, sit down at the table, and slip into deep thought. Every single thought that goes through my mind is about Matt, from our first meeting to the last kiss. How the hell is this even possible? He shouldn't be on my mind as much as he is.

My phone beeps, making me jump in my chair, bringing me back to reality. Picking it up, I see Abbie's name.

Mum is on her way over to you. Are you sure you don't want me to come and stay tonight?

I stare at the screen and sigh. Abbie would bloody stay all weekend if I let her, but I think I need to do this on my own, even though I'm sure I'll cry all night long.

Me: Okay and no. I'll be fine on my own tonight. X

Abbie: You know you're bloody stubborn. I'll see you tomorrow. X

Yes, I know I'm stubborn. I take that from my mum. Tonight, I'll probably do some work and have a glass or two of wine before falling into my bed.

"Lauren, honey. Where are you?" Sandra calls out.

"Kitchen." I swear I could easily live in my kitchen; I'm always in here when someone calls around. You would think I do a lot of cooking. If only. "There's my gorgeous girl," I say, standing and picking Kate up. "Have you been a good girl?" She giggles in my arms.

"She's always a good girl for her nana. How are you?" she asks, studying me closely.

"I'm good, although I'm going to miss the kids."

"I know. Me too. But Grant's right. If your mum was here, she would be doing this, and you know I would love to have the kids for a weekend, take them away to the seaside. But we'll see how you get on without them this weekend."

What a thought! I know Sandra would love taking them away, but I'm not sure I could handle it. I'm barely hanging on at the moment. God knows what I will be like when the kids leave. I'm swaying from side to side as Kate babbles in my arms. This is what I'm going to miss the most, moments like this.

"Okay, I'll let you get on. You know where I am if you need me but I'm sure Abbie has plans for you tomorrow. Now, enjoy the peace and don't do any work," she says, with her eyebrows raised. Am I really that predictable? Sandra gives us both a kiss and leaves.

I glance at the time. I don't have long until we need to pick up Luke. The sun is shining. I think I'll put Kate in her pram and walk to school. Too nice to go by car.

I thought I might've seen Emma as I walked here, but maybe she's running late. We've been walking to and from school most days, but I've not heard from her today. As I stand in the playground, I hope the weather is like this for the kids all weekend. It makes such a change when the sun is out.

There are already a few parents standing, talking. I don't tend to mingle with others well, especially not after David; only Emma and Patrick because of the boys. When the bell rings, there's still no sign of her. I should text and see if she wants me to take Liam home for her, if she's running late. I'm pulling my phone out of my pocket when I see Emma, but she's not alone. Matt is with her.

I frown, and Emma mouths, 'sorry.' Not as sorry as me. He looks perfect as they walk toward me. I look around, searching for somewhere else to go, but of course, there's nowhere. I need to wait on Luke.

Kate cries at the right moment and it means I don't have to focus on him. She doesn't settle and I pick her up. This is my fault. I spoil her with attention, and why not? All kids love attention. I rock her on my hip and she stops crying. Yes, my tiny daughter has me wrapped around her fingers.

"I think someone is at it with you," Emma says as they both stop. I take a deep breath and turn around, although I'm hoping the boys come out of school quickly so I can leave.

"You might be right. Matt." I finally acknowledge him. Emma smiles. I don't know why. Surely she can feel the frostiness between us.

"Lauren, how are you?"

"Fine."

"I know I'm right," states Emma, eyes dancing between me and Matt. "And not just about Kate." She narrows her eyes and I want to tell her to pack it in. "Have you finished packing?"

I don't get to answer. "Packing for what? Where are you going?" I turn away at the sharpness of his tone. There's no way I'm letting anyone speak to me like that. The boys run out. Thank God for that, because it means I can leave. Emma will understand I don't want to be around Matt.

I don't trust myself.

I put Kate back into her pram. Grumpy or not, that's where she needs to be. Luke and Liam are talking ten-to-the-dozen about plans for during the holidays. These two never seem to stop.

"Luke, come on. We need to get home. Cases are all packed," I tell my over-excited son.

"Lauren." Matt's voice is softer than it was moments ago. "Where are you going?"

"The kids are going away with Grant and Liz for the weekend."

"Oh, and what about you?"

"Don't worry about Lauren," Emma butts in. "We're going for a girls' night out tomorrow."

I can see him thinking, and when his eyes widen, I know the thought that has entered his mind. The last night I was out. He thinks I'm going out looking for a man. I know I'm not, but he doesn't. And anyway, I don't owe him anything, so if he's waiting for an explanation, he's not getting one from me.

"A night out?"

"What the hell is wrong with you, Matt?" Emma almost shouts at him. "You two need to sort this crap out."

"There's nothing to sort out," I state, firmly looking at Matt. "I don't have time for this. I have an hour before these two go away for the weekend and I'd rather not spend it with you." His eyes fall to the ground and I know my words have hit a sore point. "Emma, I'll call you tomorrow to see what we're doing."

"Okay, and I'm sorry. I just thought . . ."

"I know what you thought. It's fine."

"Lauren, please. We need to talk." Matt's voice pleads with me.

"I've nothing to say to you." My words linger as I turn and walk away. Luke holds onto the pram. Not helping myself, I turn my head and allow myself one last look at him. Emma is talking to him, but his hurt eyes are still watching me, yet he still looks so bloody perfect.

Twenty-Two

SEEING HIM HAS DONE NOTHING to help me. My flat mood is getting lower as the seconds tick by. Today was always going to be tough for me, but seeing him has hurt.

Luke is currently bouncing around the sitting room. One word: hyper. That's what he is, and why shouldn't he be? Kate looks a little tired as she attempts to copy everything her brother is doing.

I hear the car before Luke does. When he hears the front door opening, he bounces out into the hallway. "Grant," he shouts out. Kate follows behind him. "I can't wait for this holiday," he says, jumping into Grant's outstretched arms when I enter the hall.

"Hey, sport. We're all going to have so much fun," Grant says, spinning him around before putting him down and doing the same with Kate.

Yes, I know they will both have a great weekend.

"You look a little tired, Lauren."

"No, I'm fine." His eyes narrow and I know he doesn't believe me, but I'm not discussing it. We've had a conversation about Matt. Well, I had a rant because I think he should've told me from the first time he saw him in my house. "I promise I'm fine."

"Okay. What are your plans for the weekend?"

"Tonight, nothing. Tomorrow I'm off out with Abbie and

Emma, only because neither of them can take no for an answer."

He smiles warmly. "You should go out and enjoy yourself."

"Yes, I know. Grant, I've been thinking of going to visit Dad." I know he isn't my dad's biggest fan but they are both important to me, and I wouldn't feel right going without telling him.

"I won't hide how I feel about your dad, but I do think you need it. Sweetheart, I'm always here for you, no matter what." He puts Kate down and wraps his arm around me. "You and he have come a long way and I wouldn't dream of stepping between the relationship you're building with him. After everything lately, going to stay with him for a holiday will do you good, and I'm sure he would love having these two around."

"Thank you. I think I needed to hear that."

He kisses the top of my hair. "Sweetheart, you have to do what's right for you and the kids. Please don't worry about anyone else. And that includes me, because no matter what you do in life, what choices you make, I might not like them or agree, but I will always be one-hundred percent behind you. Don't ever doubt it. I know your dad will be the same. Now, it's time to get these two into the car. I told Liz I would only be a minute."

I pick up Kate, Grant takes the suitcase, and Luke skips outside to the car. Liz gets out, smiling, and picks up Luke, giving him a kiss before putting him back down on the ground. My lips are already trembling and my arms are shaking. Christ, they haven't even left yet and I'm a mess.

"Honey, are you okay?" Liz's sweet voice draws my attention.

"Yes, I'll be fine. I'm going to miss these two."

"That's natural, but try not to worry. If it helps, I can call you before they go to bed at night?" I nod, unable to speak because I know I'm about to cry. There are tears already filling my eyes. I give Kate a kiss and hand her over to Liz. She straps her into the car.

"Mummy, I hope you have fun with Auntie Abbie," says my smiling boy.

"I will. Now, you have a great time," I say, scooping him up and cuddling him.

"Come on. Let's get in the car," Grant says. Luke climbs in and Liz secures him into his seat. "Enjoy your weekend, sweetheart. I love you."

"I love you too."

Grant gets in the car and I stand in the driveway and watch them drive off. The tears I've been holding back slowly roll down my face. I'm going to be an emotional mess until they come home on Monday night.

I turn and walk inside feeling completely lost. I've never been on my own without the kids. They are what I live for. They keep me going. They are my reason for breathing.

The house is already too quiet. I don't like the silence.

Wandering into the kitchen, I put the kettle on then open the fridge door. I stare inside without taking anything out. My thoughts drift off again and I can see Matt so clearly. Why did he have to pop up today of all days? When my emotions are already running high.

The buzzing of my phone pulls me back to reality.

Matt: Please talk to me.

I stare blankly at his message.

Matt: I need to see you. Please Lauren. Open the front door.

Fuck. He's here. I blink rapidly and now I can hear banging on the front door. My heart starts pounding. I could pretend I'm not here, but my car is in the drive and I'm sure he's been watching, waiting for the kids to leave.

"Lauren, believe me, I'm not leaving until you talk to me." I walk out into the hall, stop at the bottom of the staircase, and sit down. Why today? "Lauren, please. I will keep knocking on this door. I can stay here all afternoon and night."

I cover my ears and close my eyes in an attempt to shut him

out. I feel sick to the pit of my stomach.

Please go away. This is too much for me today.

The banging on the front door gets louder and louder. What the hell are my neighbours going to say? Standing, I reluctantly walk to the door and reach for the door handle at the same time the door opens and he steps inside. *Cheeky git*. Usually, guests wait for an invite into someone's home, not just walk in.

He's standing only inches away from me. His features look strained but he's still so fucking handsome. I gulp back the lump that's forming in my throat as my tears threaten to spill again. I want to yell at him. Scream from the top of my voice, but of course, I don't. There are no words forming. The truth is, I don't have the strength.

He takes a step toward me, uncertain, his eyes holding my gaze, and in this moment, I'm weak, and he knows it. Matt holds his arms out and I allow my body to fall into his. He wraps his arms around me, holding me close.

The warmth of his body has a soothing effect on me. It shouldn't, but it does. My head is being pulled in different directions and I blame the emotions of the day. I don't want Matt or need him. So why the hell am I taking comfort in his arms?

Because I'm being torn in two.

My feelings are leaving me confused. I walked away and left him. I have no interest in the life he has led or still leads. Nothing more than a glorified pimp. If I tell myself often enough, the words might stick.

I pull myself out of his hold and take a step back. "What do you want?"

"To talk to you," he says, eyes full of sorrow and remorse.

"There's nothing to talk about. Now, shut the door on your way out." I turn my back and start walking into the living room. There is so much I want to throw his way. That night I walked away I was angry, but today, I've no fight left in me for an argument.

"Lauren, please . . ."

"Please what?" I spin on my heel. "What the fuck is it you want from me?" I shout.

"I want the chance to explain. I need you to hear me out." He reaches out his hand cautiously. I shake my head; he can't get too close.

"I'm not interested. I don't want someone like YOU being around me or my kids, so please take the fucking hint and leave." My body trembles as the anger I felt toward him that night rips through my body. "You're not welcome in my home. LEAVE!" I scream at him.

He takes another step toward me, with determination in his clouded eyes. There's no use in me fighting him. I should let him say what he came to say, and then we can go our separate ways.

He grabs hold of my shoulders, his face so close to mine I can feel his breath against my skin. "You will hear me out, even if I have to tie you to a fucking chair so you can't run away from me again."

His words shock me, but as I look at him, I think he means them, and there's not a hope in hell of him tying me to a chair, or anything else for that matter. I struggle out of his hold and enter the living room, making my way to the sofa. I sit down in a huff, curling my legs beneath me.

"You have five minutes," I state, as he sits down at the other end of the sofa. *Wise man.*

"Five minutes, huh? If that's all I've got, should we waste them talking?" His lips curl at the corners and he almost breaks out laughing. *Almost*.

"Don't start, Matt. Not today."

"Lauren, I've been a fucking mess. I want us to start again."

His words are almost laughable. "Start again? We never got started in the first place."

He looks at me, eyes full of sadness. I fold my arms across

my chest, protecting myself from the man before me. Because as much as I can say I don't want anything to do with him, my body is betraying me. I close my eyes and pray he leaves because I'm scared I'll give in to the temptation that is Matt Anderson.

The sofa dips and I feel him moving. Opening my eyes, he's there. Right beside me. "I'm going to kiss you." He prowls closer and grips onto my shoulders, holding me still. I don't have time to think before his tongue brushes along the seam of my tightly closed lips, trying to tempt them open. My anger with myself builds because I know I can no longer resist him.

My lips part and my body crumbles, giving in to the warm sensations sweeping through it. He groans, moving one of his hands from my shoulders to the base of my neck, holding me in place as his body pushes against mine, tongues rolling together as the intensity hots up. His kiss is demanding and possessive. Me? I've surrendered to my weakness.

He breaks away, and I know I shouldn't, but I want his lips back on mine. I'm panting, wanting more.

He rests his head against my forehead. "This doesn't change anything," I finally say.

"Lauren, don't say that. This changes everything. I want to explain and prove to you that my past is where it belongs; firmly behind me."

"How can you say that?" I push him away, needing some space.

"Please, hear me out?" I nod. "You already know my dad is dead. Mum ran into some difficulty shortly after he died. She thought there was enough money in the bank for her to live from, but it turns out he had a bit of a gambling problem, and there was nothing left for Mum. With me being the oldest, I felt a need to help out. Mum didn't deserve to give up the home she had lived in for years."

I shift uncomfortably.

"I had to do something, then someone offered me a way to

make some easy money. I was young and foolish, and I shouldn't have got involved, but I wasn't prepared to sit back and do nothing and watch my mum's life crumble. I did what I had to do and it was easy money."

"That doesn't make it right. What if it had been Emma selling her body?"

The muscles in his neck tighten. "It would never have happened."

"Maybe it's because I'm a mum, but I hate the thought of someone using my daughter in the way you have used women. I'm sure you will tell me those women were happy enough to do what they were doing, but in my eyes, as a parent, it's wrong."

"Lauren, I did what I needed to do at the time. I'm not proud of it. No-one was forced to do anything they didn't want to do."

"This really doesn't change anything."

"Please, don't say that. I want to spend time with you. Get to know you."

"You might but I don't think I can. You've had your say, now can you leave? I want to be on my own. I don't need your crap today. I have enough of my own to deal with."

"I don't want to leave you. You're upset and I know it's because of the kids."

And with those last words, the ache in my chest tightens and my unshed tears sting my eyes. Warm arms engulf me, pulling me close, my head resting on his chest. "I'm staying with you all weekend and I'm not taking no for an answer," he whispers.

Twenty-Three

MY BODY RELAXES INTO HIM, but I don't allow my tears to fall. I don't want him to see me falling apart. Everything about him captivates me, comforts and soothes me. I know it shouldn't and I don't want it to, but being in his company feels right. But deep down, I know it's wrong.

Matt Anderson is trouble . . . trouble with a capital T.

All weekend. There's no way I can cope with that. He can't be serious.

"Matt, you can't stay," I whisper against him.

"Lauren, you've not got the kids to use as an excuse," he says, pushing me forward a little and tilting my head so I'm gazing into those deep green eyes. "What can I do to prove to you I'm not the same man I was before?"

"I don't know."

"I'm staying and I'm spending the weekend with you, and if on Monday I haven't won you over, you won't need to see me again." His face is poker straight and I don't doubt he means those words.

I eye him suspiciously.

"I mean it, Lauren, but you have to give me some leeway."

"Okay." I sigh.

"Really?"

"Yes, really." I already sense I'm going to regret this, but I can't help noticing the smile on his face. He leans down, burying his face in my neck, and my arms fly around him. He's a temptation I can't seem to resist.

"You've made me happy. I won't fuck this up." His husky voice catches me off-guard. My skin tingles as I feel his shallow breaths against it. This is a bad idea. My body is already responding to him. "I've missed you so bloody much."

"I've missed you too." The words leave me in a breathless rush. He sits up, those green eyes blazing, hands gliding up and down my back. Shit! I suppose I already knew what to expect. The glazed look of hunger in his eyes tells me what he wants. *Me.*

I don't wait for him. My mouth crashes to his and I take the lead. I've missed this, and it's only now I realise just how much. I don't even notice the movement of his hands until I feel them resting on my breasts and kneading through the material of my top. My eyes are closed and I'm lost to all the sensations sweeping through me. His teeth nip lightly against my bottom lip. "If you don't want this to go any further, tell me now."

"I want you," I pant, pulling at his T-shirt. His hands leave my breasts, travelling south, and his lips meet mine once again. He makes quick work of removing my shorts and underwear, then I hear the sound of his zipper being undone.

I have no time at all to ready myself for what is coming. This is going to be hard and fast. He pulls me down on the sofa by my waist until I'm where he wants me. I scream as he slams into me, thrusting hard and fast. His tongue sliding into my mouth silences me.

Oh, God.

There's no time for my body to adjust. Repeatedly, he thrusts wildly against me. Over and over. Everything spins as my pleasure builds.

He pounds on, each thrust hitting the spot that will have me crying out in pleasure at any moment.

Hard and fast.

Bloody hell. He pushes my legs back and I feel more of him, if that's at all possible. The pace changes and he thrusts urgently against me, sending me closer to the deep end. I'm drowning in him and there's not a damn thing I can do to stop it.

I cry out, my body shaking uncontrollably as my orgasm takes me hostage, but he carries on thrusting, seeking his own release. He finally stills and I feel his erection pulsing deep inside me.

Oh dear God, what he does to me. My head is spinning and all rational thoughts are long gone.

"That wasn't how I intended to spend time with you," he breathes against my neck. "I'm sure I said that very first night you deserved more than a quick fumble." Thoughts of that night quickly come to light and I find myself grinning, because no matter how I feel about his past, that night was memorable.

"Well, it's what we both wanted for starters . . ."

He laughs lightly, wrapping his arms around me. "There's the woman I remember so well, with her sense of humour." He presses his lips to mine softly. "I think we should get cleaned up then decide what we're going to do with our weekend."

"I have plans tomorrow night."

"You don't, not anymore. I've already spoken to Emma and cancelled."

What the hell do I say to that? "Really? You've changed my plans just like that? What gave you the right?" I sigh dramatically as he looks on. "Well, I think I'll just work then, if my plans have been cancelled."

He readjusts his clothes. I pull my shorts up and stand, looking around. I don't like the quietness.

"There will be no working for either of us this weekend. Now, would you like to go out for dinner or do you want to stay here?

Or if you want a change of scenery, we could go to my place?"

"Can we stay here?"

"Of course. I'm sure I'll be able to keep you distracted." He looks down and then his gaze returns to me. I'm staring at him, and I'm now wondering if us spending the weekend together is such a good thing. He's demanding and controlling, and I know my heart isn't in safe hands with him.

But then again, I thought my heart was safe with David, and look where that got me. If I can keep my emotions in check, then I won't risk getting hurt. The thing is though, his past is going to cause a divide because I don't agree with it. I can't condone what he did.

Yes, his explanation has made me think, but even under extraordinary circumstances, I still couldn't have stooped that low.

But for the sake of the weekend, I'm going to put it to the back of my mind.

"Okay, so we're staying here. How about we have a shower and then we can decide what to do with tonight, including eating."

"Sounds good to me."

I had already decided I was going to make the most out of the weekend when we climbed the stairs to go for a shower. I smile, thinking about our shared shower as I watch him. He's on the phone to Emma. I don't hear a word because I'm too lost in thoughts. His rough hands pinned my body in place as we had sex in the shower.

"Emma, give me fucking peace." His raised voice catches my attention. We're in the kitchen, and he is pacing the floor. "Yes, I'll see Mum tomorrow. No, Danny will be at the club all weekend. It's fine, honestly. Do what you need to do with the kids." He stops pacing and his eyes meet mine, a slow smile forming, "I'm sure she'll appreciate your concern, but it's not needed. Goodbye."

"Everything okay?" I ask as he stalks toward me.

"Yes, Liam is sick. . . ."

"Oh no. Is he okay?"

"Emma thinks it's probably some twenty-four-hour bug, but she had promised Mum she would take her out to lunch tomorrow, and now she wants me to take her so she can be with Liam."

"That makes sense. I know what I'm like when the kids are unwell. So you can spend tomorrow with your mum."

"And so can you."

"I beg your pardon? I'm sure I misheard you."

"No, you didn't. I'm spending the weekend with you. Not even lunch with my mum will change that."

"I think it's a bit early to be meeting parents, don't you?"

"No. I've met your dad, and I know Grant and Liz personally." He kisses me, ending our conversation and distracting my mind with his tongue sweeping inside my mouth.

"What was that for?" I question him, even though I know the answer.

"Because I wanted to and I knew it would ensure your silence." *Oh.* "I won't lie to you, ever. But I do expect you with me tomorrow, and anyway, my mum wants to meet you."

"Why?" I ask, surprised by his admission.

"Because she's heard a lot about you and wants to meet the woman who has left her eldest son incapable of thinking straight since we first met." I turn away, embarrassed by his words. "I'm sure she wants to give you advice on keeping me in line."

I laugh. "I don't think you can be kept in line."

"You. Do. Have. A. Valid. Point." He kisses me in between every word. "But for you, I could make an exception. So, will you come for lunch tomorrow?" His voice is soft and his eyes plead with me.

"Yes, as long as we're not going to Martine's restaurant."

"We won't go there ever again. I promise. I understand how you feel about my past and I won't flaunt it before you. I should say, my mum doesn't know about this part of my life . . ."

"You don't need to say anymore. I sort of understand why you did it, but I don't agree with it."

"Lauren, what you said earlier about Emma hit a sore point, because yes, I would hate for her to be in that position. She's my sister and I love her, so I do understand your reaction to my past. Now." He looks at his watch. "It's almost six p.m. We should think about dinner."

I had no idea that was the time. I wonder if the kids are okay. "Dinner? I can cook for us," I say, suddenly needing to do something to keep myself occupied.

"No. Let's get a takeaway."

"How about going for a drive and getting fish and chips?"

"That sounds like a good idea. Down the coast, and a walk along the beach sounds perfect, but I'm driving."

I give up. He is a man who likes to be in control. Is there anything wrong with that? I'm not sure yet.

Twenty-Four

HE PARKS HIS CAR IN the drive next to mine. I'm sure this will give my neighbours something to talk about. The strange man that was banging on my door this afternoon is now spending the night. Matt and I have already had a discussion, and he's made it clear he's staying here with me all weekend. And the funny thing is, now that I've spent a relaxing evening with him, I want him to stay.

Matt managed to completely distract me until Liz called. I'm glad she did. I got to say goodnight to Luke. Kate was already fast asleep. Luke told me all about the cabin and excitedly told me he is going fishing with Grant tomorrow, and if they catch anything it will be their dinner. I had to laugh at that because I don't think he knows that they have to kill it once they catch it.

It was great speaking to him.

"Are we sitting out here all night?"

I turn my gaze from the window I've been staring out of. "Sorry. I was a million miles away. No, let's go inside. It's been a long day."

He offers me a smile. We get out of his car and go inside. The house is eerily quiet and I don't like it.

"Can I get you anything?"

"No. I'll grab us some water. You go on up," he tells me. I do because it's late and I'm tired. I start undressing as soon as I enter my bedroom. I grab PJs from the drawer and put them on.

The bedroom feels cold, or maybe it's just me. The weather was nice today but I should've taken a cardigan with me when we went out because it did cool down fairly quickly. Still nice enough, but still, I'll probably have given myself a cold.

His footsteps cross the bedroom floor and stop. I feel his breath against my neck as his arms slip around my waist. My body relaxes into his and it feels so good being in the warmth of his arms.

"You're exhausted, aren't you?"

"Yes," I whisper with my eyes closed.

"Come on then. Into bed." I let him guide me into my bed. He climbs in behind me and wraps his arms around me. I snuggle closer to him, wanting the warmth and comfort he provides. "Thank you for not telling me to fuck off."

"You didn't give me much choice," I say, with a smile I know he can't see.

"No, I didn't. Now go to sleep."

He presses a kiss to the top of my head and I close my eyes.

My eyes flutter open and he's gone. I suppose I already knew it, not having his arms wrapped around me, but still, I thought maybe the bathroom. There's no noise, no running water. Maybe he's had second thoughts and come to the conclusion that the single parent with two kids is just too much hassle.

I want to close my eyes again and dream sweet dreams, but the brightness shining in through the window tells me it's much later than I would usually sleep. The kids always wake me up at the crack of dawn, although in Kate's case, sometimes it can be earlier. God, I miss them. I'm glad they're only away for the weekend; there's no way I could cope with them being away from me longer.

I drag myself into the bathroom, one, because I need to pee, and two, because I need to wash, and brush my teeth.

When I'm finished, I have an internal debate on what to do. Climb back into bed or stay up? Bed wins. I climb in and sit up; the smell of cooking filters through the air. He's here. And he's cooking. I hear his footsteps coming up the stairs.

"Good morning," I say, taking him in as he enters the bedroom with a tray in his hands. Matt didn't have to cook; he looks pretty delectable to me wearing only a T-shirt and a pair of boxers. And from his wet hair, he's had a shower, but my bathroom looked so clean. Does that mean he cleans as well as cooking? Things are certainly looking up. No-one has cooked me breakfast in bed before, or tided up a bathroom after themselves.

"And what a great morning it is." His cheery voice instantly makes me feel happier than I did moments ago. "You look refreshed."

"I feel it," I say, as he puts the tray down on the bed. Fruit juice for two, and toast and bacon. Now, this I could get used to. "It's amazing what a good night's sleep can do for you. Did you sleep well?"

He leans forward and presses a kiss to the top of my head. I close my eyes momentarily, allowing the warm fuzzy feelings to flow through me. "Of course. I had you in my arms." Smooth! Real smooth. "I hope this is okay?" I open my eyes and watch him, concentration etched on his perfect face.

"It's more than okay," I reply, smiling. He sits down on the bed and we eat in silence. His gaze catches my eyes on more than one occasion. Each time, he's staring at me, his eyes smiling. "What are our plans for today?" I ask, already knowing I'm going to meet his mum.

"Well." He moves the almost empty tray from the bed, placing it on the floor. He crawls up the bed and my body slides down until I'm lying beneath him. "Interesting position you're now in. My plans revolve around you."

"And your mum?"

"You asked our plans for the day. First, I want to worship you because I didn't do that yesterday. Secondly, worship you some more. And then, hopefully, we will have time to get cleaned up before I introduce you to my amazing mum, who I'm sure you will love."

"Is that so?"

"Yes. Now, I was going to say be quiet, but today, you can scream my name without risking small ears, and by the time I'm finished with you, that's exactly what you'll be doing."

I gasp at his honesty, which I don't doubt, not even for a second.

His forehead presses against mine. Our heavy breaths mix together in the air surrounding us. His erection is hard through his boxers. The sexual tension is excruciating, but it won't be for long.

"I need you."

"I'm all yours," I tell him, as he lowers his lips to mine. Nothing is as I would expect it to be with Matt. He works his mouth against me roughly. His upper body presses firmly against me and his erection is rubbing me in all the right places. My eyes want to close but I want to watch him. See him. See what I do to him.

When his mouth leaves mine, I keep my eyes wide open. There's a wicked glint in his eye and a cheeky grin graces his lips. I would say a look of smug satisfaction, but he hasn't done anything yet to be satisfied with. But I'm sure he's about to rectify that.

His hands are resting either side of my shoulders; he's watching me closely. And there it is, that look, the one that tells me I'm done for. He leans down toward my neck and I gasp as he kisses the delicate skin just below my ear. Instinct has me tilting my head, giving him more access. I moan as I feel the light scrape of his teeth against my skin. I close my eyes.

The weight of his body shifts as warm kisses trail around my neck and then down toward my now heavy breasts. His arms rest at my hips. I open my eyes and he's watching me as he leans toward my breast and takes my hardened nipple in his mouth. Slowly, he teases it with his tongue, flicking and swirling.

I can't take my eyes off him. His eyes have darkened, although I'm sure I can still see a slight hint of brightness linger there in the background. My breath hitches in the back of my throat. He's in control of all my senses, and in my present state of pure, unashamed bliss, I don't mind that he's in control.

He divides his attention equally between each breast, driving me almost insane as I try to absorb the burning desire that is spreading through my veins like a wildfire burning out of control.

His attention diverts and he's crawling further down the bed. "Lift."

I do as he asks, although I'm not sure it was a question, more a demand. His hands are now tilting my hips and he removes my shorts and tosses them aside.

He pushes one hand between my legs and they fall shamelessly to the side, giving him the access he wants and my body desires. I'm so aroused. He slides one finger inside. My back arches as I clench around him, wanting to feel more. Desperate to feel.

Grabbing the bed sheets, I try to talk myself out of the orgasm that is close to the brink. He pulls out, and before I can miss him, two fingers are pushed back into me. My hips move in a circular motion into his thrusting fingers.

Matt is breathing hard as I moan and wriggle under his expert touch. I need to see him. I open my eyes; he's staring at me, his face flushed with lust as he watches how turned on I am.

"Don't close them. Keep your eyes open. I need to see the look in your eyes as you fall apart for the first time today."

I gasp at his words. God, I'm done for.

The wicked grin on his face tells me all I need to know. He

has me exactly where he wants me and my body is responding the only way it knows how. The pad of his thumb rubs against me and I almost cry out from that touch alone.

Everything tightens within my core, tension building as he pushes his fingers in and out at a steady pace. My gaze locks to his, unable to look away, his words ringing loudly in my ears as I cry out. Pleasure pulses through me.

"One . . ." he says, before burying his face between my legs.

"No . . . I can't . . ." I'm swollen and too sensitive; my body can't take it again. I try to push him away, but when his tongue touches me slightly, my hunger builds again.

Twenty-Five

"CAN YOU RELAX?" HE SAYS.

That's easier said than done. My body still feels like mush and my legs are still shaky. Four times . . . four times he had me crying his name, and I'm sure if we weren't meeting his mum for lunch, I would still be in my bed.

"Lauren, you have nothing to be scared of. She doesn't bite, unlike me."

I gasp hearing those words on the busy pavement in front of his restaurant and club. I should hope she doesn't, because I'm sure Matt has left two marks on the back of my neck, hence the reason I've left my hair down on what feels like the hottest day of the year so far.

"Does she know about the kids?" I ask nervously. Why didn't I ask him this earlier on?

"Of course she does." He presses a kiss to my lips. "Relax."

I've not been able to relax since we left my house. Everything has been rushed. We had to go via his apartment so he could change his clothes and also grab clean clothes for tomorrow and Monday. He really did mean it when he said he was staying for the weekend.

I also took a phone call from Abbie; she's not impressed by the change of plans. She also wanted to talk to Matt, so I put the call on speaker as he was driving. She told him in no uncertain terms that if he hurt or upset me in any way, there would be hell to pay. I really wanted to laugh as she said it, but there was a hint of a threatening tone in her voice and Matt assured her he wouldn't.

"Ready?"

"Yes."

Matt holds the door open and I step inside. I haven't been in here since the Thursday we had a business meeting. That makes me think I should speak to him and see if he has someone else to do his design work.

It's really busy, but then it should be; it's Saturday afternoon. Matt speaks to the woman at the reception desk before placing his hand in the small of my back and guiding me through the restaurant to a table in the far corner. Such a simple gesture, yet the hairs on the back of my neck stand to attention. The woman sitting at the table looks elegant as she waits. She's typing on her phone and doesn't see us approach. It's clear to me that Emma takes after her mother.

"Mum," Matt says as we step closer.

"You're early," she states, standing. Matt drops his hand and gives his mum a kiss. "For a change."

"Mum . . . this is Lauren," he says, holding his arm out to me.

Bloody hell. I'm so nervous.

"Mrs Anderson," I say, holding out my hand. Matt sniggers at my side. God, he's not making me feel any better.

"Lauren, less of the Mrs Anderson. It's Lesley. I'm so glad we're finally meeting. I've heard a lot about you and the kids. Liam talks non-stop about Luke."

I smile, and with talk of the kids, I relax a little. "The boys do get along."

"Well, come on. Sit down beside me and you can tell me what my son has been up to." I glance at Matt and try to hide the alarm that must be on my face. "I don't see much of him these days, but now I know why."

My body relaxes again.

Matt pulls the chair out for me and kisses the top of my head as I sit down. "Mum, are you having wine?"

"Only if Lauren is going to join me in a glass because I presume you have the car?"

"Of course. Lauren?"

"Yes. Wine would be nice."

"Not a cocktail?" he asks, grinning.

I shake my head. He's impossible. Between the Sheets is where this all started.

Matt orders a bottle of wine and water from a passing waiter and finally takes the seat opposite me. He hands Lesley and me menus, but doesn't bother reading it himself; he obviously knows what he wants. This thought has me smirking. He is a man who sets out to get exactly what he wants.

"So, Lauren, Matt tells me you're a graphic designer."

"Yes. I've been working from home lately, but have started looking at premises for business in the last week."

"Oh, how exciting," Lesley says, but I catch the scowl on Matt's face. Of course, this is news to him. If we had been talking he would already know this.

"Have you and Abbie found somewhere you like?" he asks.

"I think so. You could see it this week and give me your opinion, if you have time."

"I'll make time."

The waiter brings over our drinks and we order food. Matt shakes his head when I ask for a chicken salad, and he orders an extra portion of chips. Conversation flows with ease between Lesley and I as Matt sits back and watches the interaction between us. It has to be said, she knows how to make me feel at ease, by talking about my kids. And she does seem to know lots about them.

Lesley asks about David. Well, she doesn't use his name.

"Mum!" Matt snaps.

"Matt, I'm sure if Lauren doesn't want to tell me, she won't, so don't use that tone with me."

"David isn't around. When we split up over eight months ago, he chose not to see the kids."

"Oh, sweetie, I'm sorry," she says softly, placing her hand on top of mine.

"Don't be. He made that decision, not me."

"It's a shame because I think kids need two parents, whether they are together or not. It must be hard on you, having to do everything on your own."

"It's not been too bad. I have my uncle and aunt and also my best friend and her parents, who are like grandparents to my two."

"I'm glad. I think in today's society, kids need the support an extended family can provide."

"And when was the last time you helped out with Emma?" Matt says sarcastically.

"If I saw more of you these last few weeks, you would know I stayed over last Saturday night and watched the boys whilst they had a night out."

Matt sits back in his chair, sighing heavily. Lesley is frowning as I look between the two.

"I've been busy," he says.

"Yes, your sister has told me how busy you've been." Something passes between the two, although I can't put my finger on it. Does she know that I walked away from him? I think so, and I'm sure she wants to know what's been going on. "Lauren, what are your plans for the summer holidays?"

"I'm not sure yet. My aunt and uncle have taken the kids away this weekend. I'd like to go and visit my dad in the next few weeks, and then if I can manage, take them both for a week abroad before Luke goes back to school. But I'll have to wait and see."

"What the hell Lauren?" Matt's raised voiced startles Lesley and me. I look at him. He's not happy, wild eyes glaring across the table at me, lips pressed together in a tight line. He rubs his hand against his temples.

"Mathew! What was that for?"

He almost sinks into the chair under the watchful gaze of his mother. "This is all news to me. You might have told me." His voice drops as his eyes fall onto the table.

"I've not made any firm plans other than I'd like to see my dad. It's been a rough few months . . . weeks. I'd like to go and forget about recent incidents."

And there it is; a look of sadness when my words sink in.

"Matt, I'm not sure what your problem is, but I've brought you up better than that."

He nods his head in agreement with Lesley and excuses himself from the table. Part of me wants to go after him and explain, but the other part tells me he should be the one to come to me and ask the questions he wants answers to.

"Will I . . ."

"No, you won't go after him," Lesley tells me. "I know my son, and he knows he's in the wrong, but I also sense your news is new to him. Matt is used to getting things his own way, always has, even as a small boy. It won't do him any harm to go and sulk for a bit. You seem like a lovely young woman, and from what Emma has told me, your focus is on Kate and Luke. Don't let Matt push you into anything. Stay true to yourself and your kids, who, I do hope I have the pleasure of meeting soon."

"I'm sure you will. Luke is never away from Emma's house."

"She's very fond of all three of you."

"I know," I say with a sigh.

"Look, whatever happens with you and Matt won't make a blind bit of difference to Emma. But I will say this. I understand there is some sort of a problem with you both and that's none of my business. But I do hope you can sort it out. He seems happier with you. The happiest I've seen him in a long time."

"I'm sure it will work out for the best. I just think he wants more than I can give."

"Probably, but as I said, stay true to yourself and give yourself time. Yes, you come across as a very independent woman, but not all men are as bad as your ex." I look away, a little uneasy with the current conversation. "Sorry, Lauren. Too much for today. Let's change the subject. Danny said Luke is really good at football."

The pace of conversation between us is making me dizzy; I can't keep up.

Matt joins us just as our lunch is served. He's timed that perfectly. I still can't believe he would leave me sitting in a restaurant with his mum while he walked off in a huff.

"Sorry," he says, leaning down and pressing a kiss to my cheek.

"You will be," I say. He sits down, looking a bit shocked at my words, but Lesley smiles at my side. I might well be the one thing he can't control.

The rest of our lunch is great. Matt is the perfect gentleman, and Lesley, well, there's nothing to not like about her; she is very easy to talk to. She is very family-orientated; they all mean the world to her. She's also made it known that she would love to see her boys settle down with families of their own. Her eyes dart between Matt and me as she tells us she always thought Danny would settle before Matt. He smiles but I can't help but blush; I feel the heat in my cheeks.

As she speaks of Danny, I realise I've not seen him since we arrived. He must be busy. "Mum, can we drop you home?"

"Of course. That means I can still chat with Lauren." Matt takes his mum's hand as she stands. "You do know I'm not in an invalid yet? There's a few more good years left in me."

"Oh, there's more than a few," he says, with a hint of laughter.

She shoos his hand away and instantly he takes my hand in his, bringing a smile to Lesley's face.

We walk across the restaurant. I stop, gasping, causing Lesley to walk into the back of me. I run my free hand through my hair as I do a double take. With wide eyes, I take in the three people walking towards us. David, Stacey, and Martine. *Really.*

Matt's hand tightens in mine when he realises what has made me stop. Why is Martine with those two? And why do I keep running into him here?

It's just a coincidence.

The pout on Martine's face tells me she has seen us. Fuck, her look mirrors my sister's. Surely there can't be two people so alike? But as I look at them, I realise they are similar. David looks down at Matt and my joined hands before his eyes dart around the restaurant. What is he looking for? It's not what, it's who. He's looking for the kids.

"Isn't that Martine?" Lesley asks. "I've not seen her in years."

"Yes," Matt snaps. "But I'm more interested in who she's with."

"Don't be. I'm not," I say, taking a deep breath and putting on a smile. Matt's eyes are on me when I turn my head, staring. "What?"

"How the hell can you be so calm? I want to punch him for the last time he was here."

"Can one of you tell me what's going on?"

"That's Stacey, my sister, with David, my ex."

"Oh."

"It's fine. Matt, I'm okay." And truthfully I am fine with David and Stacey. It's Martine I have a problem with, and Matt's past. Because seeing her reminds me of what he's done.

"You might be, but I'm not."

I start walking again, closing the distance between us. Matt removes his hand from mine and wraps his arm around my waist, pulling me closer to him.

"Where are my kids? If you're out drinking on a Saturday afternoon . . ." David's voice cuts through the air. Matt's body tenses beside me.

"Nice to see you too. MY kids are with relatives, not that I need to explain myself to you. Stacey." I finally acknowledge her.

She takes a deep breath and plasters on her fakest of smiles. I think she forgets I know her well. "Lauren, you look . . . well."

"That's because she is," Matt hisses through gritted teeth. Oh dear. Why do I think this isn't going to end well? Martine runs her eyes up and down my body. I see the slight shake of her head as she looks between Matt and me.

"Matt. Lesley." She finally speaks. Matt doesn't say a word and Lesley seems bemused by the whole situation.

"Where the fuck are my kids?"

Matt lets go of me and I try to pull him back, but his body is shaking with rage. Lesley takes my arm.

"Your kids? Those two beautiful kids you turned your back on over eight months ago?" David is unable to meet Matt's eyes. His shoulders slouch as he stands before us. He is a weak man; there's no doubt in my mind. "What gives you the right to stand there and question Lauren?"

Martine steps in front of Matt and takes hold of his shoulders. He freezes under her touch before shrugging away from her. "Martine, move." There's a calm edge to his controlled to tone, but Martine does as he asks. "You, take your bit of skirt and get the hell out of my restaurant." He spits the words with venom.

"No." David seems to be either brave or stupid. "She needs to answer my question. Who has my kids?"

That does it. I can't hold back any longer. Lesley lets go of me and I step toward David, and even Matt looks surprised.

"SHE? She is the mother of your two kids, who, for the past eight months, has looked after them both on my own. So don't you dare stand there questioning me. Where have you been when

Kate's been teething and unwell? Or when Luke started football training? That's right, you've had my sister in your bed, not giving a fuck about YOUR kids. So forgive me for not informing you where they are. Now, get out of my way."

Stacey looks smug with herself, and to be honest, I don't know why.

"Laur . . ."

"No, David. I'm not interested. If you decide you want to see MY kids, give me a call. My number hasn't changed."

"I think that about covers it," Matt says. "Now, I want all three of you out of my restaurant."

"Matt!" Martine's whiny voice goes straight through me.

"Martine, don't. You and I have nothing to say to each other. I've already told you that." My mind starts racing. When did he tell her this? "Look, for fuck's sake, go."

Martine gasps and her mouth falls open at his outburst before she turns on her heel and leaves, quickly followed by Stacey. David stops. "Is he the new man in your life?"

"Yes, but that's none of your concern."

"No, I don't suppose it is." He turns and follows Stacey.

"Bloody hell. I need a drink," I say.

"I'm not surprised," says Lesley. "Come on."

Matt takes my hand and we walk over to the bar. Danny is there and hands me a glass of what looks like brandy. Well, they say brandy is good for shock. But the thing is, I'm angry with David's reaction, and also curious. Angry that he thought to question me, yet curious as to how they know Martine.

"Lauren, are you okay?" Matt asks, turning me to face him. Lesley looks on and Danny has a sad look in his eyes.

"Yes, I'm fine. Although, something is telling me David might cause trouble now he's seen us together."

"I'm not worried about that. He can try. But what will you do if he decides to take an interest in the kids now?"

"I don't think he will, but on the off chance, I wouldn't stand in his way."

I put the glass down and Matt takes me in his arms. My body melts against him. "I still want to smack him one on the mouth."

"But you won't, because that's the last thing I want."

"I know. Are you ready? We can drop Mum home and then try and relax for the rest of the afternoon."

"Yes. Take me home."

"Let me grab a quick word with Danny."

I stand with Lesley and watch as Matt and Danny talk at the side of the bar. Their voices are hushed so I can't hear what is said, although Danny is frowning and, if I'm not mistaken, rocking on his feet. I wonder what's wrong.

Twenty-Six

"BABE, CAN I GET YOU anything? A drink?" he asks, at the same time typing out another message on his phone. His phone has been going non-stop since we dropped his mum at home. I'm not sure what's wrong, but I do know the last two text messages have come from Danny.

"Matt, considering it's what, almost five p.m., no, I don't want another drink. Are you trying to get me drunk?" I ask, teasing, as I flop down on the sofa in my sitting room.

"No. I don't need you drunk to be able to do all the things I want to do to you."

Oh, where the hell did that come from?

"Don't look at me like that."

"Like what?"

"With those green eyes all wide and shocked. There's lots I want to do with and to you, but first, we need to talk." There's a nervous edge to his voice. The last time I heard this tone, I walked out of a restaurant and left him sitting on his own. I take some of my hair in my hand and twist it around my fingers. "Lauren, stop that," he says, sitting down beside me.

He wraps his arm around me and I feel at ease. Whatever he's going to tell me isn't going to be so bad. "Let's start with business.

Where are the premises you and Abbie have seen?"

"Not a million miles away from the restaurant and club, in Bath Street."

"That sounds promising. I already like it. I can view it any day. What are you doing about investment, business plan?"

"We both have investment and won't need to borrow funds. The rent is a bit more expensive than we'd like, but the location is perfect. And the business plan, I can work on projection figures based on what I currently have with my customers."

"You seem to be on the ball."

"I need to be. If I'm going to do this, I have to do it right, and then hopefully when we're up and running, it won't be so hard for me to fall into a routine for both work and the kids."

"And where do I fit into these plans of yours?"

I turn to face him. "I won't lie to you, I'm not sure. Yes, I enjoy the time we're spending together . . ."

"Don't say *but*. I know the kids come first. I've already told you this. I just want to know you're prepared to see where this goes. Yes, I'd love to spend every day with you but I know that's not possible. Maybe we could aim for one date night or day a week until you decide you want more."

"You might decide you want less," I say with a laugh.

"That's not going to happen. Now, you're going to your dad's?"

"I've been thinking about it for the last week and it would be good for him and us."

"Yes, it will, but it won't be good for me. I might need to join you. And a holiday abroad?"

He looks very serious. Would he really come to London? Yes, he would. I inwardly smile at that thought.

"Yes, it's something else I've been thinking about, although I'm not sure on the practical side of that with Kate."

"Please talk to me before you make a decision on that."

"I will," I say, leaning and pressing a kiss to his lips. "Now,

Martine?"

"She's not someone I want you to worry about."

"That may be so, but after seeing her today . . ."

"Danny has been doing some digging, and it turns out, she and Stacey are friends. And David is going to do some re-branding for her business."

"Oh, okay. I have a question."

"You don't even need to ask. I've already told you, I'm long gone with that business. It was something that helped my family at a very difficult time and I'm not proud of what I did, but I also can't change my past. Even though at times I wish I could. As for Martine, I can't say for definite if she's still doing it. But the truth is, what she does or doesn't do is of no interest to me."

I draw in a deep breath. "Okay."

A slow smile plays on his lips. "That one word could have a whole host of meanings."

"Yeah, I know, and it's meant to."

He sits up straight, slipping his hand around my waist, pulling me closer to him. He claims my lips as only he can. Wrapping my arms around his neck, I respond, letting him have me and letting him know the meaning of my unspoken words. That, yes, I'm prepared to give us a go. I'm prepared to take the chance.

Our kiss starts slow and sensual, but it doesn't stay that way for long. He consumes me and my thoughts as his tongue delves inside my mouth, seeking out mine. My tongue meets his stroke for stroke. I allow myself to forget about some of today's events by losing myself in this incredible kiss.

"Mmm," I say breathlessly, as he moves the kiss from my lips and places small feather kisses over every inch of my neck. He pauses at my earlobe and nips his teeth against it, sending a shiver coursing through my body.

"You're stunning."

"You're not so bad yourself."

"Mum likes you, but then again, I knew she would."

"How so?"

"Because Emma has told her all great things about you and the kids. She didn't leave me much to tell her myself. Although, she does know I've fucked up where you're concerned. She just doesn't know the facts."

"Oh."

"Don't sound so surprised. You should also know my dear mum has warned me not to mess you around," he says, smirking, his hand running up and down my back. "If I fuck up again, she won't be pleased with me."

"Well, in that case, don't fuck up and you won't be in her bad books, or mine."

"I'm going to do something I never do. I promise I'll try not to fuck up. Now, we've spent the afternoon with my mum and Emma would like to see us tomorrow, but I have tried to put her off. Because I'd like to take us somewhere, anywhere, away from everything and everyone for the day."

"This sounds interesting, but I'm happy to see Emma."

"Going for Sunday dinner with my family and the kids; I don't think either of us needs that tomorrow. No, tomorrow is about you and me. No-one else."

He's right. Seeing the boys would have me thinking of my two.

Fuck! I'm the worst mother in the world. I've hardly given them a second thought today. I slump back, allowing my head to rest on the couch, and close my eyes on a frown. I hope they're both okay. Grant would've called if there were any problems.

"Lauren, what's wrong?" I open my eyes and he's observing me, trying to work out my sudden mood change, the cogs ticking within.

"The kids. I'm a bad mother. Other than talking to your mum about them, I've been too wrapped up in us to think about them."

He reaches out, taking my face in his hand, tilting it until our eyes meet. "You are the best mother in the world to your kids, but you're allowed some you time. And *me* time. And now we're going to have some us time and all thoughts of the kids will be pushed aside for a few hours, until your call with them at bedtime."

He stands, and before I realise or can object, I'm scooped up into his arms and carried up the stairs. He kicks the door to my bedroom open and strides towards the bed. Ah, now I see what he means about *us* time.

"You drive me insanely crazy." He lowers me to my feet, looking smug. "Now, for what I want, you are wearing too many items of clothing."

I could drag this out with a strip tease, but somehow, I don't think either of us have the patience for that. Kicking off my shoes, I undress quickly until I'm standing before him in matching white lace underwear.

Dark eyes filled with lust are watching me, penetrating me. All my senses heighten. He reaches out an arm and I brace myself for the sensations that will sweep through me when his hand connects with my skin. Every nerve ending is standing on edge.

His warm hands skim my breasts. I close my eyes and arch my back, closing the distance between us, and needing to feel his body. I shiver when I feel his other hand on my back. He makes quick work of unhooking the clip on my bra. My breasts free as he pulls the straps down my arms, and my bra falls to the floor.

When I open my eyes, our eyes connect as he runs his thumbs repeatedly over my nipples. Oh dear God. Endless sparks of pleasure shoot through me.

"You were made for me. Only me," he breathes against my throat. He licks along and around my neck before working his way up my jawline. I roughly grab his hair, lacing my fingers through it, at the same time releasing the breath I hadn't realised I was holding.

"I need to taste you," he says, dropping to his knees. Holy crap.

He can't do this here. Not with me standing. There's no way my legs will take that. His head nuzzles between my legs and I can hear the sharp intake of breath. I feel his hands on the waistband of my knickers before he quickly removes them. My body shakes.

"I need to sit down before I fall down," I tell him, my voice as shaky as my body. He nods and I sit down on the edge of the bed. My body falls back and my eyes close as the first touch of his tongue circles my clit. His hands are pressed against my legs, spreading them apart, his tongue sweeping back and forth in circular motions. This is intense. Fisting the bed sheets in my hand, my body arches against him. The relentless assault on my senses sends my body in a spin. The need to press my legs together is intense, but his hands spreading my legs are restricting my movements. My hips rock.

The pace changes and my body trembles. He releases my legs and grabs hold of my arse, pulling me closer to him, all the time still sucking and licking. My thighs press toward him and my body convulses. The deep forceful throb that started in my core takes over and I tremble under his expertly delicate touch. I shatter, crying out his name.

He doesn't stop.

Finally, he moves. My body is flushed.

Opening my eyes, I watch as he unfastens his trousers and lowers them and his boxers. "Turn over," he says, eyes wild with excitement. "I'm not finished with you yet."

I roll over, lying on the bed on my stomach. He pulls me down the bed and I grab the sheets, because I know, without a shadow of a doubt, this will be rough and quick.

He enters me quickly and fully. I gasp, trying to taking in as much air as I possibly can. In this position, I can't move. He grabs my hips, thrusting against me. He pulls almost all the way out and quickly pushes back in, going a little deeper than he did before.

Lifting my arse until it's in the position he wants, he starts grinding against me. The pace is punishing, quick, like I knew it would be, but I did think I would last the pace he set. No, it's not going to take much for me to fall off the edge again.

Again, he pulls out, although this time he rams into me. I cry out as the pleasure begins to course through me. Each thrust is forceful and precise and hits the spot that sends my body spiralling out of control. One last powerful thrust has him crying out my name. He releases my arse and his body falls against me. I'm dizzy, my head spinning as soft kisses lace my back.

"See what you do to me. I lose all control around you."

He lifts himself off me and turns me back around. He's shaking almost as much as I am, a sheen of sweat across his forehead. "Are you okay?" he asks.

"I'm more than okay."

"Good. Now I think we should grab a bath and then decide what to do with our night."

"I'm not opposed to scrapping a bath and laying in bed with you the rest of the night."

A slow smile starts at the corners of his lips. He leans forward. "That could be one of the best things you've said to me." He presses his lips to mine, and in this moment, I happen to agree.

Twenty-Seven

AS THE CAR SPEEDS ALONG the motorway and takes the slip road for the Erskine Bridge, I suddenly know the direction we're going. I'm presuming Loch Lomond, but I don't want to get my hopes up. He's been very secretive since we got up this morning. His mood is light and playful, and he's not the only one who's happy.

Our evening together was blissfully perfect, and yes, I got to speak with Luke, who, by all accounts, is having a ball and has now decided he loves fishing. He pleaded with me to take him once he comes home. I didn't tell him there isn't a hope in hell of me taking him. Grant has started this so he can take him.

I spoke to Liz because I was desperate to know how Kate is. She said, as always, she's been an angel. She asked how I was coping without them; all I could say was I was being kept occupied. I'll wait until they're home and then tell Grant I've been spending time with Matt. I have an idea of how that conversation will go.

"Are you going to tell me where we're going?"

"Stewart Hotel," he tells me. Bloody hell. Stewart Hotel, in my opinion, is THE best hotel on the banks of Loch Lomond. "That's why there is an overnight bag in the back seat."

I glance over my shoulder, and right enough, there is. He's

been very sneaky.

"So, this is your surprise?"

"Yes. If things had been different between us these last few weeks, I would have whisked you away for the whole weekend, but as it is, here will do nicely, and anyway, I know the owner."

Oh, that surprises me. Although, I feel as though I know Libby Mathews personally with everything I've read about her in the papers.

"I know Libby and the Stewart family through my mum. So you can wipe that frown from your face. Green doesn't suit either of us, it seems."

I chuckle as I remember Emma using those words a few weeks ago. "So, we're staying overnight?" I ask excitedly.

"Yes, and if you're lucky, we might even manage to take in some sights other than the hotel bedroom."

I don't even bother to pretend his statement shocks me. It should, but it doesn't.

"When did you pack my things?"

"When you were sleeping."

I shake my head and now I'm a bit worried what he's brought for me to wear. Not another word is said between us. The music is on and I happily sing along quietly. The scenery is breath-taking.

"Oh-my-gosh. It's even more perfect than in the pictures I've seen," I say, with more than a hint of excitement in my voice.

"You've never been here before?"

"Nope."

"Oh, then we are going to have a lot of fun." The car comes to a stop at the main entrance. Matt gets out and quickly comes around and opens my door. I stop and turn, facing the Loch. It's beautiful. Down by the water's edge sits a seaplane. I've never been on one, but I've been told it's such an amazing experience. I fight the urge to walk down to the edge because all I want to do is stroll along and take in the magnificent views of Ben Lomond.

"Can we go exploring?" I ask.

"Of course. Let's get checked in and then we can do whatever you want." He takes my hand and hands his car keys over to an older gentleman who greets him by name.

We don't make it up the stairs of the entrance before a woman calls out to Matt.

"I thought I recognised the car," she says.

He lets go of my hand and greets the perfect Libby Mathews with a warm hug.

"Libby, you look great. Motherhood is certainly agreeing with you."

He's not wrong; she looks amazing.

"You don't look so bad yourself," she says, giving him the once over before her eyes meet mine. "Hi. I'm Libby." She holds her hand out to me, which I shake politely.

"Sorry, Lauren. This is Libby."

"Pleased to meet you," I say softly, a bit taken aback.

"Are you working today?" he asks her.

"No. Alex and I are taking the twins out for the day."

"We should make a point in catching up properly soon."

"Yes, it would be good. Now, enjoy your stay, and I'm sure my staff will take care of you. Lauren, you need to keep this one on his toes," she says, laughing, and I laugh lightly with her.

"Hey, you two, enough. We need to check in; I have plans. It was good seeing you. Tell Alex I'll give him a call soon."

"Enjoy your stay." We start walking up the stairs. "Oh, and Matt, behave. Lauren seems too good for you." Libby walks away, smirking.

"You know, she does have a point. I'm lucky you're here with me." I blush. He takes my hand and we go inside. It doesn't take long to get checked in, and then we're shown to our room by a porter, who also has our cases. I had forgotten about those.

I gasp, entering the room. Matt thanks the porter as I wander off toward the large windows that have a clear view of the Loch and the hills beyond. I'm in total awe of the view before me. This room must be at the tallest part of the building. The room itself is immaculate; finished to a high standard, but for me, the view has won me over. No wonder Stewart Hotel has an amazing reputation. I'm sure Libby and her staff play a part in that, but I can bet it's the view that guests return for.

Hands slide around my waist, pulling my body closer to his. I relax against him, happy and content in his arms. I could stand here all day and watch the world go by. Tourist boats cruise the Loch, while a few speedboats zip through the water.

"Well, what do you think?" he asks, moving my hair to the side and kissing my neck.

"I think it's perfect," I answer breathlessly. A dull ache forms deep inside me and I love the closeness we've shared so far this weekend. From the bumpy start on Friday afternoon to now, standing here, looking out at this romantic location. Tears well in my eyes as I think of how this weekend could've ended up if I hadn't given him another chance. Not that the decision was mine. No, Mr In Control had already made the decision for me.

"Yes, it is, but not as perfect as you. Now, if you want to go exploring, there is a jumper in amongst your things."

"A jumper? But it's beautiful outside."

"Yes, it is, but it will still be breezy on the Loch."

Oh my. We're going exploring on the Loch. "So we're going out on a boat?" I ask, turning in his arms.

"Yes. Just the two of us and a picnic."

"Mmm, that sounds perfect."

He presses his forehead against mine. "Come on. Let's change and get out of this room before I decide to make good use of that bed."

My eyes dart to the bed; it's enormous. I smile at the direction of his thoughts, but it's too nice a day to spend in bed, although it does have a certain appeal to it.

"No. As much as it pains me, it's not happening. Not yet, anyway," he says, with a wicked glint in his warm green eyes.

He releases his hold of me and I reluctantly step away toward the case and open it. He's not done so bad in his choices of clothing; there's even a black dress which I take out and hang up. I pull on the white jumper and change out of the sandals I'm wearing to my Converse.

"I'm ready."

"Good, we can head off then." He grabs my hand and we leave the room.

This time, as we walk through the hotel, I have a good look around, taking in all the small details. The décor is traditional with lots of modern twists.

We step outside and I stop on the top stair and take in a deep breath. The air is fresh and filled with heavy woodland scents. "Are you ready?" Matt asks.

"Yes."

We walk down the stairs and I expect to turn and walk in the direction of the marina, so I'm surprised when we walk straight down to the water's edge. The bright yellow seaplane takes up the scenery in front of us. I turn my head and glance back toward the hotel; it is truly breath-taking. And to think Libby Mathews, a woman a few years younger than me, owns all this. Not only does she manage to run this hotel and estate, but look after her twins. It makes me think of myself and what I want to achieve out of business.

"You'll have to watch your footing." I turn to Matt, not understand what he's saying.

"I thought we were going out on a boat?" I ask, puzzled, as we stand in front of the seaplane.

"Yes, we are later, but first I thought you'd like to see an aerial view."

I smile at this. His hand tightens around mine as we walk toward the captain. He introduces himself to us and advises us on our planned flight route, as well as providing us with a professional, relaxed but comprehensive safety briefing prior to boarding.

Matt instructs me to go first and I hesitate, but only for a moment. Matt follows closely behind me. We take our seats. Matt takes my hand in his as the engine starts and the seaplane pulls slowly into the Loch, ready for take-off. Neither of us speaks; we don't need to. I'm sure his smile mirrors my own.

The seaplane starts to pick up speed and it's not long until I can feel it gently lift off. I rub Matt's hand as we climb higher into the sky. The captain starts to speak, pointing out various landmarks and the stunning landscape just below the aircraft; everything looks as though it's in touching distance.

My eyes drift to Matt's and he's watching me, smiling widely. This is the most thoughtful thing anyone has ever done for me. I turn back, looking at the scene below. It's the most amazing thing I've seen; all the beautiful colours between the hills and the water. It's magical.

All too soon, we've landed by the shores of the Loch at the hotel, standing on the grass, sipping champagne with the captain. Matt has his arm wrapped around my waist. We finally say goodbye to the captain and walk towards the marina.

"Well, did you enjoy that?"

"Matt, that was the most amazing experience. Thank you."

"Don't thank me. It was my pleasure. I love seeing you happy. Your smile makes me smile. Now we go out on the Loch and we can enjoy a picnic lunch and some more champagne."

"Sounds great."

We stroll through the grounds at a leisurely pace, hand in hand. The marina is filled with boats, and as I look along at them, they seem to get bigger. Bloody hell, some of them are huge. Matt tells me Libby and Alex stay about a ten minute walk away from here within the grounds of the hotel, and that it's Libby's boat we're going out in today.

The boards squeak underfoot as we walk along to the end. "This is us," he says, as we approach a stunning boat.

"OH. My. God."

"You like?"

"What have I done to deserve all this?"

"Nothing, except being you. You deserve the very best out of life, and as long as I'm part of your life, I'll always try to do the right thing by you."

I stand on my tiptoes and press a kiss to his lips. "Thank you." He leads me on board the boat and introduces me to the captain and a member of staff. Again, we're talked through safety procedures before we take our seats on the upper terrace where we're truly spoilt for panoramic views in all directions.

I lean into Matt's body and relax as we set off. Matt keeps his arms around my waist as I lean into him; his head rests on my shoulder. He was right about the jumper; there is a chill in the air as the boat glides across the water. Champagne is served to us as we sit, taking in the wonderful scenery.

What I'm loving most about today is that it's so different to my everyday life. It's so far away from my life with the kids and all my daily struggles. That's what's making today so special. As we sip at the champagne, the captain tells us information about some of the various islands we pass. I try hard to listen to what he tells us, but to be honest, I'm in complete awe.

"Lauren, you're very quiet."

"I'm just taking it all in. Today has been amazing."

"This is only the beginning. We still have dinner tonight and then whatever happens after dinner. And, of course, you have a phone call with Luke to look forward to, to round off what I hope will be a perfect day." I turn, looking into his deep green eyes, and watch as his smile widens. He kisses the corner of my mouth. "Now, let's enjoy this experience. We'll have our picnic on-board later before we come back to shore."

We both turn our attention back to the Loch and enjoy.

Twenty-Eight

"LAUREN, YOU LOOK A LITTLE tired," Matt says as soon as we step off the boat.

"I suppose it'll be all the fresh air today." I spin around to face him. "I've loved every single minute we've spent together."

"No regrets?" I hear the meaning behind his question and I can answer him honestly.

"None whatsoever. Now, I think I should show you my gratitude." I press my lips softly to his. Warm feelings rush through me as we stand by the boat that has just docked, and now I'm wondering how quickly we can get back to the hotel room.

"That sounds interesting, but I'm not sure your plan works for me," he says, his voice teasing, his green eyes twinkling with that sexy smirk he has. "I also think you might need a nap before dinner tonight. Don't want you using too much energy."

He wraps his arm around my waist and we walk, leaving the marina behind us, and make our way back to the hotel. My head is fuzzy and I blame a combination of excitement, champagne, and fresh air.

I stop before the hotel entrance and turn, facing the water. I let his hand slip from my waist as I watch. The water ripples against the shoreline; it's soothing. Birds chirp up above and there are a few kids running about on the front lawn. Not even the noise of the kids screaming at each other can take away how calm I feel.

Glancing over my shoulder, I find Matt studying me. "What?"

"I'm not sure. You look happy."

"That's because I am."

He holds his hand out to me, which, of course, I take. "Glad to hear it." We walk back inside the hotel and straight back to our room.

There's a bottle of champagne chilling on the coffee table, with a tray of fresh strawberries. I wonder when he organised this. He has been very thoughtful and attentive, not just today but the full weekend. It's actually refreshing, someone thinking about and putting me first.

I kick my Converse off and turn to face him; he's standing in the middle of the room, gazing at me. "Do you want to lie down before dinner?" he asks.

"Not to sleep," I say, pulling the jumper up and over my head before tossing it on the floor. His eyes don't move from mine as I start to strip. The intensity in his gaze captivates me and gives me the courage to continue with the floor show I've started.

My fingers fumble with the belt on my jeans and I lower the zip. Taking a deep breath, I swallow sharply at how brazen I've become. Never in my life have I had the confidence to stand in front of a man and do this.

I leave the jeans where they are for the moment, hanging loosely around my waist with my underwear on show, and reach around my back, unhooking the clips on my bra. Matt's eyes move, this time travelling with my bra that drops to the floor.

The sexy smile on his lips tells me he approves. Matt's eyes slowly drink me in. With my new found confidence, I finally lower my jeans, keeping my eyes on him. I can't help the smug grin that must be on my face when I see him shift uncomfortably on his feet before adjusting his jeans at the groin.

Mission accomplished.

He's not the only one turned on by my sudden strip tease.

I stand motionless in front of him, in nothing more than my lace thong. His gaze has left mine and I watch as he takes every inch of my body in. Dark lustful eyes linger on my breasts, before slowly working down my body. Both hands clench into fists at his side as he struggles with what to do with them.

His gaze finally lifts and settles on my face. He takes slow, precise steps toward me and I gasp because I know I'm no longer in control.

"This was not what I had in mind. You, Lauren Trent, are a tease." His tone is low as he moves closer to me. There's an aching deep within my chest.

"I can get dressed if you're not interested."

"We're not playing games, Lauren. You make it fucking impossible for me. I was trying to ensure today was perfect."

"And is it not?"

"No, it is, but this." He's in front of me now; warm fingers run up and down my skin from the side of my breast bone all the way down to my hip and back again. "This, is totally unexpected. So, the question I have to ask myself is, what do I do with you?"

"I know what I want you to do."

"Yes, I see that." I can see the smirk on his face when he notices my legs pressing tightly together. Yes, I want him. I can't deny that. All the time I spend with him makes me feel so good. It's exhilarating.

Now he's close, I want to undress him. Glancing down at his jeans, I allow my fingers to undo his buttons before taking the hem of his T-shirt. With a quick look into his eyes, I pull it off and throw it on the floor.

He looks perfect as my eyes leave his face, travelling down his firm chest to his abs and that perfect V. I reach out, placing my hands on his chest. His eyes close and his breathing changes. My fingers trace small patterns down his skin.

"Enough. I can't let you have all the fun." His eyes snap open.

That's what he thinks.

I drop to my knees without looking at him. I'm taking back control, if only for a short time. Slipping my hands under the waistband of his boxers, I lower them and his jeans, freeing his erection. I smile when I feel a small shiver tremble through his body. Taking a deep breath, I steal a look in his direction; his heavy eyes stare back at me.

Taking him in my hand, I lean forward, kissing the tip slowly, pre-cum glistening on the tip as I draw back. Swallowing nervously, I watch him as I run my tongue along my lips. He groans when I lean forward and take all of him this time. He doesn't move. His hands hang by his side, but I already sense they won't be there for long.

Drawing my hand up and down at the base, I tease him softly with my tongue. I take him deeper, sucking him in. Pulling back, I allow my teeth to graze lightly against him. He moans on a long breath. I run my tongue over and around the tip, still teasing him before taking all of him again. I glance upwards when I feel his grip on my shoulders. I might be in control now, but it won't be long until he takes it back. His body is tense.

I continue to work my hand at the base while his body starts to move, thrusting against me. "Lauren, please, no. Not like this," he whimpers. I lift my head, dropping him from my mouth, and he pulls me to my feet. I smile, knowing I've completely unravelled the man before me. "I might make you pay for that performance."

"I'm counting on it," I say breathlessly. He wraps me in a tight embrace and kisses me hard, capturing my mouth with his. Teasing and tasting, he pushes his tongue deep into my mouth, exploring. I meet him with the same passion and force.

Slowly, he pulls back, staring intently into my eyes. "What am I going to do with you?" he whispers against me.

"Oh, I don't know. Why don't we have some champagne and strawberries?"

"Champagne seems to agree with you." His voice teases me. "But I think the champagne can wait, don't you? I want you in that bed and most definitely between those sheets."

I don't get a chance to respond to his words. He kicks off his shoes and steps out of his clothes before grabbing me and throwing me over his shoulder. I'm sure the high-pitched scream that leaves me will be heard in the bedrooms closest to ours.

He lays me on the bed and removes my now very wet thong. As he prowls up the bed, I smile. My smile quickly turns into giggling as he starts kissing me from my belly button, working slowly up to my breasts.

He pauses. "What's so funny?" he asks. I can't even answer him; for some reason, I'm so damn ticklish.

"Lauren!" He stops kissing me. My body sags in defeat into the comfortable bed. "Have you finished?"

With a deep breath, I answer, "Yes. Sorry."

"Okay, then I shall continue."

Oh, no. I'm not sure I'm ready for this again. Warm lips trail up my skin, gently kissing and nipping. I close my eyes and allow my head to fill with thoughts of only the two of us. Of here and now.

Warmth spreads through my sensitive body as he applies pressure to each kiss that he places on my skin. Awareness surrounds me. I gasp and moan loudly when he reaches my breasts, taking my nipple into his mouth and sucking hard, rolling it between his teeth. Pleasure takes over, my giggling fit of only moments ago a distant memory.

Matt Anderson makes me feel alive.

I feel wanted and desired.

"I should tease you as much as you've teased me." My eyes fly wide open, wondering what he means. "But I don't know if I have the ability to bring you that close to the edge over and over to not see that final look on your flushed face as I leave you going without."

I'm sure my mouth forms a perfect O at his words.

He leans down and our mouths meet, tongues tangling in what starts off as a slow, sensual kiss. I wriggle beneath him, trying to meet his erection that is between my legs. A hand stops me from getting what I so desperately desire. I moan as our kiss deepens and his fingers slide roughly through my wetness.

Slowly, he pushes his finger inside, moving it in and out. My hips move and I try to still but I can't. Every part of me wants him, and today, I've shown him how much.

He breaks our kiss and I open my eyes. He's staring at me intently, a slow smile curving on his lips. I moan louder as he hits the spot deeper within me. I wrap my arms around him, clawing at his back as my pleasure grows. He smirks, stops, and removes his fingers.

"Please," I whimper, wanting a release.

"Maybe I was wrong. I might be able to bring you to the brink over and over, just to hear you plead. Begging me for more. But no. I want this just as much as you."

With no warning, his erection is where I want it, pushing deep inside me. His head drops to my neck, nuzzling against it.

He grabs hold of my hips, drawing me closer to him as he thrusts into me. My hands continue to wander up and down his back, clawing him.

Every nerve ending in my body is on high alert as my pleasure builds deep within. Hard and fast I can take, but this is sending my body into a state of shock. My back arches to meet him and I'm lost, blinded by my orgasm. My body trembles as he continues thrusting, needing his own release.

I watch on helplessly as he follows through. He lifts his head, green eyes blazing with desire, but there's something else there, an unspoken promise, maybe. That I belong to him and only him.

He rolls off me and pulls me onto my side, facing him. "Maybe next time I will tease you." His husky voice sends signals to my core and my legs press together.

"Mmm, maybe," I say with a yawn.

"Why don't we go to sleep?"

"What about your plans for dinner?"

"Plans can always be changed. We can order room service later."

"Do you mind if I call Grant? I don't want to miss their call and not speak to Luke."

"No. Stay put. I'll grab your phone. Then you can relax in my arms."

"Now that, Mr Anderson, sounds like a plan."

He kisses my nose before leaving the bed, still gloriously naked. My eyes follow him to where my jeans are lying in a heap on the floor. I could get used to spending time with him, especially if this is how he makes me feel.

Twenty-Nine

"I'M NOT READY TO GO home yet," I say, as we leave the hotel and walk hand in hand to his car.

"I know, but I'm sure we can do this again."

I frown because I know it won't happen. The only reason we could do this is because the kids are away this weekend. And yes, I've missed them, but I've enjoyed my time with Matt. "Less of that frown. It won't be long until your babies are back home."

"I know, and I'm excited to see them, but I've enjoyed being with you."

"We'll have plenty of time together. Of that I've no doubts. Now, can I stay with you until they come home? You're not the only one not ready for this to end yet."

"Yes, but I want to speak to Grant."

"I'm sure you do, but I'd like to be able to speak with him too. Have a chance for me to explain myself if he will listen to me. Which he might not. He might take one look at me and swing a punch."

"He wouldn't. Not in front of the kids," I say, smirking before frowning because even I know Grant may well want to lash out at him.

We stop by the car and I turn to face him. His mouth lowers

to mine before I get a chance to speak. This kiss is perfect; slow and sensual. "Thank you for having me in your life," he whispers as his lips leave mine.

"The pleasure is all mine."

He shakes his head at my words and opens the car door. It feels strange as we drive away from the peace and quiet and head toward the motorway that will bring us home. The traffic is busy, and as I look at the time, I realise we might be home with only a few minutes to spare before the kids are back.

Conversation is light and relaxed. We talk about me doing the work for the restaurant and club, which I agree to do. It's all still saved on my laptop. And I wouldn't be happy with him getting someone else in to do the job I started. We talk about my dad, and Matt makes me promise to tell him before I decide to go and visit him, not just take off. It's actually quite nice that he wants to be close to me. He tells me, if it weren't for the kids, he would come down to London with me. My reply was to slow things down. One step at a time.

"Lauren, I know you have the kids and I don't know how the hell we'll manage it, but I do want to spend time with you."

"It's going to be hard with the schools off on holidays for the next seven weeks."

"I know and understand. I'll try to be patient, only you need to give me something to look forward to."

"All I can offer is maybe a date." He smiles, and I hope our next date is better than the last. That's something I'd rather forget. "There will be no nights together," I say, because it has to be said. I don't want to disrupt Luke's life. If and when things become more permanent between us then I will reconsider this, but for now, it's not an option.

"That's what I was afraid you would say. I'll do one step at a time, even though this might break me in two." He laughs lightly. "And I promise to be on my best behaviour in front of the kids today."

"Yes. Be sure you do that."

The rest of the journey is also relaxed, but as we turn into my street, I see Grant's car pulling into my drive. Shit! I at least wanted to be home before they got here. Bloody traffic. My body tenses as Matt stops his car behind mine in the driveway. "Lauren, please. This will be fine, and if it's not, I'll see Grant myself this week."

I nod and get out of his car.

Grant is out of the car. He smiles then frowns when he sees Matt behind me. Tension rolls off him in waves as he stares blankly at Matt. Liz is lifting Kate from the car.

"Mummy!" I bend down and pick up Luke as he runs into my arms, and spin him around. "Mummy, when can you take me fishing? Can we do it tomorrow?"

"I'm not sure about tomorrow," I say with a frown, looking at Grant. This time when he looks at me, he smiles a proper smile. He knows there's no way I'll take Luke fishing. "Maybe Uncle Grant can take you again."

"Of course I can," he says, lifting the kids' case from the car. Kate is sound asleep in Liz's arms.

"Mummy, I did miss you but I had so much fun."

"I missed you too," I say, smothering him in kisses.

"Mum! Stop it."

"Okay." I put him down and he runs toward the door. I offer to take Kate, but Liz keeps her in her arms as I open the front door. Liz puts Kate down on the sofa, while I stick the kettle on.

"He seems a nice man, Lauren. This is the second time I've seen him here with you," Liz says, catching me off guard.

Shit. That means Grant and Matt are together in the sitting room with the kids.

"He is."

"Is it serious?"

"I don't know yet."

"Well, sweetheart, you know where I am if you want to talk, or if you need me to babysit. Sandra does so much for you. It would be nice if I could help you, even in a small way."

"Thanks. You could talk to Grant. He doesn't like Matt and I can understand his reasons, but if we do continue seeing each other, I don't want my relationship with Matt to come between me and Grant."

"Sweetheart, consider it done." She smiles warmly before telling me how Kate's been today as I make tea.

We take the tea into the sitting room and I'm pleasantly surprised by the relaxed atmosphere, considering the frosty reception when we arrived. Liz and I exchange glances, both of us wondering what's going on. But the answer is clear as Kate runs around Luke, who is lying on the floor, giggling away. I hand Matt his tea before putting mine down in a safe place. Kate stops when she sees me and launches her tiny body at me. I drop to her level and take her in my arms.

"Mummy has missed you," I say, with tear-filled eyes. "I think the three of us can watch a movie tonight," I say, as Luke joins me on the floor, wrapping his arms around me.

"That sounds good, but can I go and play with Liam?" he asks.

"You don't want to stay here and hang out with me?"

"I want to play football and I've missed Liam too."

"Yes, but what do you say to Uncle Grant and Aunt Liz?"

Luke walks over to Grant and Liz, kissing and thanking them both for the weekend. Grant tells him he wants to watch his first football game with his new team, which is in only a few weeks.

"Okay, on you go. I'll text Emma."

Lifting Kate, I sit on the sofa beside Liz because, for me, she is the safe option. Liz asks what I did over the weekend, although I see the way her eyes dart between me and Matt. I tell her about going to Stewart Hotel and I catch the scowl on Grant's face.

"Okay, we should get going. I have some unpacking to do," Liz says. Grant nods. I leave Matt sitting with Kate and I see them both out, thanking them for having the kids.

"Grant . . ."

"Lauren, stop. I only want what's best for you. I've agreed to meet with Matt for lunch this week. He's told me briefly his reasons, well, you know what for. I'll hear him out." He puts his hand on my shoulder and pulls my body to his. "Sweetheart, I've told you I may not agree with some of your choices, but I'll always stand by you. No matter what. I love you as if you were my own, and for that reason, Matt and I will have a conversation because he needs to be aware if this doesn't go well, he has me to answer to." Liz looks on with love in her eyes.

"Grant, thank you."

"Don't thank me yet."

I kiss him before saying goodbye to Liz. "Everything will be fine, I'm sure of it. Now, I expect to hear from you during the week, and remember what I said. I, no, *we* will be happy to watch them any night for you."

I wave them off and go back inside. In the sitting room, I find Matt lying on the floor with Kate in his outstretched arms, giggling away.

"Having fun?" I ask.

"Yes. I think she likes me," he says, before turning his attention back to my daughter. I stand watching them; everything looks so natural for Matt. But then again, he's used to being around his nephews so it will be natural to him.

"Matt . . ."

"Yes."

I pause, thinking about what to say. In the end, I say, "It's nothing."

I'm not sure how I feel about the kids seeing him yet. This is all moving too quickly. I need to be cautious, especially where they are concerned. Luke seeing Matt around at Emma's is different from seeing him coming around our house. After all, Luke knows him as Liam's uncle. And for now, until we both decide what we want from the other, it's best for kids that that's the way it stays.

"I know you're still watching me. Kate, I wonder what's going on in your mummy's mind." He turns and looks at me, frowning.

"I'm thinking I should go to Emma's and make sure Luke is behaving."

"That sounds good because I'm going to head there myself," he says, putting Kate down and pulling himself back up onto his feet. "I'm sure my sister has a mountain of questions about us."

"I'm sure she has, but she won't get a lot of information from me. I'll change Kate and then I'll come along."

Matt narrows his eyes and frowns. "I'm not going anywhere without you."

"Okay, but please remember what we spoke about coming home."

"I know. Baby steps," he says, with some amusement in his voice.

After changing Kate, we walk along to Emma's. Matt has Kate on his shoulders and it has to be said, she's loving the attention he's giving her.

"I was wondering when we would see you two," Emma says as we enter her kitchen. "The boys are at the park."

"Playing football?"

"Yes. Matt, Patrick is in the garden."

"Emma, you could've just said you wanted rid of me."

"Well, go then." Emma is straight to the point. Matt kisses me on the cheek. Kate wanders to him, and he reaches down and takes her hand, and the two of them go out into the garden. "Okay, what have you done with my brother? And is it on? Off? Come on, this is all very exciting."

"God, what do you want me to say? Yes. We're taking it slow."

"And spending the entire weekend with him is taking it slow? When are you seeing each other again?"

"I don't know. It's the holidays. This might sound bad and I don't mean it to be, but I don't want him in the kids' lives at the moment." Emma leans forward, placing her chin in her hand as we sit at the table. "I'm scared that if the kids get too used to him and then we decide not to see each other, they will get hurt."

"Lauren, you've every right to be cautious, especially with them, and yes, Matt might not be happy about that but I'm sure deep down he must understand."

"Thank you. I think I needed someone else to tell me I'm doing the right thing."

"Of course you're doing the right thing. I'm glad you've given him another chance. He was a nightmare without you. So, when are you going to arrange a date? A proper date."

"I don't know."

"Well, for what it's worth, I think you should make it soon. I know the kids are your priority and you don't want them getting attached to Matt, but to get to know each other properly you have to spend time alone, and I don't mean in bed like you've done this weekend."

I blush at her words. "Well, I suppose I should arrange a babysitter."

"Lauren, I'm more than happy to watch them at yours for a few hours. That way the boys can play and I can spend time with Kate. We all win."

"Okay, let me have a think about it and I'll organise a date and surprise him."

"Now, I believe Patrick is going to light the barbecue, so will you stay and have something to eat?"

"Yes, only because I know he's not a bad cook on the barbecue." We both laugh and head outside.

Thirty

THE WINDSCREEN WIPERS STRUGGLE TO keep up with the rain battering against the car. Today, we don't just have rain, it's a full thunderstorm, and I'm wishing I was back home with the kids, snuggled up with them and watching cartoons instead of being out and about. Abbie is driving slowly and this short journey has taken double the time it usually takes, all because of this freak storm we have. "Lauren, I can't believe you sold me out for a weekend with Matt."

"Enough. Will you stop going on about it? Today is about business, not my se . . . personal life." She's not stopped going on about this all day. Right now, I want to choke her, but I won't because she's my best friend and I love her.

"Mmm, is that so? At least you have a sex life."

I shake my head and look back out of the window as she drives, not just the car, but me insane.

Today is exciting. This is the start of a new journey for us both. I'll be honest, I never saw Abbie leaving working for her dad. I always thought one day she would take over from him, but after he took on a business partner a few years ago, he's no longer a one-hundred percent shareholder. Abbie is as independent as me, and wants to be able to stand on her own feet without her parents' help.

Les has offered us both financial assistance getting this project off the ground, but we haven't accepted it. We will always listen to and take on board his advice in our decision making.

"I'm glad you've come to your senses and decided to see where this goes with Matt."

"Yeah, me too, but I'm scared."

"I get that and I don't want to see you get hurt, but I don't think he will hurt you. He's been honest and open with you and it's clear to see he has feelings for you. So enjoy."

"I'm going to try, and I'll start with Friday night. Are you sure you're okay to watch the kids overnight?"

"Yes, so don't worry about them. I've not seen them since last week. It will be good spending some quality time with them. And I'm sure Mum's going to come over with dinner." I laugh because it's true; Abbie has never cooked in her kitchen. Actually, I'm not sure Abbie can cook.

"They will love it."

"What have you told Matt about Friday?"

"Only that we're going out for dinner. I've not said I don't have to rush home because the kids will be with you. Thought I would leave that as a surprise."

"Well, I think he'll love it. Now I just need to remember and keep my mouth closed when we see him."

I smirk, knowing I might need to gag her when we get to the premises and meet with Matt so he can give us his opinion. Les has seen it and thinks it's the perfect size for us starting off in business.

We pull up in front of the building and Matt's car is already here.

"Should we wait or make a mad dash for it?" Abbie asks, looking outside.

"I say dash."

With that, we grab our jackets, and as soon as we step out of the car, we run toward the building. We must look so silly with our jackets over our heads. We stand in the doorway, and it's a few minutes before Matt leaves the safety of his car.

"Fancy meeting you both here," he says, smiling.

I raise my eyebrows. I texted him earlier to warn him that Abbie will most likely have something to say about him stealing me for the weekend.

"Funny that, isn't it?" she replies, as we step inside. The agent is waiting for us in the main building. I greet him and introduce Matt, but it appears they know each other. Why doesn't that surprise me? Matt seems to know everyone.

Matt has a good look around, looking in every corner of every room. I catch him frowning on more than one occasion. The agent is very relaxed. We ask if anyone else has looked at the property and he tells us not yet as it's fairly new on the market. I discuss rent and rates with the agent, but try to not let on that I'm really keen. The rent does sound steep.

After an hour of being in the property, looking around, we say goodbye to the agent. Matt has been fairly quiet the whole time.

"Can I treat you both to lunch?" Matt asks, as we stand outside. It's finally stopped raining. "I want to talk to you."

Abbie and I exchange glances before she nods. "Yeah, why not?"

We leave the cars parked and walk the short distance to his restaurant; it is literally around the corner. Matt shows us to a free table in the corner.

"Okay, so what are you both thinking?"

"I love it," Abbie says, and I can hear the excitement in her voice.

"It's a great location. There's a lot of internal decoration needed before we could move into it," I say.

"I sense a *but*," says Abbie.

"Yes. The rent, in my opinion, is steep for the interior

condition."

"You're right, the rent is steep," Matt agrees. "If you're able to get the price down, it would be perfect for you, but I don't know who owns that property so they might not be interested in lowering the price of rent."

"It's the first we've looked at," I add.

"Yes, but it's perfect," Abbie says.

"Abbie, in business you can't rush in, especially with something like this," Matt tells her. She sighs, shoulders dropping, and her eyes fall onto the table. "Look, I don't want either of you rushing into this and then finding out you've made a mistake, especially if you end up tied into a long-term lease. You need to look around."

What Matt is saying makes perfect sense. We order lunch and some soft drinks and we talk, although Abbie is pretty quiet. I get it's not what she wanted to hear, but I'm not going to sign a lease for the first property I see, even though it is in the perfect location.

Matt, sensing Abbie's disappointment, offers a short term solution. "Lauren, your office at home is more than big enough for both of you to use at the moment. Why don't you use that until you find suitable premises at the right cost? It would keep costs down at the moment while you find your feet."

"We could, although I would have to get Sandra to watch Kate at her house so we don't get disturbed, but it would work for now."

"But what about the work you've already taken on?" Abbie asks.

"Well, I would finish all projects I currently have before taking on new work under our new company name."

"That makes sense. I'm here for both of you if you need help or advice, but I do think Lauren knows a lot more about the business side of things than she lets on."

He might be speaking to Abbie but his eyes are firmly on me as he cocks his head to the side.

He's right, I do know more than I let on when it comes to running a business. After all, I ran a business with David for a number of years. Abbie really doesn't have any experience with that side of things. She is great at what she does, though.

A waiter brings over lunch and we start eating. Abbie looks a million miles away, lost in her own thoughts.

"Oh, for fuck's sake!" Matt drops his cutlery onto his plate and pushes his chair back, eyes focused firmly behind me.

"What's wrong?" He doesn't answer so I turn to see Martine standing near the doorway, taking off her jacket. "Matt, why don't you just sit down and ignore her?"

He stops, facing me. "You want me to pretend that witch isn't here? I can't do it. I don't want her here."

He stands, shaking his head. I take his hand and urge him to stay. Matt sits back down, offering me a smile before frowning. He leans back in the chair and I already know with the expression on his face that she has seen him and is walking toward us. "I shouldn't have listened to you." He throws the words across the table with amusement.

"My darling Matt, I was hoping to see you." Her voice cuts through the air as she leans down and gives him a kiss. "We should talk in private. I need your advice and opinion."

"Martine, when do you ever listen to anything I say?"

Abbie stares at Martine and turns back to me, eyebrows raised. I nod because I know what she's silently asking. I confirm this was his business partner. The one I met the night I walked away from him. "And if you don't mind, you're interrupting my lunch."

She swings her body around, long blonde hair flowing dramatically behind her as she moves. Her eyes drift from me to Abbie then back to Matt. "Interviewing new staff. These two could earn you a lot of money."

Abbie gasps, but it's Matt's reaction that worries me. He flies out of his seat, grabbing her roughly by her shoulders, and pushes her against the wall. "You fucking bitch. What is it you want? Truthfully, why are you here?"

She doesn't flinch under his hold. Her eyes are on Matt and nothing else. "To discuss business with you."

"Martine, it wouldn't make a difference what you want to talk about, I'm not interested."

"Well, in that case, maybe I should be speaking with mummy dearest."

"You bitch." His body presses against hers and all I can do is look on.

"Matt, let go of her. She's not worth it." Danny is now beside him, hands on his brother, trying to pull him back. Matt finally takes a step back and Martine's body relaxes, although she does look shaken up. "You," Danny hisses. "Get fucking out of here."

"I'm going. But, Matt? You might want to think about what I've said. After all this time, I don't think Mummy would take it well." She all but stomps toward the door, jacket flung over her shoulders, heels clipping across the floor.

"What the fuck was that about?" Danny shouts at Matt.

"Well, she now thinks she has one over me and is prepared to speak to Mum." He slumps back into his chair. Danny takes a seat.

"For a minute there I thought he was going to hit her," Abbie whispers. But it doesn't go unheard by either of them.

"Sorry." One lonely word falls from Matt's lips. I offer him a weak smile. "So much for a pleasant business lunch."

"It's fine," I say with a sigh.

"It's not fine. Martine is fucking poison and if she thinks for one minute she has the upper hand with me, she's sadly mistaken."

"What are you going to do?" Danny asks with concern.

Matt looks at him. "What I should've done years ago. Go and speak to Mum."

"Is that wise?"

"Probably not, but it needs to be done. That part of my life needs to be over once and for all. Can you cope on your own for the rest of the day?"

"Yes, but you'll need to expect Mum will more than likely fly off the handle with your news. After all, you have never done wrong where she's concerned."

Matt nods but doesn't look relaxed. No, he's dreading this conversation with his mum, and after how I reacted when I found out, I'm not surprised.

The rest of our lunch is uneventful, which is a good thing. The incident with Martine has taken Abbie's mind off the property we viewed. Abbie and I can discuss more when we get back to my house, where Sandra is watching the kids. Hopefully, when she has time to think it over and maybe talk to Les, she will feel better about everything.

"Lauren, I'm sorry," Matt says, wrapping his arms around my waist as we stand at the doorway of the restaurant.

"It's fine."

"It's not. Twice now she's tried to come between us. There won't be a third."

"I know. Go and do what you have to do with your mum and give me a call later. If you want to talk, you can come over when the kids are sleeping."

He presses his lips to mine. "Thank you. I know I'll be seeing you later now."

"Don't be getting any ideas, mister. There will be no funny business."

"I hear you loud and clear. Abbie," he calls over my shoulder. "Have a think about what I've said and I'll see you later. Now, you, I'm sure I'll be at Emma's after Mum gives me an earful, so text me."

"I will."

Thirty-One

"TOMORROW, HOW ABOUT WE GO out for the day? Just you, me, and Kate."

"Yes. Can we go to the park?" Luke asks, climbing into his bed.

"Yes." I bend, giving him a kiss, and pull his bed covers up. "Goodnight. I love you."

"I love you too, Mum."

I leave his room, check in on Kate and find she's already sound asleep, and head back downstairs. I have a few things to do then I'll text Matt and tell him to come over. When I spoke to him briefly earlier, he didn't give much away about how the conversation went with his mum. He did tell me he paid Martine a visit at her restaurant, but Kate started crying and we ended the call so I have no idea what's gone on.

I don't like being kept in the dark.

Abbie and I had a long talk when we got back here today. I looked out the business plan we had already worked on and added the rent costs of the property we viewed. It made her see sense. I'm more than happy to continue working from home, but I'm not sure Abbie is. She's going to have a think about it. Part of me thinks she might put the whole idea on the back burner for the time being, and for her, it might be the right thing to do. For me, though, I'm making a decent living working from home and over the last few weeks I've taken on new clients. Some of them have been David's and they weren't happy with the work he was doing for them. After talking to one of them, and also Grant, it would appear business isn't going well for David.

Hearing that didn't give me any sort of satisfaction. Some might argue it should, but it doesn't. I'm happy enough with how my own life is going to even give David a second thought. Well, I would still like him to change his mind and start seeing the kids, but I know it's not going to happen. Although, I did think after our run-in when I was out for lunch with Matt and his mum, David might get in touch. But he hasn't, and now I don't expect him to.

I'm sure when Luke is older he'll start asking me lots of questions, and hopefully, when he does, I'll have the right answers for him. But I'm not going to worry about that until I need to.

I open the files on my laptop and go through each one I have for Matt's business, ensuring I'm happy with the finished designs. When he comes over, we have business to discuss, as well as today's events. I just hope he's happy with what I've come up with. There is also the small matter that I think he needs to give the interior a bit of an overhaul, but I have designs for that as well.

I send him a text. *Kate is sleeping and Luke is in bed.*

Matt: Ok I'll see you in 10

Me: Don't knock the door, it's open. I'm in my office working.

Matt: I told you, you work too hard.

I decide not to reply, because if I do, I won't get everything ready for him. Instead, I print off all my designs so he can look at these properly.

Losing myself in my work, I pause when I hear the front door opening. I lift my head and he's standing in the doorway. "You can come in. I don't bite."

The smirk on his face tells me I shouldn't have said that. "Sweetheart, you can bite me anytime you like," he says, stalking toward me. "Now, why are you in here working?"

"Because I had a few things to finish up on a project."

"Should I ask?"

"Not yet. Let's go through to the sitting room. I'd rather hear how you got on today with your mum, and also Martine."

I stand, turning the papers on my desk so he can't see them. He takes my hand and presses a soft, brief kiss to my lips, leaving them tingling with want and desire. "It's all good. Come on then."

"Do you want a drink?"

"Yes. If you're having wine, I'll have some. My car can be left at Emma's and I'll get a taxi home."

I'd love to say stay, but I can't. It's too soon for Luke to be seeing a man at our breakfast table in the morning.

Matt takes a bottle of wine from the fridge and I grab two glasses, and we go into the front room. We sit down on the sofa together. Matt opens the wine and pours. He leans back and hands a glass to me.

"Well?" I press for conversation.

"Mum wasn't as shocked and upset as I thought she would be. We spoke at length about not just Martine, but my dad. Mum says at the time she couldn't see it, or rather didn't want to know how bad things were financially. But looking back, she feels bad for allowing me to get the family out of the mess my dad left behind."

"What do you mean? She wasn't shocked?"

"She had an idea of what Martine did for a living. In my mother's words, 'there's no way she could afford half of what she owned without selling her soul.' Yes, of course, she's disappointed in me, but I think after all her tears today, she's more disappointed with herself for allowing herself to be blind to what was going on."

"So you and your mum are okay?"

"Yes."

"Now, Martine?"

"Well, you've seen how she operates. I had to go and see her one last time so she knew I want nothing to do with any business proposals she has now or in the future. What I didn't bet on was her reaction." I find myself sitting up straighter because I have an idea of what he's going to tell me; that she threw herself at him. "That woman doesn't handle rejection well."

"I knew it. She wants you."

"Yes, but I don't want her and I've made it clear to her. All these years and I never knew she was interested. But I could never be happy with someone like her, not when I know what it's like to feel happy with someone."

I take a slow drink of the wine because I truthfully don't know what to say to that. "Now, is there anything else you want to know?" he asks with a smile.

I move my head from side to side, trying to think, but there is nothing else. "Unless there are other skeletons in your closet?"

"Nope, none at all."

"Well, that's fine then." I lean back, my body relaxing into his, thankful that he has nothing else to share with me. "How is Emma?"

"Oh, yes. She said to tell you she expects to see you soon."

I laugh because I can almost see the expression on her face as she said it. "I'll call her in the morning to see what she's doing. I was going to take the kids out tomorrow for the day. A park if it's nice, and if it's not, an indoor play area."

"That sounds good. I'm sure she was thinking much the same as you. Now, how long am I allowed to stay? Because I'm missing you like crazy."

"I'd love to say all night, but I can't."

"Lauren, you don't need to say. I understand."

Almost jumping from the couch, I hand Matt my glass. "Back

in a minute." He frowns. I dash into the office and grab my designs and rush back.

"What are you doing?"

"Letting you see your designs."

I sit back down and swap the papers for my drink, and watch as he quickly scans each page. "Fucking hell, these are great." He lifts his head until our eyes meet, a wide smile on his face. "And this . . ." He holds the design of the interior in his hand. "You did this?"

"Look, I'm a graphic designer, not an interior designer, but I think you need to consider doing something like this. I only did this to give you an idea of what it could look like."

"Lauren, it looks amazing and the brand is perfect. No wonder the Wrights hire you and recommend you to everyone."

I smile shyly at his words. "Is there anything you want to change or add?"

"No. I can't wait to get started on changing menus and everything else. I see us having a huge launch night once we've completed the work and branding."

I'm both excited and nervous; the rebranding of the restaurant and club is by far the biggest job I've taken on myself. All this talk of launches has me worried that no-one will like it. But the design suits what he wants to achieve.

Matt puts the designs down on the coffee table and takes my glass, putting it down too. He roughly grabs my face until our eyes connect. When they do, all I see is him, open and honest. "You, Lauren Trent, are an amazing graphic designer, but seeing how good the restaurant could look makes me think your talents are wasted. There is nothing I would change about any of it, including the interior. I think you and I need to go on a shopping expedition for soft furnishings, and I'm calling the decorator first thing in the morning."

"Really?"

"Yes, and I'll pay for that design and concept."

"You will do no such thing. You never asked for that. I did that because I wanted to. Now, how quickly can you move on this?"

"I'm going to say we will be closed from a week on Sunday for a week or two. If I phone Abbie tomorrow first thing as well, do you think she could work within my timescale?"

"There's only one way to find out. Call her. But I think you'd be surprised at what she can do."

"Now work has been dealt with, I need you," he says, licking his bottom lip.

"Is that so?" I inch closer to him, wanting to be the one to make the first move, but I don't get the chance. His mouth quickly seals mine; his tongue dips inside, teasing me, and a pang of desire shoots through my body. An involuntary moan leaves me.

"I need you too," I say breathlessly against his lips as I pull back, breaking our kiss. I stand, taking his hand, and lead him straight up the stairs to my bedroom.

Thirty-Two

"THE ONE BAD THING ABOUT you dropping the kids off with me just now is that I don't get to see how you look going out tonight. Does he still have no idea about the kids?"

"No, but then again, I don't know where we're going for dinner. He says it's a surprise."

I've not seen him since the wee small hours of Wednesday morning when he left me. We've spoken every night after I've got the kids in bed, and there have been text messages going back and forth every day. Most of them flirtatious and fun.

It still surprises me how easy going he is.

There have also been a few business calls between us because he's keeping to his word. Abbie has already started working for him in getting the word out there about the launch. The decorator is booked in and we have a shopping trip on Monday to look forward to. Sandra is going to have the kids for me for two full days a week during the holidays, and on those days, I can concentrate on work, and the rest of my days I can plan lots of trips out with them both.

There's only one slight problem for me with the launch date that Matt has picked. My dad is coming to stay that weekend to spend time with me and the kids. I think he got fed up waiting for me to pick a date for going to his, but I've honestly been so busy. I don't think I'll fit in a trip to London now. I'm re-evaluating my workload because of the kids, and maybe also Matt. I want to spend time with all of them, but if I keep taking on more work, I will be too tired to even play with the kids or take them out.

"You had better go. Have a great time, and there's no rush tomorrow, so you can have a long lie in bed, or not," she says, grinning. Trust her.

"Okay, I'm going. Luke, Kate, Mummy is going now." They both walk over. Kate jumps up, wanting a cuddle, which I'm more than happy to give.

"Mummy, are you going out for dinner with Liam's Uncle Matt?"

Oh, no. Abbie looks at me, shaking her head.

"Yes, I'm going for dinner with Matt. Is that okay?"

"Yes, I like him. Does that mean he's your boyfriend?"

"We're friends and I'd like to get to know him better."

"He likes you a lot. Really likes you."

"Is that good?"

"It's good because everyone should like you." I smile at the warmth in his voice. "He and Liam's dad sometimes play football with us."

"That's nice. Now, be a good boy and I'll see you tomorrow."

"I'm always good."

"You are." I give the kids a kiss and hand Kate to Abbie so I can get home. An hour and a half isn't a long time to get ready for a date.

I take a deep breath and a final look in the mirror. All Matt told me was to wear a dress and something sexy. When I spend my free time running around in jeans and T-shirts, anything can look sexy, but bloody hell. This green dress is stunning and elegant, yet sexy, and of course, brings out the colour of my eyes. The material hugs my body, showing off my curves. I love the back, or rather lack of it. My hair is pinned up and my make-up is light.

I'm pleased with how I look. If only I knew where we were going tonight.

A knock on the front door startles me. He's here and he's early. I slip on my black heels, grab a shawl, and walk down the stairs.

Matt spins around as I open the door. His deep green eyes bore through me. "Bloody hell, Lauren. You look incredible." His eyes travel up and down my body, taking in my appearance.

I turn and walk through to the sitting room. "Fucking hell, woman. I'm already in knots just watching you walking away."

I stop. His feet cross the floor and already my body is anticipating his touch. The first touch of his hand against my back has my body buzzing. But that's nothing compared to when he slowly starts kissing my neck. I tilt my neck to the side and close my eyes as he presses his body against mine, and I feel his erection prodding into me.

Oh God. Why are we going out?

"You smell delicious," he says in between kisses. If he keeps this up, my legs are going to buckle beneath me. Internally, I'm both begging him to stop and to keep going. All these thoughts swirling around in my head can't be good for me. He's sending me into a spin.

"Matt, shouldn't we be going out?" I ask, as he continues teasing me. My skin is burning with desire.

He stops kissing my neck and I shiver. I'm already missing his touch. "Yes, but as you can tell, I want you."

Turning around to face him, I slip my arms around his waist and smile. "Well, I'm all yours later if you want me."

The smile on his face grows and his eyes light up. "Of course

I want you. Where are the kids?"

"Abbie is keeping them overnight."

"And why didn't I know this?"

"I wanted to surprise you, and I think I have."

"Yes, you have. We can argue later about where we will spend the night. Now, I think we should go before I change my mind and slowly undress you."

Oh, but that sounds more appealing than dinner.

He leans closer, his breath hot against my face. His lips rest gently on mine in a soft kiss. Closing my eyes, I open my mouth and return the kiss, only for him to break it as quickly as he started it. "We do need to go. We have a reservation."

"Okay." I release my arms from him and watch in amusement as he adjusts his trousers. We leave the house, and after I lock the front door, he quickly takes my hand for the short walk to his car. Always the gentleman, he opens the door for me and I try to slide in gracefully, but this is me, and I'm sure I don't manage it.

After a few minutes driving, I realise we're not heading into town like I expected. We're headed into the countryside. There's soft music flowing all around me in the car, and as I look at Matt, he's smiling and everything about his appearance looks relaxed. Turning my attention back outside, the scenery is stunning; rolling hills, green trees. This is a road I don't think I've ever been on.

I ask more than once where we're going but he refuses to answer. He's enjoying teasing me. When I finally realise he's not giving in, we talk about our week. There isn't much left for me to tell him. He already knows everything, from my day out with Emma and the kids to going shopping for food.

Emma and I had a great day out with the kids. We went to the park and then took them all for a pizza. The boys, as usual, had a football to play with, and as for Kate, Emma enjoyed playing with her.

The car slows down and I gasp when I see the building before me. It's a castle. Matt gets out and quickly rounds the car and opens my door. All I see is the beauty of the old building before me.

"If you think this is good, wait until you see inside." He takes my hand and guides me to the entrance. Now I can appreciate why he wanted to keep this reservation. As soon as we enter, we're greeted by a lovely gentleman. Matt gives his name and then we're shown into the restaurant.

My eyes take in everything. This place is exquisite. The soft furnishings are all tartan and traditional with modern twists; soft greys and creams. Beautiful candle chandeliers hang from the ceiling, soft lighting creating the mood. There's nothing I don't like about it. Matt orders drinks for us, although he's only having a soft drink.

"What do you think?"

"I love it, and that's before I've tasted the food."

"Well, Mum assures me you will love the food." I smile thinking about that. Up until we stepped inside, I did think I was overdressed, but I'm not. "I've never been here but Mum recommended it, so I know the food will be good."

"I'm sure it will be. Luke asked if I was going out with you tonight. It appears he's overheard you talking."

"Sorry. Is he okay?"

"Yes. He seems to like you. Or maybe that's something to do with the small fact you've been playing football with him."

"That might be it. He's a really good kid. I've already said I want to know both of them too."

"I know, but for their sake, I don't want to rush it. He knows you're Liam's uncle and that's helping. I'm sure if I was to just introduce you as a friend, he would be upset."

I don't say another word on the subject and neither does Matt as we both read the menu. Everything on the menu sounds mouth-watering and I really can't choose. When a waiter arrives to take our order, I ask Matt to choose something for me, because

I honestly can't pick. He orders starters of smoked salmon for me and cod for himself, and then proceeds to tell the waiter to surprise us with a meat dish for the main course.

Our conversation is relaxed as we discuss everything from work to the kids. Matt has spent a lot of his time the last few days with Emma and their mum, which has meant he's been around Luke when all the kids have been playing together.

"I know what you've said about Luke, and it does make sense not rushing things with us in front of him, but that doesn't mean I can't get to know him."

"Of course not."

"Well, I'm not bad at football, considering I've not played since I was in my teens." I laugh, finding the whole football thing slightly amusing. "You do know that boy of yours would love to go to a real football match?"

"Yes, he's been hinting. Patrick said he will take him for me with the boys."

"I know, he mentioned it. I sometimes go with Patrick and the boys, so if it's alright with you, I'd like to go with them."

"You don't need my permission to go to the football with your brother-in-law and nephews."

He reaches across the table, taking my hands in his, those green eyes of his piercing through me. "No, I know that, but I don't want to make things complicated with us by spending more time with Luke."

"Thank you, but I'm sure Luke will be happy to go to the football with you. He asked if us going out means you're my boyfriend."

"And what did you say?"

"I said I wanted to get to know you."

"For now, I'll happily accept your answer. Now, no more talk of work or the kids. Tonight is about only us."

Us. I like the sound of that.

Thirty-Three

HIS EYES LINGER ON ME as we sit in the car, in the car park of his building. There was no hesitation when he asked whose home we were going back to; my reply was yours.

We've had a lovely evening so far, and from the glint in his eyes, our night is far from over.

"Are we going to just sit here in the car?"

"Lauren, I could sit and stare at you all night long. It wouldn't be a hardship for me, but as it is, I think we would both benefit from being inside because I want to slowly unwrap the best present I've had in years."

There's nothing I can say to that because I do want him to slowly unwrap me and devour me. I'm hardly the best present he's had in years, but I suppose I should learn to take compliments.

He exits the car quickly, and before I get a chance to, he's there opening my door. Taking my hand, he helps me out, and it has to be said, not very elegantly. With my hand in his, we enter the elevator and ride the journey to his apartment in silence.

I feel as though I've waited forever for this moment. The endless flirting through texts and calls has only heightened my need for him, and tonight's foreplay has been interesting. Each small touch of his had my body burning with desire for him.

We enter the apartment. He takes my bag and shawl, putting them on the sideboard in his hallway. I stand firmly, unsure of what to do now. He grabs me roughly, throwing me over his shoulder in a fireman's lift.

"Put me down," I yell, but he doesn't, only laughs as he strides through the apartment into the kitchen.

Stopping in front of the fridge, he tells me to take out a bottle of Prosecco, which I do. Next, I'm told to get two glasses from a cupboard, and again, I do. I turn the glasses upside down so I can carry them in one hand and the wine in the other.

"Perfect!" he states. "Do we need anything else before I lock us in away in the bedroom?"

"I don't think so."

"Good, because now I want you between *my* sheets," he says, before striding quickly to his bedroom.

Entering his bedroom, he finally lowers me to my feet. My head is in a bit of a spin as I stand uneasy on my feet.

"Turn around." I do as he asks, giving him a clear view of my back. I hear him inhale deeply as he gently runs his fingers down my spine. The tiny hairs on the back of my neck stand and goosebumps spread quickly across my skin. His hands move to my side and he slowly unzips my dress. I close my eyes and enjoy the warm fuzzy feelings sweeping through my entire body.

He presses his soft lips to the skin at the back of my neck. His hands slide up my back to my shoulders and he teasingly lowers the straps on my dress, letting it slide down until it pools on the floor.

I turn back around to face him, eyes hooded, mouth gaping. I place my fingers under his chin and tilt until his mouth closes. We're both desperate for the other. He reaches forward, clasping our hands together. My heart starts to thump deep inside my chest as his eyes travel over my exposed body. All I'm wearing is my lace knickers and four-inch-heels.

"You are the best gift I've unwrapped, and I thank God for all the time we spend together. And it may come as a surprise, given our present situation, but the time we spend not having sex is more important to me."

His words take me by surprise. In this moment, everything is gentle between us. He lifts our joined hands and presses them to his heart. We silently gaze into each other's eyes. The only noise I hear is our hearts beating. His lips fall to mine, and instantly, my body dissolves into his.

I moan as his tongue dances with mine, circling around and around. With slow, calculated steps, he guides me back toward the bed, our mouths still latched onto each other's. We stop. He releases our hands then folds down the bed covers before picking me up and laying me on the bed.

He stands before me and starts to undress. There's no hurry on his part, and as much as I want him to get a move on, I'm enjoying the scene playing out before my eyes. The hungry look in his as he keeps his eyes on me. I'm totally mesmerised by Matt; every last detail. He's become such a huge part of my life in a short space of time.

I can see the cogs turning in his mind. *If only I knew what he's thinking*. He removes every single item of clothing he wears and I smile when he's completely naked before me.

"Something seems to be pleasing you, Miss Trent," he murmurs, closing the distance between us and crawling up the bed. His hands stop and rest on the thin lace of my underwear.

"Yes. You're doing that a lot recently; pleasing me. I'm getting used to it."

"And so you should, because pleasing you seems to be my new purpose in life. Now, it's about time I remove the last item you're wearing." He pulls my knickers off in one quick go and then crawls back up the bed. He parts my legs and runs his tongue straight up the inside of my right thigh. I whimper when his tongue slips between my legs.

"Oh dear God!" I cry out when he plunges his tongue deep into me. There's no words for the sensations building inside. He withdraws and laps against me, circling before dipping back into me.

My eyes close as I drift off in happy bliss. He splays his hands on my stomach in an attempt to hold me in place, but it doesn't help. My hips rotate slowly in time to the pace he's set. He lifts his head and I open my eyes and watch as he looks at me with his own lust-filled eyes, before flashing me a cute smile and dipping his head once more.

The instant warmth I feel as he tenderly runs his tongue through my flesh has me arching my back, wanting more. Do I want more of this or more of Matt Anderson?

I want both.

Waves of pleasure surround me and it's only a matter of time before they come crashing down. Desperately, I try to hold back, but he knows . . . he knows how close I am. My body trembles beneath him as he changes the pace. His mouth latches onto my core as I crash; his name falls from my lips in an incoherent mumble. But that doesn't stop him; he continues lapping and sucking until my body can't take any more.

In this moment of time, my body and mind feel weak and I'm unsure if that's a good thing. I promised myself eight months ago I would never allow myself to be weak where any man is concerned. Yet, the defence I put in place has come crumbling down with Matt, and that scares me.

I've been there before and I don't want to allow myself to get hurt. But as I lie here underneath him, my body shuddering in the aftershocks of what I'm sure is only my first orgasm of the night, I already know he is capable of destroying me. There would be no way back. And that frightens me.

As my breathing slows down, I open my eyes. Matt's eyes meet mine in a hazy gaze. This thing between us is so intense and I know I'm not the only one feeling it. He slowly starts kissing his way up my body. I allow myself to enjoy the fresh wave of desire that surges through my core.

Soft lips brush lightly against mine, giving me a taste of my own release as he gazes down at me. I adjust my position, moving my hips to welcome his erection. His body feels weightless on top of me.

"I need you," he whispers into my neck.

Something about the way he says those words makes me think there's another meaning to them, and not just because he needs to be inside me. Does he need me in his life? Do I need him? I want him. Is that the same?

He drives into me and stills. Every muscle grips around him. He moves slightly, teasing me. His eyes are fixed on me, watching. Slowly, he withdraws, and I moan at the instant loss. A lazy smile plays on his lips as he slides back in.

"You and me, we are perfect together," he says, driving forward. I lose his words as I try to concentrate on the way he's making me feel. Happy. Wanted. I gasp for air as my heart pounds deep within. I'm trying not to think about the meaning of his words and my own feelings for him, but it's hard not to as he pushes me closer to the edge.

Each thrust is precise, going deeper each time.

"This, us, it all makes sense."

I moan, not only at his words, but from the internal feelings that are rushing through my body. I tense as he pushes deeper into me. Short, sharp breaths leave me in a rush each time I attempt to drag in some much-needed air.

The leisurely pace is almost unbearable. I need more. With his eyes still on me, I reach up, taking his face in my hands, and pull it down to me, capturing his mouth with my own. I roll my hips to meet his as my pleasure builds. He sinks in and out quicker now. The urgency is there for us both.

I move my hands from his face and claw at his shoulders as the pace changes once more. Gone is the tenderness as he thrusts harder and faster. He groans, biting on my bottom lip, and pushes deeper into me again.

Pulling back and thrusting forward again, we both cry out together, letting go. My body trembles beneath him with my heart hammering deep within my chest. His body finally relaxes and he places slow, sweet kisses all over my face. Tears fill my eyes and I try not to let them fall.

He shifts the weight of his body and lies on his side, pulling me with him. Nuzzling into him, I allow my eyes to close as he wraps his arms around me, holding me close.

Opening my eyes, I realise he's not in the bed. Slowly, I climb out. I hear music in the distance, or is it singing? It's four-thirty a.m. It's too early to be up; he should be in bed beside me. My body aches in all the right places as I stand and stretch. I smile to myself. I use the bathroom and brush my teeth before grabbing his white shirt that he took off. I stare in his mirror as I turn up the sleeves. I look tired.

I pad through his apartment barefoot. Stopping in the doorway of the kitchen, I watch him as he moves around, singing whilst making coffee.

He stops, standing in only his boxers, his hands pressed against the work surface.

"You sing!" I say, slipping my hands around his waist. He turns his head and smiles.

"Can I get you anything?"

"Yes. You back in bed beside me. It's too early to be up."

"I couldn't sleep and I didn't want to disturb you."

"Well, you not being in bed was enough to do that."

He turns fully in my arms and his eyes travel the length of my body. He reaches around my waist, hands sliding down my thighs and back up again underneath his shirt. "I was going to have coffee, but now you stand here before me in only my shirt, which suits you, I want you."

I smirk with a shrug of my shoulders.

He picks me up and places me on the counter. "Now, it might be too early but this could very well be the best start to any day." His mouth descends upon me.

Thirty-Four

"WHY ARE YOU SO NERVOUS?" Emma asks, as we sit in her garden, watching the kids play.

God, is it really that noticeable? Of course, it is. I've been tapping my fingers on the glass in front of me and my feet are bouncing under the table. "I'm not sure. It's not as though my dad hasn't met Matt. I think it's the thought of the whole weekend."

"I'm sure everything will be fine."

"I hope so."

"What time does his train get in?"

"Thirty minutes."

"So why the hell are you sitting here? You need to get a move on."

"No, he's meeting up with Stacey before I go and pick him up."

"Oh."

There's not much more to say to my comment. I think this is why I'm so nervous, because I have no idea what they will talk about. But Dad was right. He couldn't very well come here for a long weekend without at least attempting to see her.

"When will your dad see Matt?" Emma has been subtly fishing for the last two weeks on what's going on between us.

"Tonight. I'm cooking dinner."

"Oh." She takes a drink from her glass of water, staring at me. I know she wants more information from me.

The last two weeks have been busy and incredible. I've been able to spend quality time with the kids. On the really nice days, we've gone for days out to the zoo, the beach, and lots of parks. Sometimes I've taken them myself, although Emma and the boys came to the beach with us and Abbie. I've hardly seen Abbie. She has been tied up with everything for the launch of the restaurant and club tomorrow.

I've also seen a lot of Matt. We've managed a couple of dates, but he's been at Emma's almost constantly. He says it's his way of seeing me and the kids. He wants them to both like him. I have to admit, it's nice seeing him with not just Luke, but also Kate. She makes him work harder than Luke. She always wants his attention, and Luke, well, he's happy because when he sees Matt, he usually has a kick about with him. I swear he must be leaving Danny to do all the work at the restaurant and club.

Tonight will be the first time Matt's having dinner with us. For me, that's a big thing. It's easy at Emma's when everyone is there, but I feel as though the pressure is on tonight.

"Are you ready for this?" she asks with concern.

I sigh and shake my head. "I don't know. I know he's your brother, but everything is going so quick. My head still tells me I should be cautious."

"Oh, Lauren. I get that, given what you've been through before. You have every reason to be cautious. But Matt is smitten with you. I've known it for weeks. He wants to be with you and I also know he's desperate to spend more time with the three of you."

"I know. This is why I'm doing dinner tonight, although with how nice it is, I should have a barbecue."

"Do what you feel comfortable with, and if that means phoning and getting a takeaway, do that. Now, Patrick has tickets for next week's football match. I know Matt would like to ask Luke if he wants to go with him. What do you think?"

"Matt knows that's a sure fire way to win my son around," I say with a laugh. Who am I kidding? I know Luke likes him. He's been asking me more questions about Matt than David recently.

"I'll speak to Matt before he comes over."

"I'm so pleased for both of you."

"Why?"

"Because you both deserve to be happy, and I know Matt makes you happy."

I can't argue with that. "Yes, he does. Now, can we please change the subject?"

I turn back and watch as Kate runs around the garden after Luke and Liam. She could run around after those two all day long. Liam is almost as protective as Luke of her. Whenever she falls over or cries, both boys instantly stop what they're doing and rush to help her. She has everyone wrapped around her tiny fingers.

The conversation with Emma is easy, especially when we don't talk about Matt. The kids play well together and we have a relaxing afternoon and have lunch sitting out in the sun.

My phone starts ringing—my dad. "Hi, Dad."

"Hi, sweetheart. I'm in a cab and heading to yours now."

"I would've come and picked you up."

"Yes, I know, but I'll see you soon."

"Okay, I'll go back to the house. I'm just at a friend's."

"I should be there in ten minutes."

We end the call and now my nervous kick in. I wonder if he'll tell me about his meeting with Stacey.

"I better take these two home. They're not going to be happy about leaving. I'm sure they both think of this as their second home."

"And they should. We're practically family." She quickly throws her hand over her mouth.

"Emma . . ."

"Sorry, I'm getting carried away, but I have a feeling one day that's what we will be."

"We'll see. Luke, Kate, we need to go. Your grandad will be here soon." Luke strolls up the garden, huffing and puffing. "Luke, you can play with Liam anytime. Grandad's only here for the weekend and wants to see you, so you can stop huffing."

"Sorry, but can I come over later on?" he asks with sad eyes.

"I'm not sure. Remember Matt is coming to have dinner with us tonight."

"So does mean that he is your boyfriend now? Everyone thinks he is."

Emma stands to the side of me, laughing. "Well? I'm sure we all want to know the answer to this."

I can't believe I'm being put on the spot by my son. And he's standing patiently, waiting on my reply. "Yes."

"Hallelujah! About time," Emma says, smiling.

"Good, I'm glad. You smile more," says Luke, as he grins almost as wide as Emma. I've no words, so instead, I say goodbye to Emma, and with Kate's hand in mine, we head home.

The taxi stops outside the house and I call on the kids and go out to meet him. He looks more relaxed than the last time we saw him. I'm sure that's because this time he's not here in Glasgow for work.

"Sweetheart, let me look at you," he says, putting his case down. "You look different."

He picks up Luke and gives us all a hug together. My earlier nerves seem to have settled and I'm glad he's here. Letting me and Kate go, and with Luke still in his arms, he picks up his case and we go inside. Luke is excitedly telling him all things football, and Dad can only nod in agreement because Luke isn't giving him the chance to get a word in.

"Grandad, can you play football with me?" Luke asks as he jumps onto the floor.

Dad laughs. "Give an old man a chance. Let me put my things away and then we can play with Kate, and then football, I promise."

"Okay. You've got the spare room."

I watch, amused, as Luke takes his hand and leads him upstairs. That boy of mine; he's very excited. This is the first time Dad has come to visit, so he's bound to be.

"I'll put the kettle on," I call upstairs after them.

Kate toddles into the kitchen in front of me. She might not be speaking much, but she knows exactly what I'm saying. She moves around the kitchen with me as I make two cups of tea. I put some juice into her cup and pour out a drink for Luke, and I pop her in the high chair with some fruit I chopped up.

The thumping down the stairs can only mean Luke has finished showing Dad his room.

"Are you sure you're ready for a weekend here?" I ask, after he sighs heavily and sits down at the table.

"Of course. Luke here is going to keep me on my toes, and this little one, well, I haven't worked out what she'll do."

"Oh, she'll have you wrapped around her finger, just like the rest of us."

"Of that I have no doubt. Now, Luke tells me you have a boyfriend."

Oh, well. Better to deal with this sooner rather than later. We sit drinking our tea and I talk about Matt, and I see the recognition when I mention his name. He smiles when I tell him he will be here soon. I find myself telling him that, although he knows the kids, this will be the first time we all have dinner together.

I don't want Dad thinking that I introduce random men into the lives of my kids. Dad's happy that I'm putting the past behind me and finally moving on with my life. To be fair, he's not the only one. Everyone in my life seems to be of the same opinion.

Luke starts to pester him for a game of football. "Luke, please let Grandad have his tea. Why don't you go out and play in the garden, and we will be out in a few minutes?"

"Okay." He huffs as he leaves the table. Kate's eyes follow him and I can see she's starting to get restless too. She wants to be out of her chair and following Luke.

"Is he always so full of energy?"

"Yes. How did it go with Stacey?"

"You really want to know?" I nod. "Not great. She's not interested in anything I have to say. She is a selfish girl and I'm sorry about the hurt and pain she and David have caused you." He stares blankly into his cup.

"This isn't your fault."

"I know, but I want you to hear me out. I think you should take some legal advice over the kids."

"Why? Is he going to try and take them off me? He can't." The words rush from my mouth and I'm anxious.

"No, nothing like that. He's not interested in them; Stacey made that clear. I know he's not given you anything for them, and other than a brief meeting that night, he's not seen them in months."

"Dad, truthfully, I couldn't care what he does, but if down the line he decides he wants to see the kids I wouldn't ever stand in his way."

"Sweetheart, you have a bigger heart than I have. Now, I think we should go out and play with the kids and not talk about your sister. Although, I can only hope that one day she comes to her senses and realises what she's done."

"Come on, baby girl." I lift Kate from her chair and Dad takes her off me and wanders out into the garden with me following behind. Even if Stacey were to come to her senses, I'm not sure I would ever be comfortable having her in my life. Even as a child, it didn't matter what she had, she always wanted more. More friends, more gifts. It's just the type of person she is.

My phone beeps. A text from Matt: ***I'm on my way and I have collected your takeaway order. Be with you in 5 x***

Me: See you soon x

When I said to Dad earlier that I was going to cook dinner, he told me not to bother and we would get a takeaway, and proceeded to ask Luke what he wanted. Luke had said pizza so that's what we're having. Not the meal I had in mind, but I've promised Dad a Sunday roast with all the trimmings.

"Luke, Matt is on his way with pizza. You should go and wash up."

My son's eyes light up. Dad and Luke have been playing football on and off all afternoon, with Kate running around between them. I've sat quietly watching them with memories of my early childhood in my mind. I remember I had a playhouse in our garden. I'm sure Dad made it for me.

Nerves are kicking in now. Luke runs on back into the house while I wait for Dad and Kate. He has her in his arms and she's babbling away. "Lauren, are you okay?"

"Yes, why?"

"Because you look tense."

"It's nothing."

"Sweetheart, I can see you're not. If you're nervous about me meeting Matt, don't be. From what I can tell, Luke likes him, so this should make things easier."

I smile, but his words aren't helping.

When we finally get inside, because someone wanted down to walk, Matt's already in my kitchen with Luke, putting the food on the table.

"I did knock, and Luke let me in," he says as I look at him. He's come here straight from work and is still wearing his suit and tie. He looks handsome as he always does, but maybe more so today.

"Mr Trent, it's good to see you again."

"It's Adam. Can I help you with anything?"

"No, Luke has sorted this, leaving me nothing to do," he says with a warm smile. Kate wanders over to Matt and holds her hands up to him. He picks her up and tickles her, making her laugh. "You, Little Miss, seem to be in a very good mood." Dad looks at me and glances back to Matt. I wonder what he's thinking about this.

"Can we eat now, Mummy? I'm hungry," Luke shouts out.

"Yes, we can eat," I tell him as we all sit down. Matt puts Kate in her high chair and I hand her some garlic bread and a small slice of pizza.

Dinner is relaxed, and I'm glad we got a takeaway. It's taken the pressure off me, and of course, it's Luke's favourite, so everyone is happy. Chat is light; most of it revolves around my son's love of football. As I watch Matt interact with my kids and my dad, I don't know why I was feeling nervous. He makes everything look and feel so easy. He is great with the kids and I'm sure Dad has noticed.

"Lauren, what do you want to do about the launch tomorrow?" Matt asks.

"What launch?" Dad questions Matt.

"As you know, Lauren was working on the rebranding of my restaurant and club. Tomorrow is the official launch."

"Sweetheart, you should go. I can look after these two," Dad tells me.

"No, I'm having family and friends, including my nephews, in for dinner. The invitation is for you all."

Dad looks at me. I didn't want to dictate what we were doing all weekend. "Well, in that case, I think we should all go. You and I can take the kids out in the afternoon."

"Are you sure?"

"Of course. You shouldn't miss this because I'm here. I don't want to interfere in your life but be a part of it."

"Dad, you're only here for a short time. We want to spend time with you."

"And you will, but this is important to you and Matt."

"Okay, but I should warn you, Grant will be there," I tell him, and now I'm not sure going is such a good idea. Matt knows about Dad and Grant; we've spoken at length about our families.

"Sweetheart, I'm sure Grant and I can put our differences aside for you."

"So, that's it settled. You will all be there tomorrow," Matt says, smiling. I nod. "Perfect."

After dinner, Dad wants to get Kate ready for bed. He has no idea what he's letting himself in for, giving her a bath. Luke goes with them upstairs, and for the first time today, I'm alone with Matt as we tidy up the kitchen.

"Are you okay?" he asks, slipping his hands around my waist. My body falls into his warm embrace.

"Yes. I was nervous about today."

"You didn't have to be. Look how easy it's been. I know this is a massive step for you to take, but I'm not going to let you down. Now, are you sure you're happy for me to ask Luke if he wants to come to the game?" He tilts my head and presses a soft kiss to my lips.

"Yes, I'm sure. Ask him. I know it will make his night."

"This. Us. Everything is going to work out just fine."

Thirty-five

"SO, WHAT ARE YOUR PLANS for this weekend?" Emma asks as we stand in the playground, waiting for the boys. Four weeks they've been back at school, and I know Luke loves it. I've found a routine since the schools have been back. Two full days a week I work on designs for clients, and the rest of the time belongs to my kids and Matt.

"Well, tonight it might just be me and the kids, although Abbie has said she wants to come over, but tomorrow Matt is taking is all out for the day before staying over tomorrow night."

"Bloody hell, Lauren. You've kept this quiet. Why am I only hearing about it now?" She crosses her arms in front of her. Kate is playing with a little girl on the grass to the side of me.

"It's not a big deal."

"Not a big deal. You and I both know it is. This is a huge step for you. I'm happy. So where are you going tomorrow?"

She's right, it is. The kids are very comfortable with Matt and love being around him as much as I do. This will be the first time he's stayed over when the kids are home.

"I don't know. He says it's a surprise."

"Why are you frowning?"

I didn't realise I was. "I'm not good with surprises." The school bell rings and I call Kate over to stand with me. She holds onto my hand and we wait on the boys.

"I'm sure whatever he has planned you will all love. You do seem to bring out his thoughtful side."

I turn and smile.

Luke and Liam come running out together. Emma still has to wait on the other two. We both walked down together with Kate in her pram, and as she stands beside me, I already think I'm going to have problems trying to get her back in it for the walk home. Emma and the boys are going to the shops, so we will be walking back on our own.

I strap Kate in her pram, and instantly she starts screaming. We say goodbye to Emma and the boys, and I tell her we will see her on Sunday at her mum's for dinner. She's invited us all the last two Sundays, but Matt has worked and I didn't want to go without him, even though Emma assured me it was fine. As much as they all lead busy lives, they are a really close-knit family, making time to see each other.

Luke tells me about his day as we walk home after Kate finally stops crying when she realises I'm not going to take her out. Luke loves school and has really taken to his new teacher.

Abbie's car is in the drive when we get home.

"Hey, sport," she says, rustling Luke's hair.

"Are you having dinner with us tonight?" he asks her.

"Not tonight. But we can have dinner one night together at Nana's next week." He seems happy with her answer as we go into the house. I tell him to go and change out of his uniform. Abbie lifts Kate from her pram and gives her a kiss. My daughter smiles. I think it's because she's out of her pram and not from seeing Abbie. But I don't share this with Abbie.

"Tea?" I ask.

"Yeah, go on. I'm not staying too long. I know you want a night alone. Have you heard from your dad this week?" she asks as I make tea.

"Yes. He wants to come up again in a few weeks." Abbie knows how much I've been missing him lately since his last visit. That weekend was perfect, even Matt's launch at the restaurant. He was right about Grant. Deep down, I knew neither of them would cause trouble but they both made an effort with each other. Called a truce, so to speak.

"And what about his work?"

"Well, he asked for a transfer, so he needs to wait and see what happens." The company he works for has offices up and down the country and he asked about the possibility of transferring to either the Glasgow or Edinburgh office. I would love it if he moved here and so would the kids. Luke would love having him close.

"What are your plans for this weekend?" I ask her.

"I'm going out with some of the girls from work tonight, and Mum wants to go shopping tomorrow, so she's dragging me with her."

I laugh because Abbie doesn't do anything she doesn't want to do. She's also put the whole idea of running her own business on the back burner and she's happy with her work at the moment.

Abbie stays for another hour. We chat and play with the kids before she leaves to get ready for her night out.

I've promised Luke we can sit and watch a movie together, although I'm sure Kate will have other ideas about how our night will go. A night with these two and then the whole day tomorrow with my three favourite people. That sounds like a perfect weekend to me.

"Good morning, gorgeous," Matt says, kissing me quickly, taking me by surprise, before bending and picking up Kate then giving her a kiss. I never heard his car pull up. "Did you all have a good night without me?"

"Morning yourself, and yes, our night was perfect."

"Matt, you're here." Luke runs down the stairs.

"Luke, what have I told you?" I swear one of these days he's going to fall down them.

"Sorry, Mum."

"You need to listen to your mum. Now, are you all set for a great day out?"

"Yes, where are we going?" Luke asks.

"I thought we could go to the beach. It's meant to be a nice day and I've made a picnic for lunch, and if you behave, we can get a pizza tonight when we come home." Luke's face lights up. I'm sure it wouldn't matter what we were doing today; he's happy and content. "Do you have everything you need?" he asks me.

"Yes." I have a bag packed for Kate and a change of clothes for both of them because I wasn't sure what Matt had planned.

"Okay, then we should get going and strap these two into my car." I frown. I thought we would be taking mine. Now we'll need to take their car seats from mine. "Stop frowning. I have car seats in my car."

"Really?"

"Yes. We can't keep swapping the seats about whenever I take them somewhere." I can't help but smile, because to me, it means he wants to stick around. Luke started playing football games a few Saturdays ago, and I went to his very first game, but Matt has been going along too. He even took him last week when I wasn't feeling well. "Now, come on. We're wasting precious time standing here."

He carries Kate outside and Luke follows him while I grab my things and lock up.

Our drive is pleasant, and Kate falls asleep. Luke talks almost non-stop. Matt parks the car and he and I get out first to fix Kate's pram before we put her in it.

"Today is going to fun," he says, getting Luke from the car.

"It will. Can we go in the water?" he asks.

"I'm sure Mum will let us go for a paddle later when Kate wakes up," Matt tells him. I lift Kate and put her in the pram; she's still sound asleep.

"I won't be able to take the pram on the beach," I tell him.

"That's okay, isn't it, Luke? We can go and wander around some shops until she wakes up. Get a bucket and spade." He thinks of everything, especially where the kids are concerned.

He takes Luke's hand and I push the pram, and we make our way to the shops. I smile watching the two of them walking in front of me, chatting away. I've known for weeks that I've fallen for Matt, but there's something about seeing him with my kids—it gives me butterflies in my stomach.

We go to the shops and Matt buys the kids buckets and spades; one set blue, the other pink, and when Kate wakes up, we walk back to the car and put her pram into the boot and grab the picnic basket that Matt has brought and my bag for the kids.

I'm excited for Kate. This will be the first time she's been on the beach. Her face is a picture as she walks across the sand. I can't wait to take her shoes off her so she can feel the sand on the soles of her feet. We find a space far enough away from the water and Matt sets out the picnic blanket and towels he's brought with him. He really has thought of everything.

When I take Kate's shoes and socks off, she pulls a face that has us all laughing as she looks at the sand and her feet. Matt has his phone in his hand and snaps away, taking pictures.

"Mummy, please can we go to the water?" Luke asks, jumping up and down.

"In a few minutes."

He pulls a face and slumps down on the blanket.

"Come on. I'll take you both and Mum can sit and watch us," Matt says, taking Kate's hand. Luke jumps back up grabs the buckets.

"Be careful," I say.

"We will," Matt says, before walking toward the sea.

I lean back on my arms, watching them. I smile as Kate takes her first steps into the water, still holding Matt's hand. Luke is happy jumping about the water, and for a brief moment, I'm nervous, but as I watch the three of them together, I realise Matt would do anything for them. He's cautious when Luke wants to walk further into the water. Matt obviously tells him no because he stops and rejoins him and Kate. I could sit here and watch them all day, but I don't. No, I take my own shoes off and go and join them. Why should they get all the fun?

"Thank you," I say, as we stroll through the park, hand in hand. Luke is walking in front of us holding Kate's hand. It's been a great day. The kids loved the beach. We couldn't get Kate out of the water so we could all have lunch. We brought them to the park and they've both had a shot on the swings and some of the other equipment. Now we're getting ready to leave and go back to the car.

"What for?"

"For today. This has been the perfect day."

"Lauren, you're right, it has been perfect, but we are going to have lots of days like today. This is the first of many. Do you think they will sleep tonight?" His voice changes to a more teasing tone.

"I think so. All this fresh air and running around, it's making me feel sleepy."

"Not too sleepy I hope, because I have plans for you tonight after we get these two in bed."

"Oh, I don't know. We'll have to wait and see."

He shakes his head and neither of says anything else. "Mummy,

Mummy! What are these?"

I look at what has Luke's attention. Both he and Kate have stopped and are standing in amongst some dandelions.

"Dandelions," I tell him.

Matt lets go of my hand and bends down beside them both. "When I was little, when they looked like this, we called them wishes." He picks one and holds it in his hand. "I used to hold them, close my eyes, make a wish, and blow. Then open my eyes and watch as it flies away."

"Can we make a wish?" Luke asks.

"Of course, and I think Mummy should make one too." Matt stands and hands me one. Luke hands one to Kate and she shakes it until there's nothing left but a stem in her hand; it makes me smile.

Luke closes his eyes and does exactly what Matt did only moments ago. He opens his eyes and gazes at me.

"Can I tell you what I wished for?"

"It's meant to be a secret, but if you want to tell me, it's okay."

"I wished that Matt could come and stay with us forever."

Matt and I exchange glances and I'm not sure what to say to that. Matt smiles.

"My turn," he says. I watch as he repeats what Luke has done. "Done. Now your turn."

I close my eyes, take a deep breath, and make a wish. *I want this between us to become more.* I open my eyes and Matt stares at me.

"Mummy, will you tell me your wish?"

"No, I think I'll keep this to myself," I say, my eyes firmly on Matt. "What about you?"

Matt smiles, wraps his arm around my waist, and presses a kiss to my lips. "My wish has already come true."

He picks up Kate, and Luke takes my hand, but he doesn't start walking. His eyes hold my gaze and I wait. "Lauren, the three of you are very important to me, but I don't think you realise how much. I've know from our very first meeting that you were someone special, but it's these last few weeks spending time with all of you that I've finally admitted my feelings to myself and now it's time you hear them. Lauren Trent, I love you, I love all three of you. I want to be a part of your life. You don't need to say anything. I just wanted you to know."

I reach up, touching the side of his face. There's so much emotion as I look at him. Not only has Matt Anderson found a way deep into my heart, but he loves me and the kids.

"I love you too," I whisper against his lips.

Epilogue

One year later

"LAUREN, KEEP IT ON AND sit still." I can sense he's mumbling under his breath, probably something along the lines of, 'bloody woman. She can't do as she's told.' He has no idea how bloody hard this is for me. I don't do surprises as he well knows. So sitting here in his car with a bloody blindfold on is driving me insane.

"I can't sit still."

"It won't be long," he tells me in a reassuring voice, but it's not helping. Whatever he's up to, Abbie and Emma must be in on it because they both offered to have the kids today. Emma has them at her house and I'm sure they are being spoilt rotten.

"Please, Matt. Tell me where we're going?"

"No. You'll see soon enough." He chuckles nervously. I might not be able to see him but I hear the tension in his voice.

We've only been in the car what I think is a short time, but I could be wrong. The music is on and the windows are closed, so I have no idea where we could be. All I do know is the air conditioning is keeping me cool because it's warm outside. And I'm grateful for that today.

So far, we've had an amazing day together without the kids.

A long leisurely walk in the park with some ice creams to keep us cool. A picnic lunch that I'm sure Emma prepared for us. We've had a lovely day. We don't often get what I would call quality time like today together. So when we do, we make the most of it.

The car finally comes to a stop and I try to guess where we are, but nothing is coming to me. He opens the car door and I'm suddenly hit with the noise and the heat. It sounds like we're in town. Traffic moving, horns blaring, and voices of people going about their daily business. The passenger door opens and strong hands take mine and help me from the car. If we are in town, I must look ridiculous to passers-by as I stand here with a blindfold on.

"Matt . . ."

"Okay, just a minute."

Suddenly I'm nervous. What if I don't like his surprise? He knows me well and I wouldn't be able to hide my disappointment from him. He stands behind me, his body pressed against mine. Arms wrap around me and rest on my stomach. Such a small act sends shivers down my spine. If only he knew. "You can take it off now."

Slowly, I lower the blindfold to see we're on the pavement outside his restaurant and nightclub. So much for him taking a few days off. I knew it wouldn't last. And he says I work too hard.

"Why are we here?"

"There's just something I need to do," he says softly over my shoulder.

"Okay, can we make it quick?" I can't hide the annoyance in my voice at being here. He promised no work for a few days.

He takes my hand and we walk the short distance to the front door. Ever the gentleman, he opens the door and ushers me in first. I stop and gasp. My eyes widen as I take in the restaurant. Other than our closest family and friends, there's no-one else here. Even my dad and Uncle Grant stand side by side.

Everything looks stunning. Soft candle light and fresh flowers fill the enormous space. Carnations and lilies; my favourites. Then I notice some dandelions and my first thought is of our day at the beach. Now my mind has gone into overdrive wondering why everyone is here.

I turn to face him and all I see is his smile and love.

"What's going on?" My words come out in a whisper as I watch him.

"I wanted to come here, back to where it all began for you and me. You have been mine since that very first night here, even if you didn't realise it. Now, tonight, I'm going to make you finally see that I don't do walking away, even if you try to push me."

My breath catches and goosebumps spread across my skin. He keeps my hand in his and we move further into the room, stopping beside Luke and Kate.

"Mummy!"

"Hey, you two. I hope you've behaved for Emma." They both nod. My dad smiles at me then nods at Matt. Whatever this is, I seem to be the last one in the loop. Nothing much changes then. I stand and look around. Matt's mum is sitting down beside Emma, holding her hand. Patrick stands behind them, their kids close to mine. Danny is standing by the bar. Abbie is sitting beside her parents, grinning. She might not be grinning for much longer. My sneaky friend is getting too used to keeping secrets from me. Although, I can't give her hell for this today because she's not the only one keeping secrets. I do have one of my own.

He turns me to face him and takes a deep breath. "Lauren, sweetheart, you knocked me for six that night when you first walked through those doors with Abbie. I wasn't meant to be here. I should've already gone home, but when I saw you, I couldn't leave. Something about you kept calling me to stay. We won't go into the rest of that night. I plan on staying in your dad and Grant's good books." He shifts from one foot to the other, concentration written all over his face. My dad says something but I don't hear the words; I'm too lost in the man before me.

"Lauren, I love you and the kids from the bottom of my heart. The three of you are everything and so much more to me. Not a day goes by without thoughts of a future with all of you in it." I stare at Matt, feeling so overwhelmed by his words. "We're here because, for me, meeting you here was the beginning. The beginning of a lifetime together."

I bite nervously on my bottom lip. My eyes fill with tears.

"Sweetheart, I know your biggest fear. I'm nothing like him. There's no reason on Earth I could turn my back and walk away from the three of you. All of you are the most important people in my life."

My tears roll slowly down my face.

I watch as he steps to the side and bends down in front of the kids. He scoops up Kate and sits her on his knee. Luke eyes him curiously. I can see his mind is already ticking, thinking about what he's going to do or say.

"Luke, you might only be nearly seven years old, but you are a smart young man who has been looking out for your mum. Ensuring she's always happy and not allowing anyone to hurt her, including me. For that, you've done a great job, but I'd be very happy and honoured if you could pass that job onto me."

I close my eyes briefly, because this is all too much. Far too overwhelming. I blame my hormones.

"You see, Luke, I want the job of not just looking after your mum, but also protecting you and Kate because I love you and your sister just as much as I love your mum."

I open my tear-filled eyes and look at the three of them. They are my life.

"The job is yours only if you promise to never hurt her."

Oh, my precious boy.

Matt stands before me with Kate still in his arms and Luke now by his side. I look over at Abbie and she's crying. Matt's mum and Emma are also sobbing.

"Lauren, you are my family. You are the one I want to spend the rest of my life with. Luke is happy for me to take over his job, so marry me. I want you as my wife." He puts Kate down and drops to the floor, taking my left hand. "Lauren Trent, please say yes to being my wife?" There are gasps from everyone as they wait.

Slowly, I nod my head, because I can't form the words. Cheering erupts as he slides the most beautiful ring I've ever seen on my finger. My heart can't take anymore today. It's full of love for my man who is still on his knees before me, his own eyes filled with unshed tears.

Unable to keep myself steady, I drop to the floor and his arms wrap quickly around me.

His lips meet mine with softness and tenderness.

"I love you," I whisper as our lips part, and his head rests against mine.

He pulls the kids between us and kisses both of them. Our world feels complete. Well, almost.

"So, if you're getting married, will that make you my dad?" Luke asks.

"Luke, first and foremost, I'm your friend, but if you want me to be your dad I'm more than happy to be."

"Yeah, I think Kate and I would both like you as our dad." My tears continue to fall at my son's grown up acceptance of today's events.

"Well, does this mean we might get a baby brother or sister?"

I almost choke at his very straight-faced question.

"Maybe one day," Matt tells him.

I've blocked out the noise of everyone else. My attention is on my family. I draw in a deep breath and Matt helps me to my feet. Luke and Kate wander back over to Emma.

"Well, you're not the only one with a surprise up your sleeve," I say to Matt in a whisper, because he has to hear this before everyone else. He looks at me, puzzled, but Luke's words have given me the confidence to reveal my secret. "We will be adding to our family in six months' time."

It takes a minute for my words to register. He scoops me in his arms, lifting me and spinning me around.

"Really?"

"Yes," I say, nodding my head.

"I don't want to wait any longer than I have to for you to become Mrs Anderson."

"I don't either."

"You've made me the happiest man on the planet today. When can we tell everyone?"

"After my hospital appointment on Monday morning, when you get to see the little one I'm carrying."

We kiss again, until cheering from our family and friends separates us. I lean back and look into his dark green eyes, and I can see the depths of his feelings for me. All his love is there to be seen. He has nothing to hide, and in my eyes, he never had anything to prove to me.

Matt Anderson is my forever. He's the man who makes me feel complete. He's not just my happily ever after, but Luke and Kate's.

The end xx

About the Author

KAREN FRANCES IS A BUSY wife and mum to five kids. She currently lives just outside Glasgow, Scotland, with her husband, kids and two dogs, although she is trying hard to convince her husband to move to somewhere warm and sunny. But he's not interested. Her days are spent helping her husband run their family business, along with keeping on top of a busy home. She spends some of her free time trying to keep fit and prepare healthy meals for her family. With her kids being older the boys all lead busy lives and they don't always get times to sit down and eat together. Karen loves spending quality time with family and friends. The rest of her free time she can be found plotting or writing in her office.

Find out more about Karen Frances at *www.karenfrancesauthor.co.uk* or follow on Facebook or Twitter.

Books by KAREN FRANCES

THE CAPTURED SERIES

Family Ties a Captured Series Novella

He's Captured my Heart ~ Book 1

He's Captured my Trust ~ Book 2

He's Captured my Soul ~ Book 3

She's Captured my Love ~ Book 4

Captured by Our Addiction ~ Book 5

A BEAUTIFUL GAME SERIES

Playing the Game ~ Book 1

Playing to Win ~ Book 2

Playing the Field Novella (Coming Soon)

Moving On ~ A standalone novel

Printed in Great Britain
by Amazon

57178383R00166